SECRETS OF THE TOWERS

BY SUSAN MANSBRIDGE

Copyright © Susan Mansbridge 2022

All Rights Reserved

No parts of this publication may be reproduced, stored in a retrieval system, or transmitted in any form or by any means, electronic, mechanical, photocopying, recording, or otherwise, without the prior written permission of the copyright owner.

This is a work of fiction. Names, characters, places, and incidents are either the products of the author's imagination or are used fictitiously. Any resemblance to actual persons, living or dead, businesses, companies, events, or locales is entirely coincidental.

Cover artwork by Mathilda Parker

Author website: https://www.susanmansbridge.com

By the Same Author

Master and Apprentice

For Mum.
You taught me to read, nurtured my love of books and gave me Earthsea.
If I could, I would send my stories to you in heaven.

Chapter One

Reez woke with a start, his heart pounding and his mouth dry. His eyes darted anxiously around the dark room, searching for the familiar and safe. The candle that had shed a little light as he tried to sleep had gone out long since, but the moon was nearly full and its light was enough for Reez to make out shapes and forms. In the gloom, he recognised the long shelves of books and papers, the chest in the corner, and the desk positioned by the window to catch the last light of the day. He was home. He was safe. Reez could feel the sweat cooling on his body in the frigid air, and a sound somewhere between a sob and a moan forced its way past his lips. Sensing the protective shell within him rising to the fore, he willed himself to calm down. Breathing deeply, his panic subsided, until he could sit up and swing his legs down from the cot in his room. Shivering, he pulled the woollen blanket from the bed and wrapped it around his shoulders. There would be no more sleep for him tonight.

Wincing as the familiar ache rippled through his left leg as he stood, he limped slowly down the smooth stone stairway and into the freezing galley. With trembling fingers, he struck the tinder box until the small pile of kindling caught and flames licked the wood already stacked in the stove. Ignoring his former Master's seat, Reez sat in his own chair and allowed the warmth of the small blaze to penetrate his frozen soul.

He couldn't start a fire for a long time, the terror of the previous summer still holding him in its grip, but as the winter cycle began, and the frost set in, he had forced himself to face his fear. Despite that, the range had gaped like an open maw around the tiny blaze, and even now he had to fight the urge to run and hide from the crackling flames. His gaze roved unseeing past the familiar shelves and cupboards holding the pots and pans for cooking and the food stores which were woefully lacking. His appetite was virtually non-existent, and he ate more because of habit than anything else. He knew he had lost weight; his face, gaunt and haunted, stared back at him in the looking glass if he caught sight of his reflection. His brown eyes were dulled with remembered horrors, and his dark hair hung limp and lifeless. He had lost his hair, and the fire had ravaged his face on one side. Even though the hair had grown, it was still not long enough to hide the grotesque scarring. He had tried to hide some of them under a beard, but the hairs refused to grow properly, and the result was thin and patchy. Nevertheless, the scruff remained, as he could see no point in taking a razor to it.

Water.

Reez stood with a sigh and grabbed the half full pitcher on the pitted and scratched wooden table in the centre of the room and filled a mug with the icy liquid. The part of him that was plant was usually silent, but when it had a need, it was very insistent.

In some ways, Reez acknowledged, it had forced him to live. While he could often ignore the demands of his stomach, a plant's simple yet constant cravings for nutrients and water were nigh impossible to resist. Its need for sunlight had forced Reez outside when he would otherwise have curled up in his room and slept, trying to find peace in oblivion despite the terrors that appeared to him as he slumbered.

As the moon waxed and waned and the sun rose and set, Reez had been drawn into a rhythm that was comforting and familiar. He ate and drank, finished the mindless chores that demanded nothing from him but effort. Every other day he would walk across the meadow where he would lie down, his skin bared, and soak up the daylight before returning home and burrowing back under the covers of his cot. All else was beyond him.

Returning to the relative warmth of the small fire burning steadily in the stove, Reez sipped his water and tried to purge the dreadful memories that had haunted his nightmare from his mind. The fire devouring and scorching. The stench of burning flesh and the bubble of fat. Wicton's face distorted in death and, above everything, Verrin laughing, always laughing.

As light streaked through the dusty windows, Reez stood painfully and made his way back to his room to dress, knowing he would need to make the most of the clear skies and satisfy his counterpart's need for renewed energy from the sun. Every task took much longer now, either because of the constant pain or his physical limitations, and his plant self was growing more insistent as he finally finished.

"Maybe I should give it a name," he grumbled to himself roughly, his voice harsh from disuse.

#

The trees whispered of her approach long before he felt her footsteps on the hard earth by the tower. When everyone else had given up, she had persisted, walking up to the door every morning before the inn opened for business with a basket of food, sitting on the step in silence and stillness, or wandering around the meadow for a little while before returning to the village, leaving the offerings of baked treats and ale behind. Even though he refused to open the door at her knock or acknowledge her presence in any way, the fact that she continued to care was a comfort and a balm to his tortured mind and he found he looked forward to her visits.

This morning, however, he had neglected to place the empty basket outside the door, as was his custom. Would she worry when she found it missing? He half hoped, half feared that she would seek him out as he lay in the meadow's grass. Something was moving within him, an urge to grow and spread himself. He didn't know whether it came from the plant element, reacting to the return of spring and the promise of new life, or if it was a need from deep within his soul.

There was silence for a while. He could feel the soft breeze flowing over his ravaged face and bared chest, and he took a deep breath of the cleansing air. Then he felt her tread the path around the tower and past the glass house. Attuned as he was to the subtle shifts in the plant life, he knew the moment she stepped into the meadow, bending the stalks of grass under her feet. She moved towards him. He sensed her feet falter, likely as she caught sight of him, before slowly carrying her onward, stopping a short distance away from his prone form.

His eyes closed against the bright light, Reez tried to imagine what she would see. What would disgust her the most, he wondered? Would it be his crippled leg, mercifully enclosed in the fabric of his trews? Maybe she would shy away from the scars and tracks marring his chest and abdomen? Or his seared arm, weakened and thin, lying by his side, his hand a painful claw? Perhaps it would be the grotesque mask on the left side of his face, skin red and puckered, pulling down his eye and mouth? Or would it be the way his body was luminescing green as his plant self soaked up the rays of the late winter sun? Schooling himself for either her look of horror or of pity, he opened his eyes and stared at her.

Destry stood transfixed, wisps of her blond hair dancing across her face as the breeze caught and lifted the stray tresses that had escaped her long braid. A shawl was draped across her shoulders and she was wearing a sky-blue dress which matched the colour of her eyes, eyes which were wide and focused on him. Her pale pink mouth had opened slightly as her gaze roamed across his body. Reez watched the emotions flash across her face; sadness, concern, curiosity and then something like wonder. It was nothing like the revulsion he expected. When she finally met his eyes and realised he was watching her, she jerked suddenly and flushed, her eyes darting away from him for a moment. He observed her swallow and lick her lips before turning back to him; her face composed once more.

I brought food, she signed.

Sitting up slowly, Reez reached for his tunic and pulled it up his damaged arm and over his head, wincing at the stab of pain in his shoulder. He wished he had brought his cloak so he could raise the hood and hide his deformed face. Reez stood awkwardly and faced her. He moved his fingers stiffly, trying to remember the patterns and shapes that had once come so easily to him.

Thank you.

She smiled swiftly, and it was like the sun peeking through the clouds on a dark, dismal day. Reez sighed deeply. He abruptly realised how much he had missed the companionship of others: friends, family, the chatter of the inn and the familiarity of the village. He kept himself away from such things because he knew nothing could ever be the same again. Truthfully, he was afraid of the reaction his face and figure would garner from the villagers. It was one thing to hold himself apart, but another matter entirely to be publicly shunned or even laughed at. He looked at Destry, who still beamed at him. She wasn't rejecting him. He could turn away now and go back to the tower, shut the door and close himself off from the world once more, or he could risk a little more and reach out to at least one other human being.

How are you? he asked carefully, his decision made.

Well, she replied before her fingers flew in a complicated weave that had him floundering. Reez held out his hand, and she stopped with a frown.

Slowly, he signed.

Even though she complied, there were still parts he didn't recognise. *I don't understand,* he admitted.

Why are you...?

He shook his head and repeated the pattern with a question. Destry thought for a moment before crouching down, pulling her shawl across her head.

Afraid? He asked.

Not afraid, she signed. She thought for a moment. Rising, she looked around before running to a stubby bush on the edge of the meadow and disappearing behind it.

"Hiding," Reez murmured to himself. When she returned, Reez could only shrug, knowing instinctively she wouldn't like the answer.

We will... again, an unfamiliar word. At his confused expression, she stood in front of him and turned, drawing an imaginary knife and swaying from side to side as if watching for an attack.

Reez swallowed. She was telling him that the villagers were ready to protect him against whatever had harmed him and killed Wicton. He nodded his understanding but didn't reply. Unwilling to let her see the depth of the emotions rising in him, he motioned her to walk back to the tower. He was relieved and strangely pleased when she not only matched his stride, but moved to his left side as if his disfigurement were unimportant.

Your family is worried, Destry signed hesitantly as they walked, as if she was anxious about his reaction. *Will you come down and see them?*

Reez felt guilty. Apart from a message to say that he had returned, and that Wicton was dead, he had refused to venture from the tower and had ignored all attempts by his family to speak face to face.

Perhaps, he hedged, unsure whether he wanted to risk a meeting. They had not parted on good terms, and although he regretted the words that had been said, he had not found the courage to confront them. A picture of Aydal's face bloody from Reez's fist flashed into his mind, swiftly followed by his sister, Amily's, anguish and his father's shock. He had been a blind fool that day, smarting from Nula's rejection of him and her preference for his eldest brother. Mere days later, his Master had voiced his own opinions, forcing Reez to re-evaluate his relationship and recognise that he had been selfish. Now he bore no ill will towards either of them, but they remained in ignorance of his change of heart.

As if she could read his mind, Destry signed. *They wish to be reconciled. They don't want you to hate them.*

They had reached the tower door, and Reez stopped. *I don't hate them,* he said with a frown. *You can tell them I have forgiven them.*

They should hear it from you, not me. You have the power to mend things and put right the wrongs.

But I am not the man they remember, he argued. *Look at me. They don't need to see this.* He gestured to himself and turned away.

Destry reached out as if to touch his cheek. He flinched, and she withdrew her hand. Instead, she moved around, so he had to look at her again. *You are still Reez,* Destry pointed out. *That will never change. When they feared for you, not knowing whether you were coming back, it broke their hearts. It was such a relief to have you return. They love you, not your body or your face.*

Reez looked down the lane that led towards the village. Could he have a little of his old life back? He missed his family, he realised with a pang. The easy banter he had enjoyed with Aydal. Amily's laughter. Damino's quiet encouragements and his father's wise words. Surely it was worth venturing out to repair the damage that had been done and restore his relationship with them? Before bending down to grab the ladened basket that Destry had left on the top step, Reez made a sudden decision and turned to her. *Will you wait?* he asked.

She smiled knowingly and nodded, sitting down and leaning her back against the rough stones of the tower as she had done so often before. Pushing open the heavy door, Reez limped inside, allowing the door to close with a soft thud. He made his way through to the galley and put the heavy basket on the table. Lifting the cloth, he peered inside; fresh bread, meat, cheese, goat's milk and preserves nestled inside, along with a few nips and taters and a scroll of parchment. Breaking the seal, Reez unrolled the missive from the Margrave. Apparently, the farmers were anxious. The winter cycle was almost over, and spring planting would soon be upon them. They needed reassurance that Reez would bless the ground as Wicton had been wont to do. Would he come?

Reez let the parchment fall and stared into the cold range, the small fire long burnt to ashes. There had been no requests or petitions in the long winter cycle, and Reez had almost begun to believe that the world outside didn't exist for him anymore. Now that world was calling to him and he didn't know whether he could answer. There was no-one to guide and mentor him, no-one to prepare him for the role that he had only imagined in some far-off future. He wasn't a Master and would never be one. He was alone and ill-equipped to take on the mantle that Wicton had worn so well.

Yet, despite that, Reez felt the responsibility bearing down on him and realised not only had he been hiding from the person who he now considered his enemy, but he had been avoiding the truth of his situation. No matter how incapable he felt, he was the only person who could ever step into Wicton's shoes and continue to serve the people of Fiora province. As much as he would like to stay within the confines of the sturdy stone walls surrounding him, he knew it was time for him to emerge from the darkness that had gripped him and re-enter the land of the living. The thought of it filled him with dread.

He had never been crippled by such doubt and self-loathing before. Learning and magic had come easily to him, as if he had been born for it but had just forgotten for a time. Even when he had made some of the biggest mistakes of his life, he had bounced back with the knowledge that he was wiser for having made them. When Wicton had given him tasks to do, or problems to solve, it had never entered Reez's head that he might fail. Now he faced the awful possibility that he would be proved a fraud and be completely humiliated. Reez slumped into his chair and held his head in his hands, his breathing laboured as his mind filled with images of the villagers when they realised he couldn't help them. Would they just turn away or would they be angry? The only reason he was here was because of Wicton's foresight. His diligent study and quick thinking had saved Reez, even as Verrin's malice drained Wicton's life from him to fuel his magic.

As if he were next to him, Reez suddenly heard his Master's voice in his mind. "Everything you need is in the vault. When the time comes for me to leave, you will have the wisdom of a hundred Masters to turn to." Wicton hadn't left him without help and guidance. He had promised Reez that all the information and instructions he would require were waiting for him in the depository beneath him. All he had to do was look for it.

Feeling bolstered by the knowledge, Reez took a deep breath and stood. With a new determination, he donned his cloak and pulled the hood over his head. Taking the empty basket with him, he opened the door and stepped outside.

Chapter Two

Reez paused at the familiar door, wracked with memories of his last visit. He had been full of anger, hurt, and nursing feelings of betrayal. Last time he had entered this house, he had said and done things which he now sincerely regretted. He went to open the door, then stopped. This hadn't been his home for a long time, having left to start his apprenticeship with Wicton eleven summers ago, yet he had never once doubted that his presence would be welcome. Destry's comments had given him hope that his family would be willing to meet with him, but apprehension still filled him. He wished Destry had stayed with him, but she had continued back down to the village after giving him a smile of encouragement and a small push on his back, leaving him to face this task alone. He almost turned back, but this new burgeoning need to reconnect outweighed his fear of rejection. Gathering his courage, he knocked and waited, his heart thumping wildly in his chest.

He glanced at the small front garden, once lovingly tended by his mother. The flowering shrubs were wild and overgrown, choking the smaller plants. Her beloved rosa bush had been sorely neglected and Reez decided that, no matter what the outcome of this day, he would return to care for it, even if he had to wait until nightfall to avoid any awkward encounters.

He heard slow footsteps within and took a deep breath as the latch lifted and the door opened with a creak. As his father's face appeared, Reez could see that he had aged before his time. His dark hair was lined with grey. Deep grooves of sorrow etched his visage, and his once strong back stooped as if he carried heavy loads that bore him down. Beran's eyes opened wide with surprise when he saw who was standing before him. Instinctively, Reez pulled his hood down lower over his face to hide himself.

"Son," his father said, his voice breaking as his breath hitched with emotion.

"Hello, Da. May I come in?" Reez asked tentatively.

"Of course," Beran said, hurriedly pulling the door wider to allow Reez to pass. They moved into the parlour where a fire blazed, cheerfully heating the room from the last of the winter's chill. The small almira stood in the corner holding the crockery for the household and Reez knew the large ornate chest next to it held linens for the beds. Several padded chairs were arranged around the hearth, some displaying cushions his mother and sister had embroidered. Familiar colourful tapestries lined the walls, providing extra warmth, transforming the room into a welcoming, comfortable place. The table underneath the small window was littered with metals and tools, evidence that Amily remained in residence, still creating her jewellery. Reez moved the chair his father indicated further back from the hearth and the fierceness of the blaze before sitting across from him.

"Where are the others?" Reez ventured.

"Damino has taken permanent residence with Moron now," Beran began. As apprentice to the apothecary, his brother most likely found it simpler to live in the same place that he worked. "Aydal and Amily are out in the fields preparing them for the spring planting."

"You're not with them," Reez stated. "Are you ill?"

Beran shrugged. "I have no heart for it," he said shortly.

Reez tentatively lowered the hood of his cloak, revealing his face to his father for the first time, and winced when he heard Beran's indrawn breath.

"What happened?" Beran asked, scooting forward in his chair to look closer. Reez turned slightly to hide his left side further.

"I can't speak of it yet," he admitted. "It is too raw. I barely survived after being attacked." He thought of his long recovery wrapped in the willow roots' embrace and being cared for by the earth and the deep magic underneath the clearing. "Wicton's last thoughts were to protect me. Without him, I would have died with the others." Whatever the concoction was that Wicton had brewed had not only shielded him from Verrin's magic, but had also permanently altered him. Now he was a conglomeration of human, plant and mineral, and he had no idea what that meant for him in the long term.

"Others?"

"All the Masters are gone. Paiter," Reez paused as sorrow gripped his heart. "Paiter too. Only Verrin, Malander's apprentice, walked out of there unscathed. He betrayed us and murdered them all."

"All gone?" Beran gasped in horror. "What is to become of us?"

"That is one reason I have come," Reez said. "I had a missive from the Margrave wanting to know whether I would bless the spring planting. I know I am not a Master, but Wicton told me he left instructions about his responsibilities for me to follow. If Fiora province will have me, I will try to make up for Wicton's loss."

"I'm sure they will welcome you with open arms," Beran said with relief. "If it is true, we are fortunate to have you to take his place."

"Would you treat with the Margrave for me?" Reez asked, pointing at his face. "I can't face meeting with the council. I'm not yet ready to be widely seen."

"Of course I will," Beran said, his shoulders rising slightly. He reached across and laid a hand on Reez's arm. "Does it hurt, son?"

"A little," Reez admitted, not wanting to worry his

father further. "Mostly it itches and aches. I have nightmares," he said, swallowing loudly, "and I cannot tolerate being close to fire. It brings back memories that haunt me."

Beran glanced towards the hearth and nodded slowly. "Scars like that go deep beneath the skin and into the heart. You may never be entirely free of them." The two men sat in silence for a while, deep in their own thoughts.

"Tell me about the family." Reez ventured, breaking the quiet. "I have heard no news. How are Aydal and Nula? I imagine they are handfasted by now."

Beran looked at Reez and shook his head. "They both felt guilty after you left. It was in their minds to clear things up with you when you returned. When you didn't return home, neither of them felt at ease and stopped seeing each other for a while. As time passed, we feared you were..." he swallowed audibly. "Aydal was tortured with remorse and blamed himself for hurting you. He pushed Nula away, saying he didn't deserve to be with her. They barely speak, although I see them watching each other when we go to the inn. They are both dreadfully unhappy."

"But I didn't die, and I've been back home for a while now." Reez pointed out.

"Injured and secluded," Beran replied. "In some ways, it has only hardened Aydal's belief that he should stay away. I think he torments himself, thinking that maybe he was the cause; that you would have been alert and watchful if he hadn't hurt you that day." He gestured to Reez's face. "Their scars may not show like yours, but in their own way, they both bear wounds that run as deep as your own."

"What about Amily? Why is she still here? She seemed excited at the thought of apprenticing to the jeweller I met in Minra province."

"Losing you devastated the family," Beran said in a low voice. "We were all adrift and barely able to function. I couldn't bear to let her go. Besides, she was adamant she didn't want to leave us when we were so desolate. To be honest, I don't know what we would have done without her. She has been the twine binding us together."

"I'm sorry," Reez said softly. "I thought by keeping my distance I was being kind to you, but it didn't help at all, did it?"

"You're here now, son. That's all that matters."

"And you? It seems to me as if you have been as affected as everyone else."

Beran sighed and shrugged his shoulders. "I felt useless. I couldn't fix the hurts and I couldn't bring you back. I felt more lost than when I stood over your mother's resting place. At least then I understood what I needed to do. My responsibilities were clear. Your Ma would have counselled you all, but nothing I said or did helped. As a father, you want to guide and protect your children, even when they are grown, but I was useless. It broke my heart, in truth."

Reez reached across and held his father's hand. "Perhaps between us we can make sure things get better. After all, it's an auspicious time of the cycle, with new beginnings and growth after the long sleep of winter. It's a time for life to flourish and thrive. I'm sorry. I should have visited a long time ago, but I was too wrapped up in my own sorrows and sufferings. I didn't think about what it was like for you. My only thoughts, when I had them, were that you would hate me or despise my face."

"Never," Beran said fiercely. "You are my son. Nothing in all creation would stop me from loving you and wanting the best for you. Perhaps I should have remained outside your door and insisted you see me. It was my responsibility to be there for you."

"I should have had more faith in you," Reez replied. "I ought to have known you would never turn me away."

"All that is in the past, son. I'm a fervent believer that we can fix anything with a bit of effort." He patted Reez's hand and smiled. "Let me make a brew, and we can speak more."

While Beran went into the galley, Reez sat and allowed himself to get lost in memories of his childhood. In every one, Aydal was a constant presence, teasing, playing, teaching, and protecting him. His heart constricted at the thought of his lively, carefree brother punishing himself unfairly for so long. He would need to correct the wrong as soon as possible.

When Beran returned, the two of them spoke of more trivial things as they sipped a hot drink. As Beran apprised him of the gossip from the village, Reez relaxed. Apparently Amily was still a fount of knowledge about the minutiae of village life and kept the family apprised of everything that was happening. It was heartening to hear familiar names, and the ordinary complaints and celebrations that made up the day-to-day life of the village. He even laughed loudly as Beran related how

Tazar's grandson had complained about digging up the taters. When they insisted he help with the back-breaking work, he had grumbled that they shouldn't have bothered burying them in the first place.

Eventually, Reez winced and rubbed his leg as his wasted muscles cramped. "I should go back," he decided. "The walk down is the most I have done since getting back. My body isn't used to such activity. It may take me a while to get back up the hill."

"I could find a wagon in the village…"

"No. It's time I worked on recovering what strength I can."

"You know, we had a fire in Nain's barn ten or so cycles ago. Youngsters thinking to keep warm whilst impressing their girls. Most of his winter wheat was destroyed, and he was burnt some trying to save it. Wicton gave him an ointment to put on his arms to soothe the wounds and help with healing. Maybe he wrote it down somewhere."

"I'll look," Reez said. They both walked to the door. Reez was pleased to see that his father's spirit seemed lighter and his frame a little taller. "Da…" Reez said, pausing for a moment to take a breath. "When he returns, would you ask Aydal if he will visit me tomorrow at the tower? I think it is long past time we spoke."

"Of course." Beran pulled his youngest son in close, holding him carefully, as if afraid his touch would hurt him. "It's good to have you back. You'll come again, won't you?"

"Now that I know I am welcome, I would like to visit

often." Reez wrapped his right arm around his father, noticing how he, too, had lost weight. He was not the only one in need of healing. With a nod, he moved out of his father's embrace and limped out of the door to begin his journey home. He knew his father stood watching him until he finally turned the corner and disappeared from sight.

#

The light was fading when Reez finally pushed open the heavy wooden door and dragged himself into the cold tower. He looked at his meagre supply of firewood and groaned. He needed to source some more if he wanted to keep warm. His store of firestones was low too, and he had never sent word to the Margrave requesting that it be restocked. He made a mental note to take an inventory in the morning and make a list of his needs. Despite the ache in his body and the chill of the air, Reez felt content as he pottered around the galley. For the first time, his heart had eased, and he felt a peace within. Feeling stronger, he decided to tackle one more barrier while he had the courage to spare.

#

After eating a frugal meal, Reez tentatively lit a lantern and used it to light his way up the worn, winding steps, stopping outside the study door. He hadn't been inside since returning home, preferring to stay in his own room or spend the long evenings down in the galley. His hand shook slightly as he grasped the handle and turned it before stepping inside.

His breath caught in his throat as he choked back the sudden tears that threatened to overwhelm him. Wicton's papers littered the desk alongside pots containing the brown, withered remains of plants long dead. All the glass boxes lay dark and silent, devoid of life. Several books were piled up on a small table within easy reach of the fireside chairs. Logs lay ready in the hearth for the fire his Master would never light. Reez wandered over and reached for a taper on the stone mantle above the hearth and set it to the kindling. As the flames grew and caught, dancing in the grate, Reez sank into his old chair and looked over to where Wicton would have sat.

"I miss you so much," he said to the silence. "I don't know how to carry on without you." Reez closed his eyes and imagined his old Master leaning back from warming his hands by the fire to give him his attention, his green eyes alight with merriment. He missed having his Master to talk to, but here it was as if Wicton was close by, listening to his apprentice talk about his day, or share his worries and frustrations. Reez spoke his thoughts aloud.

"I'm so afraid all the time," Reez continued. "Scared of living in case I am ridiculed and rejected. Scared of dying as I relive the fire every night. I'm worried I'll fail these people who are looking to me to restore their hope. I'm terrified that Verrin will come for me if he finds out I survived," he admitted in a small voice. Voicing that fear aloud made it seem even more real. Perhaps that was the main reason he had remained hidden inside the tower for so long. The shade of Wicton seemed to nod at him, encouraging him to explore these fresh revelations. When he recalled that dreadful day, he had focused on the events themselves, but as he forced his mind to replay it over, there was one thing that stood out. Verrin had incapacitated all three Masters before they could stop him, and had used them to fuel his magic as he destroyed Malander and tortured Paiter until he died writhing in agony, but he had all but ignored Reez.

"I know, I know, he doesn't see me as a threat," Reez responded as he imagined a small smile on Wicton's face. "At least that was a success." Although it had chafed, Reez had pretended to be ignorant, and sometimes even stupid, in order to dissuade Verrin from unearthing the secrets of green magic. "The fear remains, though." He imagined Wicton's brow furrowing in frustration. "I didn't say any of it made any sense," he said defensively. The fire crackled loudly in the hearth, punctuating the quiet of the room, and Reez jumped. "See! I'm a mess. How can I serve these people when I start at my own shadow?" His eyes filled with tears and his breath hitched. He watched the flames leaping in the hearth for a while, forcing himself not to retreat from the heat that washed over him, struggling to slow his breathing and heartbeat down. Eventually, he felt in control once more.

"I know what you would say. You would tell me to do my best and face my fears, wouldn't you?" He sighed. "It sounds a straightforward thing to accomplish, but from where I'm sitting, it all looks terrifying. Where am I supposed to start?" He chuckled then, as he remembered how Wicton would merely gaze at him, his eyebrows lifted, waiting for him to figure things out on his own. "Of course," he conceded with a crooked smile. "I'd better sleep on it then."

Reez allowed the fire to die down before taking the

lantern and making his way up the stairs to his own room. Wrapping himself in a blanket, he crawled under the counterpane on the cot and closed his eyes, his breathing slowing as he succumbed to the exhaustion of mind and body.

For the first time since the horrific events at the Tower of the Mages, he slept soundly until morning.

Chapter Three

Reez looked around at the devastation in the glass house, and his heart sank. The carefully nurtured plants of the previous cycle were gone. Brown, dried leaves littered the floor, and the plethora of pots were either empty or held dead stalks. Any life growing there originated from the weeds encroaching through the door or blown in by the wind. It was a sad reflection of his own life. Everything he'd ever thought important seemed dead or lost to him. Worries and memories overwhelmed the rest.

"What would Wicton tell you to do?" he asked himself. He smiled as the memory resurfaced. That was a simple question to answer.

#

"Welcome to the glass house," Wicton said as he led his new apprentice through the door. Reez looked round at the large space in wonder. Tables and shelves lined either side, all full of pots and trays of different shapes and sizes. Underneath were bags of dirt, tools, and more pots stacked in neat piles.

"The glass allows sunlight to reach the plants," Wicton continued, "yet shelters them from the elements outside, protecting them from winds and frost. We can grow things here that wouldn't survive outside. We can also grow seedlings earlier so that they are ready to be transplanted in the garden when the seasons change. From now on, you'll be in charge. I leave the care of all the plants in your hands. Remember to water them every day, because the rain cannot reach them in here, and you will need to decide whether to ventilate the glass house if the air grows too hot. You also need to keep it clean and tidy and check all the plants to make sure they remain free from blight. Do you think you can manage it?"

Reez had nodded eagerly, keen to impress his new Master. When the first fungus growth took hold, he was dismayed, but instead of berating him, Wicton had taught him the proper way of watering the plants and keeping them moist but not wet. His favourite plants by far were the fragrant orchids. Wicton was growing several of them, all of which had their own scent; lemon, jasmine and even cinnamon that reminded him of the raisin buns his mother baked occasionally. The warmth of the glass house lured him in often until it became his favourite place to sit and work.

#

Letting the memory fade, Reez sighed as he wandered over to where the precious flowers had stood. He had killed them once before when he was learning how to use magic, inadvertently draining them along with the rest of the plants as he worked to grow a daisy. Then Wicton had merely smiled and handed Reez some seeds. It had taken many moons before the initial shoots broke through the covering of earth, and long cycles until the flowers appeared, but eventually he had replaced the orchids. Now, once again, they were all gone.

For the rest of the morning he busied himself despite the constant pain in his limbs from his injuries and the long moons of inactivity, clearing the dead foliage, cleaning the pots and the glass, sweeping the benches and the floor and throwing out the earth. Only one plant had survived the many moons of neglect, and that barely. Somehow, the apprentice plant still retained some life, although most of its leaves had dropped and the soil was barren and dry. After re-potting it and soaking it with water, Reez had used his skills to encourage the plant to draw up the life-giving liquid and nutrients before allowing it to recover on its own. It seemed wrong to force too much upon it at once. Like him, it needed time to rest and heal before taking on the vigorous task of growth again.

He was planting the last orchid seeds when a familiar voice interrupted him.

"You wanted to see me."

Reez put down the trowel and turned slowly around,

careful to keep his injuries shadowed. Aydal stood in the doorway, his face lined and pale. His ready smile was absent, and he stood with his arms crossed over his chest as if holding himself together. The brothers watched each other warily, and Reez's heart dropped. Gone was the easy-going boy who had taught Reez to embrace life joyfully. Aydal was guarded and serious, unsure how to act around the baby brother who had once adored and worshipped him. Reez pointed to two stools in the corner of the glass house, and Aydal sat. Reez limped over to join him, careful to keep his disfigurement turned away, but Aydal saw it anyway. Reez noticed him wincing and bunching his fists tightly at the sight of the drooping eye and puckered cheek. He stared over Reez's shoulder; his jaw clenched hard. Reez saw a muscle tic under his left eye, which was bruised and black. He frowned and glanced down at Aydal's hands. He could see cuts and bruises on the knuckles.

"What happened to you?" he asked. "Have you been fighting?"

"It's nothing," Aydal said, waving his hand dismissively. "Just a minor disagreement."

"About what?"

"Do you really want to talk about insignificant matters? Because I have more important things to say."

"You're right. I'm sorry." He took a deep breath. "I want to apologise to you," Reez began slowly. "My last words to you were unkind and spoken in anger."

"I deserved it," Aydal replied tersely. "I was wrong. I shouldn't have…"

"No, you were right," Reez interrupted. "I was blind and stupid. I couldn't see the reality because I was so focused on my dreams. Nula wasn't happy, but I refused to listen. In fact, that day I had gone to the inn expecting her to be full of remorse and eager to continue our relationship. Not once did it occur to me, she might not agree with my plans, or that hers were just as important. She deserves much better than that. She deserves you."

Aydal shook his head. "She's yours, Reez. I never should have come between you."

"Nula isn't my property. She should decide who she wants to be with. It's time I listened, really listened, to what she has to say." Aydal didn't reply, but Reez could see that he was absorbing his comments. "I've done a lot of reflecting over the past few moons," Reez continued. "When I thought my life was ending, all I could think about was our last meeting. Facing your own mortality suddenly puts everything into perspective, and you realise what is really important in life. I hurt you, and for that, I am truly sorry."

"I hurt you first," Aydal said.

"Only my pride," Reez admitted, "not my heart."

"But you'd been walking out with Nula for many cycles. You loved her."

"I think I loved the idea of having a wife waiting for me and it fitted into the perfect plans I had imagined for my life. To be honest, I don't believe I really knew Nula all that well. I certainly didn't want to factor in her dreams and wishes because it would upset my orderly schedule. Wicton even advised me as we travelled to the triumvirate that we weren't suited to each other. He could see much more than I."

"He was a wise man and will be sorely missed," Aydal said softly. "Funny, but I never imagined that we would ever be without him. I thought he would live forever. Even though he grew older, he never seemed to age, if you know what I mean. He still kept a twinkle in his eye, especially when he looked at you and made you feel as if he could guess all your deepest secrets."

They both sat in silence for a while, their thoughts full of memories. "I miss you, Aydal. I miss laughing with you and talking to you. There should be no barriers between us."

Aydal took a deep, ragged breath and swallowed. "I miss you too, Weet," he said shakily.

Reez smiled at the use of his old nickname. Aydal rubbed his palms over the soft material of his trews and looked around the glass house. "So," he ventured, his voice stronger, "you're the Master now."

Reez shook his head. "I haven't earned that title yet, but I mean to work hard to provide for the village the way Wicton did. He told me all the information I needed was here, so if I don't know the answers immediately, I can search in the archives."

"You'll do fine," Aydal assured him. "We were desperately worried when you were both gone for so long. We knew things were bad when neither of you appeared for the celebration. A Master would never miss such an important ceremony in the past. The villagers will be relieved to know you will continue to serve us, like Wicton did."

Reez nodded. "I returned too late for the ceremony, but I could bless the seed, though no-one saw me."

Aydal let out a huff of breath. "It'll be a relief to the villagers to hear that. It didn't seem right to plant without the blessing." He paused for a moment. "Da said that another apprentice attacked you," Aydal said, gesturing vaguely at Reez's face. "Do you think… I mean, will he come for you here? To hurt you again?"

Reez paused before replying. "It is one of my biggest fears," he admitted in a low voice. "It plagues me at night, but in truth, I don't think he will. There is nothing here for him. He doesn't even see me as an equal, let alone a threat. I should be safe enough."

Aydal nodded fiercely. "Well, if he tries, he'll soon find himself on the wrong end of a pitchfork. I suppose its best if he stays away. I would hate to add murder to my list of shortcomings."

Reez grinned wryly. "Always ready to defend me. I'm glad you are on my side."

"I wouldn't be anywhere else," Aydal replied. "If I'd been with you, I would have stopped him."

"You wouldn't have stood a chance against him," Reez admonished bitterly. "He bested three Masters without difficulty. You would have just been another source to fuel his hate."

"Is he that powerful, then?" Aydal asked, his face pale.

"He draws on living things to maintain his power,"

Reez explained. "He has no compunction in using a man and draining him dry to suit his own purposes."

"Then should he choose to turn on us, he can't be stopped?"

"I have no idea," Reez admitted, "and the only people who might have tried are dead."

Reez watched as Aydal struggled with these revelations. Supremely confident, his brother had never come across a situation where he felt helpless or ill-equipped. He didn't know what it felt like to fear for his life and he was finding it hard to imagine himself defenceless and weak.

"Honestly, I don't think you need to be anxious," Reez said. He took a deep breath and let it out slowly, feeling the truth of the words deep inside him. Verrin was as far away from Maston as was possible without crossing the Endless Sea. He would never journey through all of Bestra and Fiora provinces just to find Reez.

Aydal nodded and smiled before glancing up at the sky. "I ought to go back," he said wistfully. "The fields need preparing, and I still have a great deal of work to do."

"I'm glad you came."

"Me too." They both stood, and Aydal frowned as he watched Reez limp to the glass house door. "It's a shame you've nearly finished that wall," he mused.

"Why?"

"You need to build your muscles back up again."

"I suppose…"

"I could help," Aydal continued, "if you want, that is."

Reez shook his head. "As much as I might wish to be stronger, if I exert myself too much, the skin splits and bleeds," he admitted. "Getting back home was difficult." Aydal winced. "One step at a time, eh?"

"Of course." Aydal had started across the grass towards the lane when he span round and clicked his fingers, his eyes lighting up for the first time. "Before I disappear, you ought to be aware that Amily is very upset that she couldn't come with me today."

Reez groaned. "That's all I need," he groused.

"Take my advice and meet with her soon. It will be worse the longer you leave it."

"Then you'd better ask her if she'll come up tomorrow. I'll find something to stuff in my ears beforehand, so the shrieking doesn't deafen me."

The brothers clasped arms, and Aydal grinned. "I wish I could watch her welcome you home, Weet," he said. "I would pay good coin to witness it."

Reez rolled his eyes. "I suppose I should be grateful that this place is so isolated. It wouldn't do for the villagers to witness their potential new Master being castigated by his little sister."

"I doubt it'll be the last time," Aydal replied as he began to walk back to the village. He looked back once and gave a jaunty wave before disappearing down the lane.

#

Reez shivered and pulled the long, heavy cloak tighter around his body to ward off the bitter wind. A door slammed and several men left the inn, laughing together. He moved further around the trunk of the old tree to better shield himself. As the men neared, he could hear them talking.

"Don't be ridiculous. You make it sound like we've been cursed."

"Mayhap we have. I heard he's nought but a shade, not a true man at all."

"Man?" another scoffed. "He's just a boy, and not fully trained at that. What can he do for us?"

"Master Wicton wouldn't leave us without help," the first man insisted.

"Well, perhaps he didn't have no choice. Maybe it was him killed Wicton."

"Shut up, Fane. You've already got one bloody nose from running your mouth off."

"That Basta jumped me. He took me by surprise."

"The only surprise was that he kept his temper that long,"chuckled one of them. "We all know he's hotter than hay in a bonfire these days. It's not wise to rile him like that."

The men wandered further out of earshot and Reez slumped against the tree, his head bowed. Aydal had been fighting over him. He wondered what else the villagers were saying and how far-reaching the rumours were. Did they really believe him capable of murder? His throat felt thick, and he rubbed his chest as he tried to keep his breathing steady. He pushed away from the tree, suddenly desperate to return to the safety of his tower, but stopped after only two steps. Was this how he wanted to live? To cower away from everyone? What would his Master say if he could see him? A door opened, and he heard men wishing each other a pleasant evening as they made their way back home. He pressed his back against the tree as hot tears streamed down his face. Verrin had taken his Master, and had almost killed him. Was Reez going to allow him to destroy the rest of his life, too?

#

Eventually, the lights finally dimmed, and the last patrons drifted away. He heard the back door open and hurried towards it as Destry beckoned him inside. He made straight for the hearth to warm himself by the banked fire. Destry moved to stand next to him.

Nula will be here soon, she signed.

Thank you.

She hesitated for a moment. *Are you here for her?*

Reez made the sign for a question.

Like before. Do you want to walk out with her again?

He shook his head. *No. She doesn't want me, especially now. I'm just here to talk.*

Destry nodded and huffed out a breath. She glanced up at his face as if there was more she wanted to say, but eventually turned and left through the door into the taproom.

It seemed like an age before Nula finally appeared, and Reez was thankful for the dim light that hid his features under the cowl of his cloak. He watched as she slowly crossed the room to stand on the far side of the hearth, keeping her gaze down as if afraid to look directly at him. Reez could see that she was miserable. Her face was drawn and pinched and his heart clenched at the sorrow he had caused.

"How have you been, Nula?" he asked softly.

"Well," she replied.

"I met with Aydal today,"

"You did?" she asked, looking at him for the first time. "How is he?"

"He's been better, I warrant. He's been fighting."

Nula's lips thinned, and she crossed her arms. "If I had been a man, I would have joined him," she said tersely.

"Will you tell me what happened?"

She stayed silent for a moment before glancing at his face again. "No."

Reez sighed. "It's about me, isn't it? He's doing it for me. Because of the rumours." Nula looked away. "You should tell him to stop."

Nula glared up at him and pointed her finger at his chest. "No, you need to…" she stopped and covered her face with her hands.

"I need to what?" Reez asked quietly. She shook her head. "Nula, I know I have shown little inclination to listen to you in the past, but I am willing now. You have something on your mind. Tell me what it is."

She wrapped her arms around her body and faced the hearth. There was enough light from the embers to see the emotions racing across her face. "The villagers need to see you. They need to hear you tell them exactly what happened, not just vague reports and made up stories. They need the truth."

"The truth," Reez said scornfully.

"Surely that would be better than lies and half-truths?"

Reez grabbed his hood and pulled it back with a jerk. Nula gasped and took a step back, her mouth wide and her eyes full of horror as she stared at his ravaged face.

"Is this what they want to be confronted with when they wander the lanes or walk into the inn?" Reez spat. "Can you imagine the screams and the fear as I come into the village? I can. It's what haunts my dreams at night. It's better that I stay away."

Nula swallowed and took a deep breath before moving closer once more. Reez flinched as she laid a hand on his chest. "It is a shock, I admit. Even after Destry had told me. I'm sure it will prove difficult for people to begin with. Perhaps some may be afeared in the beginning, but they will become accustomed to it, to you. Think about it."

He shifted slightly to better hide his disfigurement and nodded. He went to pull his hood back up, but Nula caught his arm. "No, leave it," she whispered with a small smile.

Reez looked at her. "I'm sorry for scaring you."

She shook her head. "That's all right. I get that you're afraid of people's reactions. Perhaps be a little less dramatic when you meet the rest of them, though."

Reez chuckled. "Point taken." He took a deep breath. "There was a reason I wanted to talk with you," he continued. "I came to give you and Aydal my blessing. He'll prove a more attentive husband than I could ever be. He loves you dearly and misses you. I know you miss him, too."

"Thank you," Nula said, her eyes shining with unshed

tears.

"I'm sorry for hurting you and not listening to you. I was so full of my own plans that I didn't stop to think that you had dreams of your own," he admitted.

"No," she said firmly. "I share the blame. All my friends envied me for being with you. It made me feel good to be seen on your arm. I should have been firmer when I realised it was no longer enough; that I wanted more than you could give me."

Reez sighed. "Can we be friends?" he asked.

"Of course."

"Can I ask one boon of you?"

"Anything."

"When you and Aydal have your first child, will you name it after me?"

"No!" she whispered fiercely. "I already have the names picked out."

"You have?" Reez said, realising it was yet another thing he was ignorant of. "I'll just have to petition Aydal, then. He loves me enough."

"Don't you dare," she said with a grin.

"I'll have time. I'm sure I can wear one of you down. You know, I am famed for my persistence."

Nula lifted her hand and laid it on his arm. "Are you sure?" she asked tentatively.

Reez knew she was referring to her being with his brother. "In my mind, I have pictured you together these past six moons," he said. "It was a surprise to me to learn you had not held a ceremony. I am content. All you need to do is send him one of your saucy looks, and he'll be wilting at your feet, and I shall be there to laugh at his poor protestations of love."

"Perhaps you will lose your own heart one day," she said with a soft smile.

Reez shrugged. "I'm too busy for romantic dreams, even if there were someone who could stand to look at me without running in horror. I have much to learn over the next few cycles if I am to assume Wicton's position in the village."

Nula glanced towards the door, which led back out to the taproom. "Love may not be as far away as you believe."

"That remains to be seen. As it is, I should return home before I am tempted to stay in front of your warm fire."

"Thank you for coming, Reez," Nula said, "and for your blessing."

Reez nodded and went to the door. "Be happy, Nula," he whispered. He pulled up his hood and slipped out into the chilly night. As he limped back to the tower, he smiled, his heart lighter and his mind clearer. Making peace with those he loved was strangely liberating, as if someone had removed a weight from his shoulders that he hadn't known he was carrying. Now, instead of being surrounded by darkness, he could see the dawn appearing. He huffed out a breath. Nula was right. He needed to allow the villagers to see him, and the Council deserved more than a short missive about Wicton's final day. His days of hiding were over, but instead of the crushing fear of earlier, he sensed a small flicker of hope. He allowed the feeling to warm his heart, even as he wrapped his cloak tighter against the wind. Spring was on its way.

Chapter Four

Reez pulled the notebook towards him and squinted. Wicton's normally neat penmanship was woefully lacking. Instead, the letters were scrawled across the page almost illegibly, with lines crossed out and rewritten in a terrible hurry. It was going to be a concerted effort to decipher it fully, but Reez recognised enough to know this was the research Wicton had been working on in order to discover a way to combat a possible threat from Verrin.

Using the sea plants as his base, he had been experimenting with their attributes, trying to determine how they could display all three disciplines in one form. It seemed he had hoped the concoction he had derived would enable them to call upon the properties for themselves, masking their animal nature and allowing them time to counter an attack. Although he had anticipated the shielding qualities of both mineral and plant, it seemed unlikely that he had intended a fusion into the existing host. Instead of a temporary solution, Reez now bore within himself a permanent synthesis of all three magic traits. Controlling the symbiotic relationship and calling them up at will was a skill Reez was still refining.

He had managed to get the plant side of himself worked out. When its basic needs were satisfied, it was content to lie dormant. By simulating a hunger for sunlight or water, Reez could tempt the plant to the fore, causing his skin to glow green and masking his animal nature. His mineral self was harder to control. Until now, it would only rouse when threatened, and Reez had jerked awake often at night, his lungs burning with the need for air as the hard shell arose to protect him. He remembered how he had struggled as Wicton wove the magic, desperate to take a breath and believing he was going to die, not understanding what was happening to him. Somehow, he had to utilise it without it constricting his organs so that he could function normally within its guard.

Reez closed the book, labelled it and walked over to one of the far shelves. Sliding it into its new place, he turned and stared at the vault. Light flickered across the myriad tomes lining the walls as the small flames danced in the lanterns set on surfaces throughout the room. He had tidied the tower and vault. Wicton's books had been collected from the rooms above and replaced on the shelves, and Reez had cleared the tables of all evidence of his Master's project. The glass box and its contents had been removed, and the floor swept. Nothing remained to grab his attention, and his delaying tactics had reached an end.

"Time to face my responsibilities," he whispered to himself.

After adding a new card to the filing system, Reez searched it for the manuscripts that would explain in more detail what his duties as Master would entail. He smiled when he found the index card written in Wicton's hand. *Duties and Responsibilities of a Master.* There was a long list of references, but Wicton had marked a few titles with an asterisk and the word 'important'. It was a good place to start, Reez decided, and he wandered off to collect the first book.

A good while later, he sighed and groaned, aching after remaining hunched over the table for so long. There were rituals to perform, rites to observe, festivals to mark and feasts to attend. Blight, fungus and a myriad other problems needed to be controlled or eradicated; seeds and bulbs were to be infused with magic and crops strengthened. Rotation of produce and yield were to be monitored and balanced so the province could grow enough for the populace of Zelannor without depleting the soil, but not too much that there was a waste of foodstuff or a reduction in nutrients. Any new plant specimens had to be painstakingly studied to ensure they were not a threat to those already established and to discover their properties. An entire section of the library was comprised of books about poisons and how to counter them if ingested.

Pushing aside the book before him, listing the division of land rights, Reez decided to finish for the day. The left side of his body protested as he tried to stand, pain arcing down his neck, arm, and leg. He stumbled slightly and, leaning back, steadied himself with his right hand on the case behind him. After regaining his balance, he looked down at the dark cabinet that had once caused him many sleepless nights and such anguished shame. Reez stroked the top of it almost affectionately. He had learnt long ago to put it out of his mind and it no longer featured in his thoughts or dreams. He recalled Wicton's face when he had discovered Reez in the middle of the night trying to open it, a study in controlled anger, so different from the kind, patient visage that he usually saw. By disobeying his Master and attempting to access the forbidden knowledge, Reez had caused a rift between them that had taken a long time to fully heal. Wicton had never given him permission to study the contents of the cabinet, and now Reez would never know what lay within. Sighing, he ran a finger down the wooden handle. Lost in his memories, he almost missed the quiet click of a lock disengaging. Reez pulled back his hand and watched as one door moved slightly ajar, inviting Reez to open it and explore the secrets that had been barred from him for so long. Slowly, Reez pulled it wider and peered inside.

Books lined the shelves. In fact, it looked the same as all of the other cabinets. Reez traced his fingers over the spines, feeling the smooth covers of tanned skins and the more rigid buckram bindings. Although part of him was eager to discover their topics and determine why they were considered so taboo, he was keenly aware that he had no business looking at them. He had made a promise to Wicton that he would never attempt to open the cabinet and he intended to keep his oath.

He was closing the door when he spied a piece of parchment laying across the books on the top shelf. It was too much for his inquisitive nature to ignore. Taking it down, he turned it towards the lamp burning on the table so that he could see the words clearly.

Reez,

If you are reading this, then I am gone before my time, and you are alone. It is, unfortunately, one of the many things I have tried to prepare for. On a few occasions over the long cycles an apprentice has been left prematurely, and as a result, each Master must be sure to anticipate every need and plan accordingly. I have tried to ensure everything is available to you, including the contents of this cabinet. I had hoped to introduce you to them properly with my guidance to temper you; instead I must trust you to use caution. Remember, at all times you are a Master of green magic.

In this cabinet are the forbidden books. Over the centuries, many Masters have overstepped their mandate and dabbled in other areas of magic, myself included. Here are the collected memoirs of discoveries and experiments made by your predecessors. As you can imagine, some are more interesting than others. You must never reveal that you have these in your possession and on no account must either of the other Masters ever suspect that you know their secrets.

Only you can open this door. You may wonder how I

knew to leave this accessible to you. The truth is, you could have opened this cabinet at any time over the past few cycles. Once I was sure that you would try none of your late-night foolishness again, I reset the locking mechanism. In time, when you eventually take on your own apprentice, you must judge when it is best to allow them to access the information here. My own Master waited many cycles before allowing me to peruse this knowledge, and it is imperative that you judge your successor carefully. Such knowledge could be devastating in the wrong hands.

Your curious nature and your insatiable thirst for knowledge are both admirable and dangerous. I cannot prevent you from making forays into areas of magic outside of your charge: indeed, I am well aware if I banned you entirely, it would only stir you to greater subterfuge. All I ask is that you think long and hard about the decisions you make.

I am no longer there to watch over you. Instead, I must trust you to be wise. Don't let me down, Reez. Make me proud.

Wicton.

Reez took a deep breath and blinked back the moisture gathered in his eyes. Turning back to the cabinet, he shut the door firmly. One day, far in the future, he would explore its contents and learn the secrets within. Today he must remain a Master of green magic and do his duty for the people of Fiora province.

#

Thankfully, the inclement weather meant that Reez reached the Margrave's house without being stopped by anyone.

Most people remained indoors, and the few that he had passed were too intent on reaching shelter than trying to see who was under the heavy cloak. He knocked at the door, but nearly lost all courage when it swung open and he looked into Bilan's face. His old tormentor frowned for a moment and then his eyes widened. "Reez?"

Reez nodded and swallowed before trusting himself to speak. "I heard the council was in session. I should like to address them."

Bilan opened the door wide and stepped to one side. "Of course. They are in the meeting room." He gestured across the hall to a partially closed door. Bilan followed Reez as he pushed open the door and walked into the room. All eyes turned towards him and he felt the fear rise within.

"Father, it is Reez. He wishes to speak to the council," Bilan said as he closed the door. He went to sit on the only vacant chair before pulling it out and moving to the side of the room, indicating that Reez should take his place. Reez cleared his throat as he sat down, and the murmurs ceased.

"I want to give you a detailed report of what happened last summer and to offer my services." He glanced at his father, who nodded firmly. "I understand some people are making up their own version of events, so I have come to give you a full account of what truly happened. I told you in my letter that I was almost killed, too. It has left its mark on me." He took a deep breath and dragged his hood down, keeping his eyes trained on the table in front of him. He heard a hiss and a cry. A chair scraped and fell back as its occupant stood up suddenly.

Someone moaned softly to his left.

A hand rested lightly on his shoulder. "Beran already told us the extent of your injuries, although it is still a shock to see them," Bilan said gently. "We are just grateful that you survived and returned to us." Reez turned his head and looked up into the face of the man who had once tried to drown him. Instead of scorn in Bilan's eyes, there was compassion, and Reez felt relief flood through his body.

A throat cleared at the head of the table. "Thank you for coming, Reez," the Margrave said. "I must admit, we have many questions, but perhaps most of them will be answered after you relate the events to us. Would you like something to drink before you begin?" Reez was tempted to ask for one of the bottles in Phalen's bar, but instead accepted a cup of water. When Bilan had pulled in another chair and everyone was settled once more, Reez took a deep breath.

"Wicton saved my life," he began. As the rain continued to batter the window and the candles flickered in the wintry gloom, Reez told them everything that had happened. The day was almost done when he finished. After reassuring them he had access to everything he would need to look after the province, and answering questions from several council members. He was exhausted as he trudged up the hill that evening, but also strangely relaxed. After their initial surprise, the council members had ignored his scars. By the end of the meeting, Reez had almost forgotten them himself. The hope in his chest flared brighter, and for the first time, he looked forward to the future.

He was watering the seedlings in the glass house when Aydal found him the following day. Weary of study and feeling overwhelmed by the responsibility he now carried, he had wandered out to his favourite place to allow the instructions and rituals ricocheting in his head to quieten in the mundane tasks of caring for his plants. Thanks to his Master, he could find some order to the duties and responsibilities facing him. Wicton had continued his meticulous directions from the grave, and Reez was grateful for his foresight. Despite that, there was much to learn. He had never really appreciated the burden of care his Master carried, and he was sorely afraid that he would prove woefully inadequate.

"Here," Aydal said without preamble, tossing a large pot towards him. Reez caught it in his right hand and looked at it.

"What is it?"

"Salve for your scars. Apparently, Wicton gave the instructions to Morron. I asked Damino to make some for you. He'll ensure he sends a regular supply."

Reez twisted open the lid and looked inside. Dipping his finger in the yellow lotion, he rubbed some against his left hand. It was oily and smelt of lavender, but it was immediately soothing and eased the itching that he had to fight to ignore.

"Damino says it will help to keep your skin supple so that it doesn't split and bleed."

"Thank you," Reez replied.

"As soon as it eases your scars, we can work on getting

you stronger," Aydal said with a grin.

"Why does that not fill me with joy?" Reez replied with a grimace.

"You could start by using your other arm more."

Reez held up his arm so that Aydal could see his hand. "My fingers are curling up. It's difficult to do anything with them."

"All the more reason to move them. Maybe I could help," Aydal said, closing the gap between them. As the shadows moved across the floor of the glass house, Reez bit back his groans of pain as Aydal massaged the cream into his hand and worked on each finger, moving them through the joints and flexing his wrist.

"How was your visit from Amily?" Aydal asked with a sly grin. "I don't see any bruises on you."

Reez chuckled. "I've never seen her so conflicted," he said. "She didn't know whether to hit me, hug me, or harangue me." His sister had appeared as soon as it was light and had waited impatiently for Reez to answer her summons. When he finally appeared, she had been so overcome, she immediately burst into tears, sobbing indecipherable words that sounded like a mixture of protestations of love amid remonstrations and rebukes. It had taken her some time to calm down enough for them to have a genuine conversation.

As Aydal finally finished his ministrations, Reez had to admit that he could feel an improvement. "You should do this first thing in the morning, and again before you go to bed," Aydal advised.

"Yes, my Lord!" Reez said with a smile as Aydal worked his way up his arm.

"I, er, went to see Nula this morning," Aydal ventured, his eyes observing his brother's face. "She said you had paid her a visit."

"I owed her an apology."

"If you are really sure…"

"I am. You make her happy. In fact, just hearing your name brought light to her eyes." Reez grinned as his brother's cheeks flushed red. "You have wasted a lot of time, you know. You should be handfasted after the spring planting."

"You don't think it's too soon?"

Reez laughed. "Too soon? I think it is long overdue, in fact"

Aydal smiled softly, his rough hands firm but gentle as he rubbed in the salve. Reez watched as a frown appeared on his brother's face. "She loved you, you know," he said slowly.

"I think she loves you more," Reez replied firmly. "The kind of love a woman can give, not the fancies of a young girl with an eye to impressing her friends."

Aydal snorted. "I don't find you impressive," he joked.

Eventually, Aydal finished and peered into the pot. "I think Damino needs to make up a lot more of this," he mused. "He might need you to grow him some more ingredients. The calendula won't bloom until summer, and I doubt he has much stored."

"I'll see him tomorrow," Reez promised, flexing his fingers slightly. "This feels so much better."

Aydal stood. "I should go," he said. "Da wants me to help him inventory the seed so we are ready to plant."

"Is he back in the fields again?" Reez asked.

"He is," Aydal said. "I'm glad, too. It's been a long winter."

"On your way back, would you do something for me?" Reez said, reaching inside his tunic and pulling out a piece of paper. "I have a list of supplies I need. Can you convey this to the Margrave and have him organise a delivery for me?"

Aydal perused the items Reez had catalogued that morning. "Chopped wood?" he asked.

Reez shrugged. "Not a task I can manage for myself," he said, gesturing to his crippled arm.

Aydal grinned. "I don't know. I think it would be excellent exercise and a way to strengthen those muscles. Tomorrow, you can start work on the first load."

#

As time passed, Reez fell into a new routine. He scoured the archives for all the references on Wicton's card and became more confident in his dealings with the people. He memorised the rites and rituals for all the ceremonies and learnt to harness the magic and use it for the health of Fiora province. By utilising the power in the fast-growing weeds and transferring it to the seedlings and crops, he was able to quickly take up Wicton's mantle and reassure the Margraves that life would continue largely unaffected.

As his confidence grew, so did his forays from the tower. The villagers grew used to his twisted features and after their initial curiosity, and the occasional gasp of horror, he was treated much the same as before, although Reez still preferred to hide behind a cowl when he walked abroad, unwilling to face their stares no matter how accepting they appeared. In some ways, his scars accorded him a gravitas that made up for his youth and inexperience, which he found particularly useful when the Margraves from the province made the journey at the beginning of the summer to formerly inaugurate him as Master, although he felt ill-prepared for the title and unworthy of wearing Wicton's ring. Although the ceremony had been performed and the formal promises spoken, Reez still felt as if he had been given the role by default and not by right.

Between Damino's constant supply of the healing salve and Aydal's dogged persistence, Reez's physical condition slowly improved. Aydal had him chopping wood, carrying heavy sacks, pulling the little cart to and from the village and even running up the hill to the tower until Reez was forced to stop, lungs heaving and limbs screaming. But each day saw him getting fitter and stronger and the horrors of the previous summer eventually faded to a dull memory.

Chapter Five

"I heard the Bestrians are crossing over into Fiora," one villager groused, "wanting food and having no way of bartering or paying for it."

"Morron was told they steal anything they can get their hands on. The people in Boreton are barring their doors and keeping watch over their outbuildings at night."

"Kromar says his supply of metals has diminished," observed another. "He says the guilds are claiming the ore is running low and they can't open up new seams. They are demanding more coin for the stuff they have. If that's the case, tools are going to become expensive to replace. Mayhap it's time we started asking more for our produce, too."

As the villagers continued to ruminate over the latest rumours, Reez sat quietly in his settle and listened while sipping his cup of ale. He was more aware of the affairs of the neighbouring provinces, but he wasn't sure what to do about the knowledge.

Frequent missives had arrived from Minra province six moons earlier from the guild leaders, who were getting anxious. They begged Reez to make the journey north and meet with them to solve their problems. In the two cycles or so since the deaths of Chrisos and Paiter, they reported that seams had dried up, and they desperately needed more sites. The guilds had begun to husband their existing supplies rather than trade, threatening to charge more for a product that was becoming scarcer by the day. Reez, however, wasn't convinced, and suspected that the situation was less dire than they claimed. On his travels north as a journeyman he had spoken to miners who had worked seams for decades before they were spent, and he couldn't imagine Chrisos leaving the province in such a dire situation that they would be depleted in the relatively short space of time since his death.

Although Reez was not a Master of earth magic, the guild leaders seemed to look to him as their only hope, especially as he had been the one to inform them of their Master's demise; not surprisingly, all their missives to Bestra had gone unanswered. Reez had tried to explain that he had neither the knowledge nor the skills, but they either didn't understand or refused to listen.

As for the issues in the east, they worried Reez much more.

The rumours of wild animals roaming the outer reaches had resurfaced. At first, the Margraves had followed the same advice Wicton had given many cycles earlier, but as before, the new Master of Bestra ignored their increasingly agitated letters. So far, there were no reports of attacks and despite the rumours, the Margraves were not unduly worried. Reez believed it was only a matter of time. Verrin's attempts at enhancing the normally timid wolves roaming the forests had been curtailed when Malander had learnt of his actions. Coupled with the fact that Verrin had intercepted all communication about the issue, including messages from Wicton, Reez suspected that Verrin's practises had been tightly controlled ever since. Without Malander to impede him, Reez guessed that Verrin's experiments had not only restarted but gained pace. He vaguely hoped that the results would stay far away from Maston.

Reez had written to Castor and Merrylee for news, but their reply had been brief and unremarkable, although Reez detected a note of tension under the concise words. In case they decided to leave Etheradia, Reez had renewed his invitation to come to the village and stay as long as they wanted. For a while, they had swapped letters regularly; Castor spoke of his family and his work in the inn, but news of Bestra's new Master were strangely absent. Reez had written asking for information when the rumours surfaced, but he had heard nothing since.

He raised his eyes at a laugh from the doorway and watched his father and brother entering the taproom. On seeing his wife, Aydal strode over and picked her up, making Nula squeal with delight. He kissed her full on the lips before setting her carefully down and laying his hand on her still flat belly. The whispered comment in her ear resulted in a playful slap. Reez smiled.

Beran approached Reez and, after greeting his youngest son, sat heavily down opposite him. The lines on his face were tanned from the summer sun and the physical labour in the fields had resulted in him regaining much of his former strength.

"It's been hot out there today," he said. "I'm looking forward to wetting my throat." He looked towards the bar, but Destry had already started towards him, carrying a mug of ale, which she set before him. Beran signed his thanks before lifting it and gulping the cool liquid, draining half the cup before placing it back on the table. Destry signed a more complex pattern and Beran looked across at his son.

"She wants to know whether you want soup, pie or stew," he translated for his father.

Frowning in concentration, Beran moved his fingers slowly to indicate the pie, receiving a kiss on the cheek for his efforts.

You never kiss me when I ask for pie, Reez signed.

Destry shrugged. *You are not as handsome as your father.*

Reez clutched the tunic above his heart. *You wound me.*
You'll heal.

As she left, Reez turned back to his father, who was looking at him with admiration. "How do you manage that?" he asked. "In all this time, I have still only mastered a few words, and yet you picked it up in less than one cycle."

"I suppose the patterns just make sense. It comes easily to me."

Aydal joined them with a loud groan, picking up the mug that Destry had left for him and chugging the contents down. He lowered it with a sigh and wiped his lips with the back of his hand. "I needed that," he exclaimed.

Nula sauntered over with a full mug and placed it in front of her husband, who grinned up at her, his blue eyes twinkling.

"How are you and little Reez today?" Reez asked.

Nula rolled her eyes. "It doesn't matter how much you try, you are not getting your way," she said with a smirk.

"You can't fault my persistence," Reez replied. "One day, I'll wear you down."

"What makes you think this time will be different?"

"I was too lenient before. Now I have a strategy."

"Face it, Reez, she'll never back down," Aydal interjected. "Besides," he said, caressing Nula's stomach, "it might be another girl."

"I don't see why Reez can't be a suitable name for a girl," Reez replied, forcing his face to remain serious. "You might start a trend."

"Where is my granddaughter, anyway?" Beran asked fondly.

"Lileth is with Da," Nula said. "He needed to rest, so he took her upstairs to sleep."

Phalen had struggled after suffering an injury to his mind. He had woken one morning with a weakness down one side and difficulty in speaking. Although he had recovered somewhat, he found daily tasks difficult, especially when tired, and had taken to retiring upstairs, leaving more and more of the work for the two girls. Reez knew Aydal was concerned, and the family now lived at the inn rather than the farmhouse to ease the burden, but it was still a lot to undertake. Thankfully, most of the villagers were understanding, and some had even learnt basic words so that Destry could serve them without waiting for Nula to translate their order.

After delivering their food, Nula picked up the empty tankards and left them, stationing herself behind the bar to serve the steady stream of workers now trickling in for some sustenance and rest after toiling all day in the unrelenting sun.

"Have you received any messages from Amily?" Aydal asked his father before spearing a tater and gobbling it down.

"Nothing since her last letter. They were travelling into the mountains to search for gems. I don't expect to hear word until they return home."

Aydal snorted. "I'd like to see that. She's always been so finicky about cleanliness. Her pretty dresses aren't going to stand for that kind of treatment."

"From what I learnt, it's not too bad," Reez replied. "Chrisos would open the seams to make an easy passage and light work. When I met Faradan, he had mined enough jewels in just two moons to last him through the rest of the cycle. With both of them mining, even considering his need to teach Amily, their work should be completed much sooner."

"Even so, give me good clean air and open skies any day. I wouldn't want to work underground." Aydal eyed Reez's hands. "Change over," he instructed, waving his fork in the air.

With a small sigh, Reez swapped his utensils over and continued eating. As part of his rehabilitation, Aydal made Reez do most of his work with his injured left hand, meaning he could now use either with ease. Despite his progress, Aydal insisted he alternate between left and right as much as possible.

As they lingered after the meal, talking of the farm and Reez's latest project, a man entered the inn, turning his head and searching the room.

"Da," Reez said quietly, "do you think he wants you?"

Beran peered around the edge of the settle and waved at him. "Everything alright, Dreken?" he asked as the man made his way over to them.

"The Margrave is calling an emergency meeting of the council and is asking for your attendance. Can you come immediately?" he asked quietly.

"Of course. I am finished," Beran said, standing with his forehead furrowed. "I'll see you later, Aydal."

As they watched him stride from the taproom. Aydal turned to Reez. "Any idea what that might be about?"

Reez shook his head. "Whatever it is, I doubt it's good news," he murmured.

"Maybe you should go too. You could find out," Aydal suggested.

"Me? I'm not part of the ruling council. If they have

need of the Master, I'm sure they'll send word."

"Aren't you curious?"

"Of course," Reez laughed, "but knowing how closed mouth Da is about council business, I wager I'll get to know all about it long before you do."

"Well, as long as it doesn't affect my harvest, I'm not interested," Aydal declared. "Speaking of which, I have a bit more work to do before I can stop for the night." He spotted Nula and waved before blowing her an exaggerated kiss. She shook her head and pointed to the door, but Reez noticed the light flare in her eyes and the lingering smile on her lips. Chuckling, he bade his brother farewell and leant back with a contented sigh, unwilling to leave the ambiance of the inn for the trek back to the tower and the isolation of his work. Happy to linger for a while longer, he closed his eyes and listened to the low hum of voices punctuated by a bark of laughter and the clink of crockery. Familiar sounds. Comforting sounds. Safe sounds.

Life had reached a pleasant norm for Reez. Physically, although not as able as he once was, thanks to hard work and a constant supply of salve, he had regained movement and strength in his body. He was no longer plagued with pain and itching, and he could easily ignore the deformity of his skin. He didn't even earn a second glance from the curious now and felt no need to cover his face under hoods and cowls. Because of Wicton's foresight, Reez could perform all the tasks expected of the Master, although he often referred to the tomes in the vault for advice and information. The ring he wore felt comfortable on his hand at last. The village was thriving and, most of the time,

Reez could pretend that there was nothing amiss in the world.

He sighed and opened his eyes; the moment gone. Between fabricated tales and hastily convened meetings, reality was intruding into his bubble of contentment, and with it came the whisper of unease that usually only disturbed him in the dead of night. Trouble was coming, and as hard as he might wish it, Reez knew he could not avoid it for much longer.

#

In truth, the initial sign of unrest sought him out immediately after quitting the taproom a little while later. Across the square, Reez saw several villagers gathered outside the Margrave's house and he wandered over to see what was amiss. As he approached, he heard voices getting louder as several men began arguing with each other. He spotted Aydal in the crowd and headed for him.

"I say they know something, and we should be told," a deep voice bellowed. "Didn't you see them all sneak inside? Why do they keep everything a secret, as if we are children?"

"I worked hard for my harvest," another shouted. "If they think they can come and take what I've earned, then they'll meet my fists."

"As if you need an excuse to get into a fight, Fane," Aydal retorted. "Maybe it's time you started using your brain to think with instead of your arse."

With that, all the men shouted at once. Reez saw Fane shove Aydal hard enough to send him staggering back, and Reez groaned as he picked up his pace, knowing that his brother would need no further provocation. Just as he feared, Aydal immediately took a swing at the man and bloodied his nose. In moments, the massed gathering became a melee as punches and kicks flew in all directions. Reez saw the Margrave, and the gathered council, pouring out the door and staring in horror at the brawl taking place outside the house.

"Stop this at once!" Reez shouted. "I said stop!" he repeated as his command went unacknowledged. The ground erupted around the fighting men as vines snacked across the village green and wrapped themselves around legs and ankles. The shouts of anger changed to cries of alarm, and they forgot the brawl as fearful eyes turned towards Reez. Only when they were quiet once more did Reez wave dismissively, letting the vines wither away.

"What madness is this?" he roared. "Have you no shame? You are grown men, not children. Such behaviour should have been left behind long ago." To their credit, the men appeared embarrassed and none but Aydal could meet his gaze. "Since when does the council have to give an account to you?" Reez continued. "You have trusted them implicitly before now."

"What are they doing about the thieving Bestrians?" Fane slurred. "Maybe they won't stop there. We could wake up one morning and find our throats slit." Someone laughed, but quickly stifled it as Reez glared at them all with contempt.

"You are drunk, Fane. Go home. All of you," Reez said, addressing the men, "go home. Perhaps when you have clear heads, you'll be ready to be rational."

"But we have a right to know," someone shouted from the back of the group.

"No, you don't," Reez replied angrily. "The Margrave and the council are tasked with running Maston as they see fit. Until they make a decision, their discussions are private, not for our ears. A Master has more right than any of you to be privy to their debates, yet I do not force my presence on the council. Be patient. If they deem it necessary, you will be informed eventually. Now, I will not repeat myself. Get yourselves off or I will be forced to make you leave."

Unwilling to argue with a Master, the men dispersed. Reez nodded to the Margrave, who ushered the council back inside the house to deal with whatever business had warranted such a hasty meeting. Aydal shambled over, a sheepish grin on his face. "Why do you look so pleased?" Reez grumbled.

"I haven't had a good rumble in an age," he replied.

Reez could see a cut above his brother's left brow. "You'd better let Nula look at that. As it is, you'll have a black eye by morning."

Aydal shrugged. "I bet Fane looks worse."

"You could pretend to feel a little chagrin. Why were you here anyway? I thought you had work to do."

"You know me. I like to stick my nose in. When I saw them gathering, I wandered over to discover what was happening." He touched his face and grimaced. "I'd best receive my tongue lashing."

Reez watched him walk away, whistling a tune, and chuckled, thinking it would take more than the thought of robbers and murderers to dampen Aydal's spirits. He glanced at the Margrave's door and his smile faded. He wondered again what tidings had merited such a hasty meeting, his face awash with concern. Sighing, he turned his own feet towards home. If it was serious, and his heart told him it was, the bad news would catch up with him, eventually.

Chapter Six

"Master Reez," Kromar said with a smile. "What brings you to my door?"

Reez wandered into the building and cast his eye around the smithy. It was a much smaller affair than Blane's forge in Stonaven, but he recognised the neat racks of tools and the heat from the blazing fire. The huge anvil stood on top of a thick log for added height and a nearby bench was strewn with metal implements and half-finished projects. A whetstone stood in one corner, ready to sharpen the edges of a knife or blade. Kromar himself was stripped to the waist, wearing a long, old leather apron over his trews. Although he was getting on in summers, his arms were still thick and corded with muscles.

"I know this might seem like an unusual request, but I was wondering if you would teach me about the shaping of metal," Reez asked.

"I'll do me best," Kromar replied, putting down his hammer. "What do you wish to know?"

"Everything."

Kromar's dark, bushy eyebrows drew together. "I don't understand."

"Think of me as an apprentice, if you will," Reez said. "I want to learn your trade."

"You want to become a smith?" Kromar asked in astonishment.

Reez laughed. "I doubt that will ever happen, but I'm keen to learn the skills involved. Put it down to curiosity, if you will."

Kromar scratched his head. "Certainly, Master, if that's what you want, but it's 'ard, dirty work."

"I'm prepared for that," Reez replied. "So, where do we start?"

#

Later that evening, Reez relaxed back into his warm bath and groaned in relief. After learning about the myriad tools and their uses, Kromar had put him to work. He had stoked the fire and pumped the bellows until the flames roared. He had hefted lumps of ore and firestones until his back and shoulders were screaming in protest. And tomorrow, he planned to do it all over again.

He had been mulling over the missives from Minra for a while, trying to come up with ways of helping them, but his complete lack of knowledge was an impassable barrier. Hoping to find something in the forbidden archives, he had gone down to the vault to see what his predecessors had discovered about earth magic. Unfortunately, there was very little. Stone and metal were difficult to work with, and neither were in abundant supply in Fiora. Most of the volumes concentrated on animal magic, and although his interest was piqued, he ignored them.

Master Heeva had done some studies on soil properties under the guise of searching for ways to enrich the earth for his plants. He had compared samples from across the region and learnt to identify the richer loams by magic. Master Denza had obtained gems for the elaborate jewellery she wore and had listed her findings. Unfortunately, her affinity for magic was the same as Wicton's and her discoveries were written in terms of frequency and pitch, which was of no use to Reez. Master Farlan had apparently discovered how to quarry stone, having found a source some days' journey further west from the tower. He had never identified the place, however, and Reez had shut the book and thrown it down on the table in frustration. None of the books tackled the problem of identifying ore or how to shape metal.

He had quit the vault in vexation and returned to the galley to prepare his evening meal. The air was still warm, despite the seasons slowly cycling towards winter, and he took his meal out to the glass house. After enjoying the cold meats and fresh bread, he spent some time pottering around the plants, dead-heading the flowers and harvesting the sweet pomadoro, popping some of the smaller, yellow fruit into his mouth as he worked. Outside, the finger beans were still growing and Reez watered them along with the snow berries. When he finished, he sat on the steps of the tower with his back leaning against the stones that were still warm from the heat of the day. Sipping from a cup of berry wine, he watched the sun as it slowly lowered in the sky and dipped beyond the horizon. As the stars appeared, he smiled to himself as he spotted the constellation of the little owl.

His mind wandered back thirteen cycles to his first days as an apprentice. He shook his head fondly at the images of the careful notebooks and the thoughts of a boy of twelve summers who was desperate to impress. Even though he hadn't seen it at the time, every seed, every plant and monotonous chore had been building the foundation for his skills as a wielder of green magic. Idly, he wondered what Paiter's apprenticeship had been like. If it had been anything like his own, he would have had to start from the very beginnings and understand how things worked in the world before learning how to manipulate them.

Perhaps, he mused to himself, that was the place to launch his own investigations. He wasn't ready for an extended journey north, but the village had its own blacksmith. Kromar could teach him his art.

#

"If you were a true 'prentice," Kromar said the following day, "I would keep you workin' like this for a few more moons, but somehow I don't think that's what you need from me."

Reez put down the bucket of water and wiped his forehead with a piece of rag. "I think I understand the labour part of things pretty well. I would appreciate moving on to the next lesson."

Kromar chuckled as he wandered over to his workbench and picked up a hammer, stroking it fondly. "The first thing any smith needs is a set of tools. By makin' your own, you'll get to learn all the skills and techniques of the trade. Metal workin' isn't about strength, but control. Most people think you just get it 'ot and 'it it 'ard, but the trick is to be precise in your 'itting." He walked over to the anvil in front of the forge. "'Ere," he said, making an x on the top with a piece of firestone. "This is where you put every strike. Don't chase the metal around, it'll just get ruined. Instead, move everythin' to this point. Don't worry about makin' mistakes. The beauty of metal is that it can be re'eated and reshaped until you get it right."

Reez glanced over at the rack of tools. "Which one do I start with?" he asked.

"Tongs. If you can't 'old it, you can't 'it it."

That first day of true smithing was a frustrating one for Reez. He was taller than Kromar and so they had to work on adjusting the height of the anvil until he could stand properly without putting a strain on his back. When he started to hammer initially, Kromar admonished him for using tiny blows; not lifting the hammer high enough; trying to use brute strength instead of relying on the swing; holding the hammer too tight and sliding the blows instead of hitting them fair and square. At one point, he threw both metal and hammer across the forge with a loud curse and stormed outside to the sound of Kromar's raucous laughter. When he eventually calmed down and walked back inside, all Kromar said was "Again," as he handed him the tools.

On the second day, he burnt himself when he picked up the metal he was working on with his hand instead of the tongs. Kromar had feigned shock as the curses streamed from Reez's mouth. "I never thought I'd 'ear words like that from a Master," he chuckled as he made Reez hold his hand under cold water and fetched a healing salve.

On the third day, he started to understand how to use the weight of the hammer and the swing of his arm to hit efficiently, and his body worked to a rhythm. He still had to be reminded to move his work to the centre of the anvil instead of chasing it, and more than once, Kromar had to stop him. "Reposition," he scolded. "Two 'its in the wrong place won't make it right. You need to stop and move the metal."

For the rest of that week, Reez worked hard shaping the jaws, flattening the pivot and punching the point before setting the pivot pin. When he finally plunged it into the cold water to harden the metal and adjusted the grip, he felt an amazing sense of achievement.

"Not bad," Kromar said when he inspected it. "See how much better these are to your first attempt?" They compared the two tools. "I think in time I could make a decent smith out of you."

Reez laughed. "You flatter me. What's next?"

"Let's try a chisel," Kromar decided. "You'll learn different techniques makin' one of them."

#

Reez was working on drawing out the metal edging on his third attempt when a loud whistle interrupted his labour. He looked up, his long dark hair slicked down with perspiration and falling across his face. He was stripped to the waist, sweat glistening across his chest and back, and streaks of soot and dust from the firestones patterning his skin. Kromar jerked his head towards the door and Reez turned. Over the past sennights, many of the villagers had wandered into the forge on one pretext or another to glimpse their Master as he hammered at the anvil. It had been a source of entertainment to see him at manual labour, especially for Aydal, but once they got over the initial surprise, they stayed to dissect the various strands of gossip floating around the village or occasionally news from outside. Reez soon realised that it was a better way of gathering information than sitting in the corner of the inn eavesdropping on the nearest conversations.

This time, however, it wasn't one of the farmers intent on passing on his newfound knowledge. Destry stood by the door gripping a small basket, her eyes moving slowly over his naked skin.

Reez straightened and dropped his hammer on the bench beside him. *What brings you here?* He signed.

Nula told me you were working. I thought you might be hungry.

You brought food?

With a nod, she walked further in and uncovered the contents. *Pie?* He asked with a grin. She shrugged.

Kromar wandered over and sniffed appreciatively. "In all the long cycles I've been 'ere, my Morah's never brought me a meal. Says the place is too dirty and 'ot for her." He glanced between the two of them and cleared his throat. "I think I'll just go round to the 'ouse and see whether she's got any food ready for me yet," he said. Whistling loudly, he took off his apron and walked out the door, closing it firmly behind him.

Out of the corner of his eye, Reez saw Destry lift her hand as if to touch the puckered skin that ran down the left side of his body before disappearing underneath the trews that sat low on his hips. He flinched and turned so that it was hidden as he grabbed his tunic and pulled it over his head, covering his maimed side. She watched him carefully, a frown on her face.

Why did you do that?

What? he replied, feigning ignorance.

You know what. I won't hurt you.

That's not it.

Then why not let me touch it?

Why do you want to? I'm ugly.

It's just skin, she said. *Please.* He hesitated, unwilling to expose himself to her rejection or ridicule. *Trust me*, she signed.

Slowly, he lifted the bottom of the tunic until she could see the scarring. Reaching out, she laid her hand on his side, resting it there for a moment before gently stroking along the ridges. Reez squeezed his eyes shut against the sudden hot tears that threatened to spill over. He was still ashamed of his body, which had once been strong and flawless, and the scars were a visible reminder of how weak and helpless he was, and how a good man had died to save him rather than protecting himself.

He hadn't realised he had started shaking until Destry pulled his tunic back down and gripped his arm. He opened his eyes, blinking rapidly, and looked at Destry, who was smiling softly at him. When he had regained his composure, she patted his chest. *I think I was wrong*, she signed. *You are more handsome than your father. Time for your dinner.*

She whipped round and headed towards the bench, her long braid swinging down her back, and balanced the basket on the edge. Reez followed and moved some tools to clear a space before grabbing two wooden stools from the front of the forge and placing them at the corner.

Lifting out the pie wrapped in a cloth, she laid it in front of him, followed by a hunk of fresh bread and churned butter, a jar of pickles, and a bottle of Phalen's summer ale.

Eat, she said.

Sit.

She lowered herself down so that their knees were almost touching. Reez took a bite of the pie and chewed.

This is good.

Destry smiled. *I do the cooking now. Nula is busy serving and looking after Lileth.*

How is Phalen?

She shook her head slowly. *Da is getting worse. I think he no longer has the will to live. After his last episode, he keeps himself abed. He won't eat unless I push and cry.*

I'm sorry, Reez signed before laying his hand on her arm and squeezing gently. It saddened him to think of the once vital innkeeper laid low. He wondered if talking about his own recovery might help Phalen realise that there was still hope and life, even if it didn't look the same as before. *Would you like me to visit him?*

Destry nodded. *Mayhap you will get him to see sense.*
I can try at least.

She smiled and swept her gaze around the interior of the smithy before turning back to him with a small frown. *Why are you here?* She asked.

Learning, Reez replied as he took another bite and reached for the bottle. Tilting it back, he swallowed half the liquid before setting it back down on the bench.

Learning makes you thirsty, Destry observed. *Why are you learning here?*

He hesitated for a moment before replying. Those few people who had asked him outright had been easily put off with platitudes, but Reez knew Destry wouldn't be content with half-truths and vague answers. *The people in the north have no Master. They keep asking me for my help, but I have no skill. I thought maybe I could understand things better if I had more knowledge.*

She looked puzzled. *Are you trying to learn the earth magic here?*

Not earth magic yet. Just how to shape metal and work the ore.

But you think you can do magic once you know these things?

Reez shrugged. *I don't know,* he admitted, *but it seemed a good place to start.*

I thought you only possessed green magic.

In the old days, before the war, Mages used to wield all three magics together. Later, they felt it was too dangerous for one person to have all the knowledge, so the three disciplines were divided.

Destry's eyes widened. *Dangerous to you?*

Reez shook his head. *To the people. To Zelannor.*

Destry was still for a short while. *If you learn, will you leave us and be Master in Minra?* she signed.

No. This is my home. But if I can help, then I will have to spend some time in the north.

She thought for a moment. *It took you a long time to learn green magic. It will be many cycles before you can be Master there, too.*

I don't need to be a Master. I just need to learn enough to find the metal for them and maybe work with stone so that I can be of use.

Destry paused and huffed out a breath. *If they need you, you should try your best.*

Reez smiled. *So, if you brought pie, does that mean I also get a kiss?*

Destry wrinkled up her nose. *You smell and you are filthy. Why would I want to kiss you?* She stood up and gathered the empty bottle and swept the crumbs off the bench before folding the cloth up and placing it back in the basket.

Perhaps you could bring me some dinner tomorrow, Reez said, his eyes wide with innocence. *I'm sure it would help me work better.*

Destry's eyes flickered down his chest for an instant before they narrowed. *Perhaps you could clean yourself up and come to the inn. I don't have time to serve you every day.*

Please? You could join me. Surely, Nula can spare you for a short while.

Her lips twitched. *Perhaps,* she finally signed.

Reez grinned as he watched her leave, appreciating the swing of her hips. After she had gone, his smile faded. He had no business being troubled by his old dreams of a wife and home. Experience had shown him he was unsuited to be a husband. The demands of being a Master of one province were hard enough, but if he eventually became anywhere near proficient in earth magic, he would have two to oversee. It was no wonder that many Masters remained alone. Rightly, a wife would demand time and attention from her partner and would likely not tolerate long separations. He forced the image of Destry's smile away and got up from the stool. Picking up the hammer, he turned back to the anvil and concentrated on his work, deliberately pushing all thoughts of a future with Destry from his mind.

Chapter Seven

Reez had barely begun firing up the forge the following day when the Margrave arrived with the council elders. He nodded sagely to his father and waited, but it quickly became apparent they were not there to speak to him.

"What can I do for you gen'lemen today?" Kromar enquired, a small frown on his face.

"In light of recent news that the council has been privy to, we have decided that we should start securing our stores and buildings," the Margrave began. "We need to commission locks for the communal barns and other outbuildings. Although it may not seem much, you may be inundated by work afterwards. I'm sure as soon as the villagers get wind of it, they will ask for similar devices to be fitted on their personal sheds."

"I can make a hasp for you," Kromar replied, scratching his balding head, "but if you need anythin' more complex, then you will have to apply to the guild heads in Minra. Only the Mastersmiths know how to make the more intricate devices."

"Something simple will suffice for now," the Margrave said. "Bilan thinks we won't be bothered as we have a Master in residence, but I don't want to take any chances."

"Are things that bad?" Reez asked in concern as he wandered closer.

"It's difficult to say for sure," the Margrave admitted, turning to Reez. "Facts are mixed up with hearsay and speculation. I've written to the border villages for more information, but rumour travels faster and spreads quicker than the truth. You saw what happened outside my house. More than a few people are worried, and I would rather take precautions than be caught unawares."

"There are tales of beasts roaming the forests at the edge of Fiora and people disappearing," his father whispered. "It is said that some in Bestra have crossed into the province seeking refuge."

"Many cycles ago, there were reports of enormous wolves," Reez said slowly. "Wicton spoke to Malander about it."

"Well, as things stand, we have no-one to appeal to," the Margrave said. "From what you say, the new Master won't listen to us now. I fear we must fend for ourselves. I don't see how green magic can help us here," he finished with a look of apology.

"Perhaps you're right," Reez mused.

The council left soon afterwards, but Beran hung back and gestured to Reez that they should speak. Kromar mumbled about checking his supplies before wandering off and leaving them alone.

"We've been debating the reports for nigh on a fortnight," Beran said in a low voice. "If even half the rumours are correct, then something dire is happening, but we can't seem to find the truth of it. We are concerned that if things continue, folk will take matters into their own hands. We want to head off the worst of it without worrying the villagers unnecessarily, but we have nothing specific to tell them."

"You are all wise people," Reez said reassuringly. "I'm sure you will prepare well."

"I would give a great deal for some factual reports."

Reez hesitated for a moment. "I could go," he mumbled. Immediately, his hands went clammy, and he forced himself to breathe normally. He had not ventured out of the village since limping back home after Wicton's death, and the thought of leaving the place he felt safest was disturbing. He wished he could unsay the words, but his father was looking at him with a mixture of hope and fear.

"I can't deny that it would be an enormous relief to the council to have someone reliable bring us back news," Beran said reluctantly.

"But you don't think I should go?" Reez asked.

Beran sighed and glanced at the wall behind Reez before meeting his eyes again. "I lost you once," he said gruffly. "I'm not sure I could do it again."

It was the excuse Reez needed to back out without losing face, and yet something within him rebelled. Deep inside, he knew the world outside Maston was calling to him and it was only a matter of 'when' not 'if' he would begin his travels again. If they left it up to him, he would likely never step outside Fiora, let alone go to Minra or Bestra, but he owed it to his own people to ascertain how much danger, if any, was coming their way. To do that, he would have to travel to the borders.

He laid a hand on his father's shoulder. "We were all taken by surprise that day. Wicton was the only one who had anticipated Verrin, and even he wasn't fully prepared for what happened. I'm not the same man I was then," Reez said, realising the truth of the words for himself even as he spoke them. "Wicton has inadvertently given me a gift which can protect me, and I will not be travelling in ignorance. I will take precautions and be very careful, I promise."

Beran lifted his own hand and laid it over Reez's. "I'm sorry. I shouldn't be doubting you. In many ways, you will always be my little boy. I don't think I will ever stop fretting over you." He sighed. "I wish your Ma were still here. She would have had some wise words to offer, or advice to give. I'm proud of you, Reez. You are a great Master and I know Wicton would agree with me." He patted Reez's hand affectionately. "Well, I'd best return to the Margrave and let him know your plan. The news will comfort him."

"I'll leave tomorrow," Reez said.

Beran nodded slowly before drawing his son into a tight embrace. "Safe journey," he muttered before turning and walking outside.

Reez was washing his hands when Kromar returned after watching Beran leave.

"I'm afraid we will have to put my lessons aside for a while," Reez said.

"Is there trouble?" Kromar asked with a frown, glancing back out at Beran's figure striding away in the distance.

"No. I'm going to make a journey out to the border villages to see the truth of what's going on for myself. I won't be gone forever, though, so I'll be back to bother you again before you know it."

"You're no bother," Kromar said with a grin. "In truth, I've enjoyed havin' you around. It's a shame I can't take on a 'prentice of my own. I didn't know 'ow good it would feel to be passin' on the principles of my craft to someone else."

"I'm sure you could find somebody who would be willing to learn if you put the word out."

"Nay, Master Reez. Only a fully licensed smith can take a 'prentice. I would have to be vetted by the guild and go through the standard trials before they would allow it."

"I didn't realise," Reez said.

"They only allow the best to take on a 'prentice," Kromar informed him. "It ensures that the work is held to the 'ighest measure. A shoddy smith is a disgrace to us all. That's why only certified work has a guild stamp on it, so you know you're gettin' fine craftsmanship."

Reez nodded. "Why did you decide to move here instead of staying in Minra to take the trials?"

Kromar rubbed his chin. "My Pop was a tough man and believed that a belt was the best form of teachin'. I wasn't keen on returning there after my 'prenticeship finished and jumped at the chance of coming 'ere when the old smith sent a request to the guild."

"Did you ever consider going back?"

"Not once. These mild winters agree with me, and the work is easy enough. I have my Morah to warm my bed and fill my belly with 'ot food. It's a good life."

"I thought I would be living in Minra now," Reez mused, "but it didn't work out. I would have liked to see the snow falling."

Kromar shivered and rubbed his arms. "Take it from me, Master Reez. You're better off 'ere with a light frost and an early spring. After thirty summers without it, I can promise you I 'ave no 'ankering to slog through deep drifts or feel my 'ands go numb when I step outside."

Reez chuckled and moved the tools he had made to one side. "Now, don't be discarding these as scrap," he warned Kromar. "I should be loath to have to make them all again."

Kromar laughed and clapped him on the back. "Don't you worry," he said. "They'll be right here waitin' when you return."

#

Reez was striding through the silent village before

dawn the following day, his journeyman's bag full, and a stout stick in his hand. Although he was much stronger, He didn't know how much effect an extended journey would have on his body, and he feared he might need the extra support.

His sleep had been fitful, and nightmares had plagued him when he had finally succumbed to oblivion. The thought of venturing out into the countryside had fuelled the fear in his dreams as he ran through dark corridors seeking escape from the unknown terror that hunted him. He had woken tired and tense, and it was with great effort that he donned his travelling cloak after a light meal to break his fast. He refused to contemplate what might be ahead, instead keeping his mind busy with remembering Kromar's instructions as he shaped the hot metal and reviewing what he had learnt about the nature of ore.

As he neared the edge of the village, a figure rose from the shadows and stood waiting in the predawn light for him to approach.

You always leave without saying goodbye, Destry signed. Although she had wrapped herself in a large coat which had once belonged to her father, Reez could see she was still wearing her nightgown. Her legs were bare, and she wore boots. Strands of hair that had pulled out of her braid in the night floated across her face with the breeze.

Reez smiled. *You always have to have the last word. How did you know?*

Destry shrugged nonchalantly. *Your Da.*
He told you?
Not all. I guessed some. She handed him a hemp bag. *In*

case you get hungry.

Reez looked inside. *You made me pie?*

Will you be gone long? She asked, ignoring his observation.

I don't know, he admitted. *I need to find out the truth behind all these rumours.*

Will there be danger?

Perhaps. Perhaps not.

You will come back.

Reez recognised she wasn't asking and nodded his assent. Destry indicated he should move closer. Puzzled, he leaned down. Destry reached up and wrapped her arms around his neck before pressing her lips to his. Startled, he stood immobile. By the time his brain had processed what was happening, she was gone, running back up the street towards the inn and leaving him alone as the sun finally appeared over the horizon.

#

As Reez came in sight of Boreton, he sighed with relief. He had cut a wide swathe through the countryside, visiting every village and hamlet along the way. Every Margrave had heard terrible rumours, but at each stop Reez discovered there were no first-hand accounts, just hearsay and anxiety. His report to Maston's council was going to be very short, indeed. At each village, Reez had reinforced the existing hedges and thorn bushes, weaving them tightly together to form an impenetrable barrier. For some, it would mean a longer walk round to gain access to their fields, but the security it offered was worth the effort. Reez had spent the majority of his time reassuring people who felt vulnerable and urging that the wild stories stop. His authority as Master ensured the villagers listened to him and he felt confident that the rumours would die away. He recommended the Margraves send regular factual reports back to the other villages to scotch the tide of fear and distrust that was bubbling in the province. He also advised them to secure their outbuildings. Although he could ascertain no immediate threats, he knew the villagers would need to take some action in order to feel safer, and it would do no harm.

Situated on a direct route between Maston and Etheradia, Boreton had grown into a small town nestled in the rolling hills that separated the two provinces. Although their principal source of income was still produce from the fields and orchards, it had also adopted some of the animal husbandry practised across the border. They held a weekly market incorporating both, as well as welcoming traders in jewels and metals. As Reez wandered through the lanes to the large inn at the centre, he noted several old wooden buildings were being replaced with stone constructions.

He entered the inn and made himself known to the landlord and asked that a message be sent to the Margrave requesting an audience. He was looking forward to a hot meal, a soft bed, and an early night. His leg was aching after his constant journeying, and the scars on his arm were itching. He had only just begun to eat when the Margrave himself bustled into the inn followed by his wife.

"Welcome, welcome, Master Reez," the portly man

gushed as he hurried over, his balding head shining from his race to the inn. Reez reluctantly put down his utensils and rose to meet him.

"Oh, Master Reez, there is no need to lodge here," the Margravine simpered as she joined her husband. "You must stay with us. I insist." Like the Margrave, she was also short and plump. Her white hair was piled on her head and secured with a jewelled band, and her face was painted. Both the Margravine and her husband wore richly brocaded clothes and Reez noticed a great many gems on their fingers.

"I don't mind," Reez began, but he got no further.

"Nonsense, I won't hear of it. You are an exalted guest of the town and deserve the very best."

Reez shot an apologetic look at the innkeeper, who just shrugged. "I'm sure the inn is more than sufficient for my needs," he said.

"Oh, but we have the finest linens in the province and I always demand the very best provisions," the Margravine asserted, laying a hand on Reez's arm. "I wouldn't feel right knowing you were here when you could enjoy the warmth of our home."

"There's no gainsaying it, Master Reez," the Margrave said with a chuckle. "I've learnt it best to do as I'm told if I want a quiet life. Once my lady wife decides something, there is no changing her mind."

"I already have my girls making up the bed," she said with a smile of triumph. She slipped her arm into Reez's and manoeuvred him towards the door.

"But my bag…"

"I'm sure someone will bring it over, don't worry. Now tell me, have you ever been to Etheradia?"

On the walk to the Margrave's residence, they bombarded Reez with details about the Margravine's trips to the city, and it soon became obvious that she was especially keen to emulate their more affluent residents. As a result, she had demanded her husband build another wing to their already opulent house to incorporate a separate dining area and receiving room and was the primary driving force behind the changes in the town. When Reez idly commented on the similarity of the drapes to those hanging in the Falcon Inn, she had been thrilled. After Reez explained how he had exploited his rank as journeyman to reward Castor and his wife for their hospitality, she became quite excited until Reez made it perfectly clear that he had no intention of draining Maston's coffers to refurbish her house. Over the lavish meal that was eventually served, finally quietening Reez's grumbling stomach, she interrogated him about the furnishings and fabrics in the Falcon as well as the latest style of clothes and the material used. She didn't seem impressed with his ignorance of lady's fashions or the lifestyles of the richer patrons. Reez suspected that, if there were no hint of trouble in Bestra, the Margrave's purse would have been a great deal lighter.

It was late when she reluctantly took her leave, finally allowing Reez to consult with the Margrave about the situation across the border.

"Yes, we have a few families," the Margrave

confirmed. "Terrible time they've had of it. We didn't know what to do with them, so they are staying in one of the bigger barns," he admitted. "They have very little money or possessions. People have been contributing food and so forth, but I'm worried about what will happen should more arrive. I doubt whether folk will be so generous then." He rubbed his belly and belched loudly.

"I will want to speak to them," Reez said. "It will be good to finally hear the truth of what's happening."

"I can take you after breaking our fast on the morrow, if you like."

Eventually, Reez had made his escape and retired to his room. Lying back on the soft bed with a groan, he resisted the urge to scratch his arm. He had run out of the burn salve and was already feeling the effects as his skin dried up. His body ached, and he yearned to be back home. Reaching over, he doused the lamp and closed his eyes. Despite the dire rumours, there were no ravening packs of wild beasts roaming the countryside, nor were there hordes of people streaming in to the province. All seemed quiet and orderly for the moment. Thankful that his journey had been surprisingly uneventful, Reez slipped into a dreamless sleep.

#

There were five families living in the barn, and Reez was pleased to see that, despite the Margrave's assessment of their belongings, they had in fact been able to salvage enough to be fairly comfortable. Mattresses newly stuffed with clean straw were arranged in sleeping areas that had been separated with drapes and linens. They had organised themselves well so that some collected wood, whilst others cooked, washed, tended the few animals that they had rescued, or fetched water from the river nearby. The children played happily outside, mostly ignorant of the worry straining the faces of the adults.

After introducing himself, Reez took a stool by the fire and turned to the men and women ranged around him. "I'd like to hear your stories if you would be so kind," he said, "and then we can make some plans about what happens next."

"I'm not sure we can be of much help," one man began. "None of us have seen the things that are attacking the farms up close."

"I say it's those massive wolves," another interjected. "What else could rip apart a full grown cou like that?"

"Even the wolves didn't kill like these do," a woman said, her voice small. "It's as if they are sent mad with the smell of blood and go into a frenzy."

"What do you mean?" Reez asked.

"They don't just kill the animals," the first man said. "They tear them to pieces. I woke up one morning to find all the kine dead, the field awash with blood. It made me sick to look at it."

"We got so scared," the woman next to him said. "I was worried about the children. We couldn't stay."

"Everything was gone, all my herds. I had nothing to send to market or see us through the winter cycle. We lost everything," an old man said tersely.

"They came for my family," another voice said. Reez

turned to see a wiry man with his arms wrapped protectively around another woman, who was weeping quietly.

"What happened?" Reez asked gently.

The man took a deep breath. "I was just finishing up for the evening. One of the cou's had birthed, but it had been a difficult delivery and I had been with her most of the day. We had her secured in the stalls near the house. When I came out, I heard a commotion in the fields. The kine were stampeding, some of them making a terrible noise. I saw a shape bring one of them down and the sound…" he swallowed loudly, "like a dreadful ripping. I wasn't going to wait around. I'd heard tales of predators, but I'd dismissed them as fanciful stories. I ran into the house and slammed the door, calling to Maeve to get the children. We'd just got the bar across the door when something big and heavy smashed into the wood. It must have seen me running and followed me. I thought we were all going to die.

"We have a cellar. It's not very big, but it keeps the meat cold after Maeve salts it down. Before the creature broke through, I pushed my family down the steps and closed the hatch. I've never been so frightened in my life. We could hear its claws scrabbling over the floor and the furniture being upturned. I was holding on to the handle, but I figured it wouldn't be enough if the thing wanted to get to us. It didn't growl or roar, not even a bark. It just rampaged over our heads, smashing pots and destroying everything. I daren't move after I thought it was gone. It was only late the next day when my neighbours saw the fields and came to see if we were safe that they found us still in the cellar. We packed only what we could carry and left the same day. My children still have night terrors."

There was silence for a moment. Reez looked around at the faces surrounding him and could only guess at how they must feel, running from their homes with no idea what was to happen to them or how they would live. "Do you think others will follow your example and leave Bestra?" he asked.

"It takes a lot to make us leave our land," another voice said." I haven't heard of them attacking anyone else, but it may only be a matter of time. When there are no animals left, the beasts might look to the people for sport. Then folk will be too afraid to linger. Whether they come here or try for the city, I can't say, but you ought to be ready."

After checking that the families were being looked after and had all they needed, Reez left them and returned to the Margrave's house, advising that he call a meeting of the council. After much debate, they made preparations in case a large number of Bestrians crossed the border. Reez suggested they look at erecting temporary shelters for any refugees who were fleeing the province, as they would soon need the barns to store the harvest. He then wrote to the nearest Margraves, encouraging them to do the same. Someone suggested it would be better for the newcomers to move further into Fiora, where they could build homes, barter their goods, or find work to support themselves. Between them, the council drew up a proposed network plan so that no one village would be overwhelmed should the tide of refugees increase. All in all, Reez was satisfied that there was no immediate threat and was confident that the border villages could deal with any people fleeing Bestra province. As there was nothing more for him to do, he decided he would return home the following day. He rubbed his leg and stifled a yawn as the council continued to debate. Taking advantage of a break in the conversation, he hastily excused himself and made his escape, returning to the guest room to rest before the evening meal.

Although he had affected an air of confidence in front of the Margrave, the news of the ravening creatures had greatly disturbed him. These animals were not killing for food but slaughtering mindlessly. Reez wondered what alterations Verrin had made to the wolves to transform them from shy pack hunters to lone predators who would even attack humans. As he lay down on the cot, he tried not to imagine what fresh horrors Verrin might inflict now that he was Master.

A knock on the door roused him, and he realised he had fallen asleep.

"Yes?" he called, rubbing his eyes and sitting back up.

"Dinner is ready, Master Reez," his host called through the door.

"Thank you. I will be out directly."

When he opened the door, however, the Margrave stood outside waiting for him. "I wonder if I might have a quiet word before we eat?" he ventured.

Reez nodded and walked back into the room. The Margrave followed, shutting the door behind him.

"I want to thank you for your help today," he began. "I feel relieved to have a plan in place."

Reez sat on a chair and waved a hand dismissively.

"I'm sure you would have managed admirably without me."

"Nevertheless, it has been an honour to have you here, and to be able to garner your wisdom."

"Is this what you wished to discuss?" Reez asked, his face puzzled.

The Margrave took a deep breath. "Those people…" he paused for a moment; his face troubled. "That is the first time I have heard their stories in such detail. I am worried, Master Reez. When I approached Master Wicton five summers ago and told him of the wolves on our border, there were no attacks like the ones I heard of today. We were wary, yes, but only because they seemed unnaturally large and I was worried that one of them might make off with a child rather than one of the herds. These creatures are something else entirely. We can guard ourselves if a hungry animal thinks to try easy prey, but if they break into our houses and attack us in our homes, then we have no defence. If folk hear of it, they will panic."

"I fear you may be right," Reez said with a sigh. He leant forward in the chair and rested his head in his hands. The Margrave waited patiently while Reez tried to think. "All of them spoke of the attacks happening in the early evening or at night," he pondered aloud. "What if we say that both animals and people should be indoors well before nightfall, especially in the more remote farms? It may be the stampeding of terrified animals is the very thing that sends the creatures into a frenzy. It attacked the family after the farmer ran, so maybe such behaviour triggers a hunting response. If there is nothing living abroad to catch their attention, the creatures may leave well alone."

"Your deductions make sense," the Margrave agreed. "It shouldn't take much persuasion to make it happen. Folk are already afeared and unwilling to venture far."

"Other than barricading everyone behind stone walls, I can think of no other options." Reez paused and stood. "We should join your lady wife, otherwise she will be vexed. If things change, or you hear any other news, be sure to send word at once."

During the meal, despite the Margravine's pleas for him to stay longer, Reez insisted he would be leaving.

"But I feel so much safer with you here," she simpered

"Your husband is a capable man," Reez reassured her. "He has everything under control."

Neither man voiced their fervent prayer that it would remain that way.

Chapter Eight

Reez was frustrated. He had tried the scrying tool, but that had revealed only what his own eyes had shown him, and he was no nearer discovering anything more about the metals in his hand. Kromar had obtained both raw ore and smelted metals for his inspection, but unlike plants, close examination failed to give him any clues to unravelling their secrets, or how to mould them with magic.

Leaving the samples scattered across the table, Reez rose and made his way out to the glass house. Tending to the plants soothed his spirit, and he soon lost himself in the familiar chores.

"There must be a way," he mused to himself as he worked, imagining his mentor standing at the doorway watching him with emerald eyes full of amusement. "I mean, you told me that magic doesn't adhere to the boundaries we give it. I should be able to manipulate minerals just as I do plants."

He fetched the broom from the corner and swept away the remnants of earth and plant debris scattered across the floor. "I know it takes heat to shape metal, but I can't carry a forge around with me. I need to generate it somehow within the material itself." He leaned on the handle. "None of that helps if I can't even identify the ore with magic, like you made me classify all those plants." A fleeting memory of Wicton speaking to him popped into his head and he tried to concentrate on the thought, but it disappeared again. He furrowed his brow, desperately searching his mind for the elusive information, knowing instinctively that it was the key to unlocking the puzzle. Why would Wicton have even mentioned earth magic to his young apprentice, let alone given him the tools to understand it or use it? It didn't make sense. The feeling, however, wouldn't leave him.

Sighing in frustration, he finished his work and wandered back to the tower to prepare his evening meal.

#

It was a few days later, as he worked in the patch of earth outside, that the memory returned to him, as if his mind had continued to mull on the issue independently of his own thoughts. He remembered sitting with Wicton in the hut talking about the myriad sensations in his body when he had first realised that the Masters were using their magic, and Wicton had identified that he was reacting to the different magic disciplines. Earth magic, instead of affecting his skin and making him itch, had resonated far within him as if his very bones were affected. Somehow, he needed to channel the magic deeper within him to utilise its power.

Excited by the revelation, Reez let the vegetables he had been harvesting fall from his hands as he stood and closed his eyes in order to concentrate better. He felt the magic circling him like a soothing caress across his skin, and he gathered it as if to use it as normal. Instead of releasing it, however, he fought to change it and move it further inward. At first there was no difference, and Reez was starting to wonder if there was something else that needed to be done, when suddenly the metal shifted, as if he had smashed a barrier open. He felt the magic alter as it hummed deeply within him. Tentatively, he released it, feeling the slow vibration like a heart thrumming deep inside. He turned slowly, following the direction of the flow, and opened his eyes. In front of him was the tower, stone on stone, reaching up to the scudding clouds overhead.

He took a deep breath and let it out with a huff of surprise, before his face stretched into a huge grin. Abandoning his task, he dashed inside the tower as quickly as he could, eager to find out more. He climbed the steps two at a time in his rush to get to the study where the shards of metal and nuggets of ore lay where he had left them, waiting for him to unlock their secrets.

Forcing himself to breathe slowly, Reez sat at the table

and arranged the metals in a line, calming his mind and his body so that he could better concentrate. When he felt ready, he began again. For the longest time, he could detect nothing other than the stone surrounding him and had almost decided to take the experiment out into the meadow when he felt the resonance change, as if his newly born senses had discovered something different. Reaching out, he picked up the metal and turned it over in his hand. Iron. For a while, he switched between the two substances, to familiarise himself with the subtle variations in vibration and become accustomed to their feeling. Eventually he stopped, hunger and thirst reminding him he had missed his noon meal completely. Before he went down to the galley, Reez reached for a new journal and, out of a habit born of many cycles of study, wrote down his findings.

It was a slow process, being so alien to everything he had ever known, but gradually over the following fortnight, Reez learnt to recognise the slight variances and locate each of the different metals as well as several rock types. As his senses became adjusted to the changes, he could identify smaller objects, like the iron nails in the door frame or the tools in his glass house. With trial and error, he even found the glass itself, having remembered a throwaway comment that Paiter had made regarding the origin of glass and how hot the forge needed to be in order to create it.

#

At first he gathered the magic from the plants and re-channelled it, which took time and effort, but eventually he detected a dull vibration beneath his feet and recognised the call of earth and stone. After that, he found it much easier to pull the magic directly from below. He even experimented with changing earth magic to plant magic, becoming quicker and more proficient as he practised until he barely thought about which magic he was utilising. He understood how the Mages of old could seamlessly wield their power by just taking what was closest to hand rather than search out a suitable source.

Eventually, he decided he was ready to attempt manipulating the metals, and carried them across the meadows and fields until he felt safe enough: the last thing he wanted to do was destroy his tower in his fumbling attempts. The winter cycle was almost upon them and the wind was chill as it blew across the open space. Reez walked to the edge of the woods where the trees would shelter him from the worst of the weather, put down the cloth he had brought and laid out the differing fragments of metal and stone side by side. He picked up the iron and weighed it in his hand. This was the easiest of the ores to locate and Reez reasoned it would be the best place to start. Setting the others aside, he gathered the magic and focused it. As he pushed harder, the vibrations in his body seemed to increase, but nothing else happened. He tried to envisage what he wanted the metal to do, remembering the way he could mould it and shape it with his smithing tools, attempting to force it with his will. The reverberations were making him feel nauseous and his body shook. Suddenly, like the explosion of a viola seed pod, the metal popped and liquefied, spreading out over his hand and slipping through his fingers on to the cloth like water. A sudden burst of heat made him cry out as the liquid oozed over his skin and he jumped up, dropping the metal onto the cloth. As soon as he withdrew the magic, the metal solidified. Amazed, Reez stared at his hand where a few fragments of the metal now rested. He flexed his fingers and stared at the pink skin, unharmed by his experiment. He knew first hand how hot metal burned. Somehow, the magic had altered the metal without the searing heat usually needed to melt it. The molten iron sat in a silver pool on the cloth. He tentatively placed a finger on the smooth surface and found it cold and hard to the touch. Picking a piece up, he turned the flat shape over and over. He had managed to change the iron from a solid to a liquid and back to a solid again. He whooped in celebration, knowing that he had finally discovered the way to mould and shape metal.

For many days he worked, gradually learning how to melt each substance. He even turned stone molten, although with significant resistance. Reez knew he would need a lot of practice before he could control the flow of magic in order to soften the metal without dissolving it entirely, but he was ecstatic with his discoveries and eager to learn more.

Although there was no-one to criticise or censor him, he continued to lock his journals away in the forbidden archives. The strictures that had stood for millennia on attempting magic outside the disciplines were deeply rooted within him and he was reluctant to share his findings with anyone. It felt wrong to dabble with this new magic, despite the fact that Minra had no Master and was seemingly desperate for his presence. When guilt crept up on him, with the books safely hidden away, he could almost pretend that such provocative work didn't exist, and he was just a simple Master of green magic.

#

As he shut the vault door and made his way back up the stone steps from the basement, Reez's stomach growled loudly. Confident in his abilities, he now worked down in the archives as the winter rains tumbled down and the frost covered the grass like ground wheat flour. Today had been a good day, and he had finally grasped the intricacies of softening metal, having successfully bent a strip of iron, but as often happened, he had neglected to feed himself and he discovered he was ravenous. The small fire in the galley had extinguished itself long ago, and he felt too tired to clear out the ashes in order to rebuild another. Looking outside, he realised the rain had finally stopped, so he decided to walk down into the village and eat at the inn instead. It had been some time since he had last ventured down, so focused was he on understanding the earth magic, and even longer since he had spent a pleasant evening with friends and family.

A small part of him admitted that he also wanted to spend time with Destry.

Neither of them had mentioned the kiss she had bestowed on him as he left for the border villages. In many ways, nothing had changed between them; she treated him the same and never seemed to expect anything from him. Reez, unsure what to do about her display of affection, was happy to let it lie, but it didn't stop him from thinking about it occasionally late at night as the light leached away and he huddled under the padded quilt on his bed.

He did not know what Destry dreamed of in the deep places of her soul. He had no business encouraging her if her aspirations were the same as Nula's. His position and future were more uncertain than ever before, and he couldn't promise her security or a family home. If his efforts to come to grips with earth magic were as successful as he hoped, he envisaged having to travel extensively into Minra province, which would mean long absences from the village. He rubbed the puckered skin on the left side of his face. He had once been handsome, but he no longer had even his looks to recommend him. Verrin had taken that away, along with everything else. He shook his head. In truth, he had nothing to offer a wife except a life of loneliness.

Donning his winter cloak, he walked down to the inn and, foregoing his usual seat in the corner, made for the fire. There were only a few gathered in the taproom. Many had stayed at home rather than face the chill of the night, and others had already been and gone. Destry was behind the bar, washing out mugs and returning them to the shelf. She hadn't noticed his arrival, and he was able to watch her openly. All her movements were quiet and careful so as not to draw any attention, allowing her to fade into the background. Reez wondered how someone who had no concept of sound could be so adept at creating none herself. She wiped her hands on the stained apron she always wore that had long since lost its pure white newness and succumbed to age and extensive use. She flicked the long braid of blonde hair off her shoulder and turned to wipe down the bar. Her eyes widened momentarily when she spotted Reez, and two spots of red bloomed on her flawless cheeks. Reez nodded and smiled, noticing the deep breath she took before answering with one of her own.

Ale? She asked.

Please.

After delivering the mug and finding out what he wanted to eat, she disappeared into the galley and Reez settled back in the comfortable chair, glad of the warmth and the chance for some company. When Destry reappeared and placed the food in front of him, he held her wrist to stop her from leaving.

Sit with me?

She glanced around the taproom to check for other customers before nodding and sliding gracefully into the chair opposite.

I don't see anyone else. Are you alone today? he asked, while picking up the spoon and taking a mouthful of the warm stew.

Nula went up with the children a while ago. Lileth has been difficult today and Lina is fretful. Nula thinks another tooth is coming.

Reez smiled. Naming their second daughter after his mother had been a wonderful tribute by Aydal and Nula that the whole family had appreciated. *What news of your father?*

Nothing. He won't come down. He sits in his room all day and only seems to come alive when the children are there, although he tires of them quickly.

That's hard for you.

Destry shrugged. *We manage.*

Reez knew Aydal helped when he could, but he was

needed in the fields. They had already compromised by living at the inn instead of moving in to the family home so that Nula could be available as much as possible to help Destry in the taproom and take care of their father. Having small children had made everything even harder to manage, and both girls were visibly tired. It was a shame that Phalen had no sons to take over the running of the inn.

He finished his stew and turned his full attention to Destry. *We should talk.*

I thought we already were, she retorted.

Reez grinned momentarily before he remembered the point he wanted to make. *I mean about us,* he signed. Destry said nothing. *I like you very much.* Reez continued, watching her closely.

I like you too, but you know this.

Reez sighed. *What do you want from me, Destry?*

She frowned. *I don't understand.*

I have nothing to offer you, he said, trying to explain. *You want a partner? Children? I can't give you those things. There is so much to do in Zelannor, and I am the only person with the skills. My duties as Master of Fiora are extensive, but now Minra is begging for my help, I will probably be gone for long periods of time.*

I know, she countered. *I will miss you, but I am also patient.*

Reez shook his head and tried to think of another argument. *I am not the man I was. My face...* he paused, not knowing how to tell her of his self-loathing.

Destry slapped the table in front of them, jolting him in surprise. She looked angry. *I don't see your face. I see inside,* she signed in agitation. Reez stared at her, almost missing the words as she continued. *You are good. You are kind. You tend to us all.* Reez recognised her frustration as she struggled to make the few words that she had describe her thoughts and feelings. *I want nothing more than to live very small in your heart. I want to care for you. Who else does that? I'll watch out for you while you look after the rest of the world.* She reached across with her right hand and stroked his scarred and puckered face.

You will always be in my heart, he admitted.

Like Nula?

No, not like her. Destry's face fell, and she dropped her eyes to the floor. He tipped her chin up, so that she was forced to look at him. *Nula was a fantasy. She wasn't real to me. I only thought myself in love with her. You are different.*

How?

I think you might be the flower that Wicton wanted for me. Even so, it would be wrong for me to hold on to you when my life is so uncertain.

I can wait.

I made your sister wait. I won't do that to you.

One day you will understand that it is my choice to make, not yours, she said before sliding out of the chair. *I'll be here when you stop being so stubborn.*

"I'm being selfless, not stubborn," he muttered as he watched her walk out to the galley. His head fell back on the settle as he groaned. No matter how much he might wish it, he was right not to pursue Destry. He refused to hold her back the way he had Nula. He rubbed his face and stood up. She might not agree with him now, he reasoned as he left the inn, but one day she would be grateful that he had given her the freedom to make another choice. She could have a full life with someone who would stay with her, someone without a hideous face and crippled body. He only wished the idea of her handfasted to another didn't hurt so much.

Chapter Nine

Reez stared at the stone edifice in front of him. Fashioned from the rock face that surrounded it, it looked like a half-finished sculpture hewn from the mountain itself. Black windows high in the walls stared down at him as he traced the lines of the ancient keep back until it blended seamlessly with the stone. Three stories high, the stronghold was a testament to the craftsmanship of the Masters of Minra and was an imposing building. Pillars and turrets were carved from the rock face and the walls were highly decorated. A heavy double door studded with metal was set back behind large metal gates, which could be closed and secured to render the place impenetrable. The doorway was the only opening on the lower level. On either side of it, lifelike stone figures flanked the gates, frozen in the act of hammering, shaping, and digging.

After his success with identifying and bending metal, he had finally contacted the guild leaders and arranged to meet with them. They had heralded his arrival at the bustling town of Rudsmede with a formal reception. Amidst endless speeches and presentations, they had introduced him to all the town's dignitaries and their aides, as well as prominent guild members and citizens, all effusive in their thanks for his timely arrival. Tired and hungry, he had been relieved when the three leaders had finally finished and offered to show him to his rooms so he could rest. He had taken little notice when they led him away from the streets and up the mountain, thinking only of a warm bed and a bite to eat. Reez turned back to the three men ranged behind him.

"What is this? I thought you would take me to an inn."

"It's the Master's residence," Hobart, the stone guild leader, said. Dark of skin, what he lacked in hair on his head, he more than made up for in his long bushy beard and wide moustache. He was a large man and once he would have made an impressive figure, his muscles huge and powerful, but age and lack of use had reduced his strength and mass.

"I can't stay here," Reez objected.

Samine from the jeweller's guild frowned. Shorter and leaner than Hobart, he was the most garrulous of the three. His simple manner and open face gave him the appearance of sincerity and candour, however Reez noticed his smile didn't quite reach his eyes. His mousy hair was cut short and his beard trimmed into a neat point. "This is the best we have to offer you," he explained.

"I don't have permission to enter," Reez said.

"But we give you permission," Jodrel replied, his face confused. He was the guild leader for the metalworkers and younger than the others by several summers. His fair hair and pale skin made him the opposite in every way to Hobart.

"To enter a Master's dwelling, you need a blood ritual," Reez tried to explain, "otherwise you are barred from entering." The three men looked at each other in puzzlement. Reez sighed. "Look, I'll show you."

He strode forward to the huge wooden panelled portal with its filigree tracery and pushed firmly. The door swung open silently, and Reez stopped in surprise. Warm air rushed out of the hall beyond, bathing Reez in welcome. Stunned, Reez turned back to his companions, his mouth agape, only to watch them disappearing down the track towards the town of Rudsmede below.

Shaking his head, Reez stepped inside the keep before pushing the door to. It slid quietly back into place and closed with a barely audible snick. In the gloom he noticed hooks beyond the door, some of which held cloaks of soft black fur. Shrugging off his own thin wrap, he hung it next to them. Sturdy black boots stood in regimented lines underneath, along with various other footwear; two of each, Reez noted. He took a deep breath to ease the tightness in his chest, imagining Chrisos and Paiter walking out of the door for the meeting of the triumvirate, unaware that it would be for the last time. There was also a pile of felt slippers which Reez guessed were indoor shoes. They looked very comfortable. He glanced down at his own grubby boots, filthy from the long trek to Minra. With a shrug, he pulled them off and was pleasantly surprised to find the floor warm beneath his feet. Reez bent down and touched the stone flags, marvelling as he discovered that the entire floor was heated somehow.

Curious now, he quickly donned a pair of grey felted slippers and made his way to another doorway opposite the entrance. Pushing gently, he moved through the equally silent portal and into the room beyond. A massive stone table dominated the centre of the room, surrounded by chairs, enough to seat a dozen visitors. A large ornate wooden cabinet to the side was filled with goblets and bottles of different shapes and sizes. Crossing over to it, Reez scanned the contents, choosing one at random. He pulled out the stopper from a clear bottle and sniffed.

"Taklar," he murmured softly before setting it back on the shelf, shaking his head. "No, thank you."

The ceiling of the room was high, and several windows carved into the rock let in light from the south. Sconces were fixed around the walls, the candles newly trimmed and ready to be lit should the dark encroach. Whorls, flowers and fruit were carved in the stone around the top of the walls and a large tapestry hung from the back wall, depicting various aspects of earth magic. Reez recognised a blacksmith's forge with tools on a bench, what may have been a jeweller hunched over a table with a scrying glass before her, and a giant wielding a massive hammer. Above it all, dark storm clouds swirled around a mountain and below, the earth fires flamed.

In the far-left corner, a small door was the only other exit. Opening it, Reez found it led to the rest of the stronghold. It took Reez a little while to search the remainder of the keep. Several rooms took up the rest of that floor. His first discovery was a bathing area, similar to the one he had enjoyed at Stonaven, but on a much smaller scale. Three small pools stood inside, two of them full of steaming hot water, and Reez resolved to make good use of them after his initial explorations. A large galley, fully stocked with a variety of fresh and preserved foods, was next, and a side door opened to an extensive cellar full of wine, as well as several racks of spirits. Another door led into an impressive workroom filled with an assortment of tools stored on racks hung on the walls or laid carefully in boxes on the benches, many of which Reez now recognised after his short apprenticeship with Kromar. A stone stairway led down from the workroom into the depths of the keep, where a huge forge sat banked but still burning, constantly fed by the earth fires themselves. Vents and pipes led away from it, and Reez wondered if it could be the source of the heating in the flooring above. A huge anvil richly decorated with a complex pattern dominated the floor. Pieces of half-finished work lay across a table to the rear and Reez wandered over to examine them. He slowly stroked a finger across the highly burnished plates that appeared to be shaped like a tunic. Picking it up, he was surprised at the lightness of the metal; it weighed less than a change of winter clothes. Judging by the size and shape, Reez concluded they had made it to fit Paiter's larger form. He carefully placed it back on the table and, after another look around the room, climbed back up the wide stairs.

Moving upwards, Reez arrived at the first floor, which housed a comfortable seating area with deep cushioned chairs and matching footstools, and a second cabinet stocked with liquor. There was a hearth, but it was empty of wood and Reez assumed it hadn't needed to be used in a very long time. The warmth from below continued in the upper rooms, negating the need for a fire. A few books were scattered on a nearby table, ready for their owners to return and continue reading, and Reez lifted one up to flick through it. The contents indicated it was a tome about the properties of different jewels. He laid it back down, resolving to read them all later. His decision, however, was quickly forgotten when he pushed open the next door. Inside were shelves of books lining the entire room and crammed into free-standing cabinets. On a table underneath one of the large windows was a detailed map of Minra province with letters and numbers annotating it. More sconces around the walls meant a person could sit long into the night studying and learning. Reez's fingers itched to pull down the volumes and peruse their contents. His excitement built with the prospect of discovering much more than his own paltry experiments had yielded. He hoped the tomes held the answers he needed to satisfy at least some expectations of the guild leaders.

The top floor held the two sumptuous bed chambers, each housing enormous beds piled high with soft pillows, blankets and furs and surrounded by thick red drapes. Large ornate chests were filled with clothing, cleaned and ready for use. Heavy curtains covered the large windows, all of which faced south, making the most of the daylight. Rudsmede lay below. When Reez wandered across, he could see the town clearly, lamps flickering to life in the houses as the darkness of night encroached. Peering closely at the frame, he noticed that the panes of glass were doubled inside, presumably to further insulate the keep. Holding his hand out, he could detect no errant draughts creeping in; it was tightly sealed. He thought of the chill that trickled into his bedroom at home when the wind blew, especially during the winter cycle. He could make improvements to his own tower by learning the secrets of this place.

Reez retraced his steps to the galley to plunder the store cupboards and pantry, making himself a hearty meal. He was curious to discover how so much fresh food was available and determined to ask the guild leaders during his meeting with them the following day. After eating, he eagerly stripped off his clothes and eased into the hottest pool, luxuriating in the heat while rinsing away the grime of the long journey north. He ignored the cold bath, choosing instead to dry himself on the thick towels hung on the wall and after choosing a bottle of berry wine from the vast collection in the cellar, he made his way back up to the library. As he bathed, he had had concerns that the books on display were not really important, accessible as they were to anyone wandering the keep, but he soon discovered they were full of knowledge invaluable in his forays into earth magic. Nevertheless, the number of books was far less than his own vault in Maston, and he reluctantly deduced that there was probably another archive, much like his own, that he may never locate, let alone gain entry to. Despite that, he read long after night had fallen, keen to exploit this unexpected opportunity to learn as much as possible.

#

The next morning, Reez reluctantly shrugged out of the luxurious bed and dressed. He had taken Chrisos' room as his own for the duration of his visit. Paiter's was cluttered with tools and fragments of metal as well as what seemed to be his old childhood toys. Clothes lay across the chairs, and the easy disorder was a painful reminder of his old friend. Chrisos, however, had been more systematic with his possessions, and Reez felt nothing more than a detached sorrow as he scanned the tidy room. The keep itself kept surprising Reez. He marvelled at the luxury of a basin for washing in the bedchamber's corner. When Reez moved the metal lever, hot water came splashing out, a rare pleasure indeed. He couldn't help contrasting it with his own home, bathing in a chilly room in front of a fire after hauling buckets from the stove, or the chore of boiling water for washing each day. He remembered Wicton saying the other Masters were disinclined to linger at the little hut in the clearing, preferring to return to the comfort of their own residences. Reez could well understand it now, having experienced a little of it for himself. Despite that, it surprised him to realise that he still preferred the simplicity of his own home and felt a familiar pang as he thought of Maston and the tower on the hill.

Returning to the galley, he enjoyed a meal of eggs,

fresh bread, and cold meats before deciding to make his way down to Rudsmede in order to meet with the guild leaders. When he opened the door to the meeting room, however, he found they were already there, seated at the large table. They stood and bowed respectfully when he entered.

"I hope you slept well, Master Reez," Hobart said, his black brows raised.

Reez nodded. "Thank you. I did."

"We tried to anticipate your needs, but if there is anything you require, Magda can get it for you."

"Who is Magda?" Reez asked, taking a seat opposite them at the table.

"She is the keeper of the house," Hobart explained. At Reez's puzzled look, he elaborated further. "She keeps the galley and cellars fully stocked, cleans the rooms and washes the clothes and linen. She also mends and cooks if required."

"Does anyone else come here?" Reez asked, shocked that she had unrestricted access.

"The lads who help shift the ore, although they haven't been needed since..." Hobart stopped and looked down at his hands.

"Magda would bring some local girls up when the Master was in residence to help with the extra chores," Jodrel added.

"It seems to me that people can come and go as they please," Reez said, aghast. "Has anyone taken anything from here?"

"No, Master Reez," Samine said smoothly. "Everything

is here for you, I assure you."

"How can you be so sure when the whole town can enter at will?"

"No one would dare come here without the Master's permission," Hobart blustered loudly.

"Well, the Master has been absent for almost four cycles," Reez pointed out. "Who is there to deny them entrance?"

"No one would dare," Hobart insisted.

"What about the library? Has anyone been in there?"

The three guild leaders glanced at one another. "When you first refused to come, we were at a loss," Samine began. "We didn't know who to turn to, so we tried to glean some information ourselves."

"We wanted to see if we could do the job ourselves," Jodrel finished, his arms crossing his chest and his chin thrust forward.

"I see," Reez said stonily. "Because I am here now, I assume you learned nothing useful." Jodrel's neck went red, but he refused to look away. "Are any of the books missing?"

"Of course not," Samine soothed quickly. "We can account for all of them for."

Reez took a deep breath and studied the three men one by one. It was a useless exercise to probe them further. They may be right and respect for their Master's old residence had discouraged the curious. But even if books had been taken, Reez could do nothing about it. As antagonising the guild leaders was foolish, especially as it would prove necessary to work closely with them in the future, he decided not to pursue the matter further. It would do no good to dwell upon the past. "I asked you to make a note of the seams you want opening," he said eventually. "Have you been able to compile a list for me?"

"Yes, of course," Samine said, his relief palpable. He pulled out a piece of parchment from his tunic and pushed it over to Reez.

Reez scanned the list. "So many?" he murmured.

"Necessary, I assure you," Samine replied. "If you wish, I could explain each one to you."

"No," Reez said distractedly, "I'm sure it's all in order. It may take me a while to familiarise myself with this and to work out a plan. Perhaps you can leave it with me and return in, say, two days' time?" He glanced at the men, who nodded eagerly and stood.

"Thank you, Master Reez," Samine said. "I feel so much better knowing you are here to help us."

Reez mumbled something vaguely and watched them leave. He smoothed the paper in front of him as the door closed silently behind them. It seemed odd that so many seams needed to be breached this early. There also appeared to be an inordinately large number of gold seams required, which further raised his suspicions. He remembered Blane, a blacksmith in Stonaven who had helped him when he visited as an apprentice, mentioning that gold mining was restricted and that Chrisos was very careful to only open a few mines in different communities. He rose and headed out of the meeting hall and into the keep, hoping that Chrisos had been as meticulous in his work as he was in his living space.

Chapter Ten

Reez stood straight and eased his back, surprised to see that the light was already fading. He had been poring over the large map in the library, which he now knew showed every mine opened in the last decade. A fortunate discovery of a stack of notebooks in one cabinet was the key to finally being able to decipher the annotations made by Chrisos. Each mine was listed by two letters denoting either metal or gem and a number which related to the amount of mines currently active in the province. All of them were documented in depth in the notebooks along with the date of opening and estimated length of duration expected with judicious mining of the ore detected. There were even sites labelled for mines to be opened in the future dotted around the entire area. After studying it carefully and comparing it to the list given to him by the guild leaders, he had reached the conclusion that he was being thoroughly duped.

As he had suspected, Chrisos had left the province well supplied apart from one or two seams, which he had marked in red, suggesting they would need to be replaced within the next few cycles. Reez's anger spiked, hot and swift, and he crumpled up the list and threw it across the room. His first reaction was to return to Fiora immediately, leaving them to fend for themselves. He thought of their fawning and words of welcome and cursed. How they must have been laughing at him as they left the previous day, thinking that they could fool him into giving them everything they desired. His stomach protested loudly at that moment and he made his way down to the galley to prepare some long overdue food, allowing the familiar chore to soothe him slightly. As he ate, his mind worked furiously, trying to decide on the best course of action.

The guild leaders needed to be brought to task, but the rest of the people were likely ignorant of their greed and duplicity and should not suffer. They didn't deserve to see their livelihood damaged or destroyed by a few self-serving men. He was glad he had asked for a couple of days before meeting with them again; it would allow him to calm himself and formulate a plan. He was a Master and deserved respect, and by the First Mage, he would get it.

Pushing away his empty plate, he stood, his resolve firm. There was still a mountain of knowledge to catalogue in the library, and he intended to use the opportunity to familiarise himself with the workings of the province, but first, he had a task to do.

Gathering a knife and bowl from the galley along with other ingredients, Reez walked into the meeting room and stood before the small door leading back to the rest of the keep. He paused for a moment, mentally reviewing the process he had read in the archives back home to make sure that he missed nothing out. At first, he had considered using the ritual on the outer door but had decided against it. It seemed fitting to have a place for the leaders to come and seek him out, or for a few of them to gather as they had done the day before. Knowing how brutal the winter cycle could be in the north, it was a kindness to allow visitors to enter the warmth and comfort of the big room. However, it felt wrong that they could proceed further. Nodding to himself, he nicked his finger, letting the blood drip onto the mixture of herbs and minerals in the bowl before smearing it on the lintel, posts and handle, fusing the mixture within the framework and creating the lock that only he could open. Satisfied that the secrets in the keep were now safe, he returned to the library to continue his research.

#

"Good morning," Reez said as he walked into the hall, letting the door shut behind him before moving to the head of the table and sitting down. A portly woman with yellow hair rose and bustled to the door. Reez was pleased to see that the locking spell had worked, as she pulled vigorously without effect. "You must be Magda," he said carefully.

Realising that she had completely ignored him, the woman faltered, her face turning crimson, and hastily dipped a curtsy in his direction. "Yes, I'm the keeper of the household."

"Well, Magda, I want to thank you for your work, especially in preparing this place for me. I am very grateful for all you have done. However, I won't be requiring you to enter the keep any longer."

She frowned at the locked door. "But the rooms. My galley," she argued.

"Any laundry will be left in here for you to collect, and you can return it the same way. You have been very thorough in stocking the larder, but if I need more supplies, I can either leave a list, or walk down to the town to buy them for myself. From now on, no-one will be allowed through that door except for me."

"But Chrisos liked me to…"

"Unfortunately, he is no longer Master of this place," Reez interrupted. She seemed very proprietary about her position in the keep and was obviously used to having the freedom to come and go as she pleased. By the look of sadness that suddenly crossed Magda's face, he suspected she had done more for Chrisos in the bed chambers than just laundering the sheets. He would have to make some enquiries and discover if she had any deeper claim to Chrisos' affections. If so, he would ensure she was comfortably settled before he left. "I value my privacy," Reez continued softly, "and I have no need of a housekeeper. You may go."

She glanced across at the three men sitting at the table,

who were watching the conversation in puzzlement. "Very well," she said reluctantly. She span round, her head held high, and walked back through the entry hall, collecting her coat on the way out. As the doors closed silently behind her, Reez turned his attention back to the guild leaders. Two days ago, he had sat opposite them, as equals. Now they had to turn in order to see his face. He carefully laid the creased piece of parchment with their list of requirements in front of him and made sure to catch each man's eye before he spoke.

"Gentlemen. I hope you'll forgive me if I seem a little ignorant, but I have some questions I hope you will be able to answer," Reez began. He noticed that they all relaxed at his words.

"Of course, Master Reez. We are happy to assist you in any way," Samine said with a smile.

"Thank you. Firstly, this copper mine near Screeton," Reez said, pointing to the first item on the list. "Could you tell me why you need another seam opened so soon?" Jodrel swallowed. "Perhaps it slipped your mind that Chrisos renewed that particular mine only two moons before he left here?" Reez prompted, keeping his face impassive and his temper in check. When no one spoke, he continued.

"I see. Perhaps you can explain these requests for basalt and granite," he said, pointing to other items. Hobart flinched slightly. "They seem to be superfluous when there are already opened quarries in those areas that are still being worked. Can you justify that to me?" he asked innocently. When no-one spoke, Reez raised his voice slightly. "Please, gentlemen. I am trying to understand, and you are not being very forthcoming."

"Perhaps we made some mistakes," Samine ventured.

"Obviously," Reez said, his eyes narrowing. "Next, there is the small matter of the gold. According to Chrisos' meticulous notes, no other gold mines were to be breached for another decade, and even then, he decided it would be around Adiby." He paused and watched as all three men shuffled uncomfortably in their seats. "You disappoint me," Reez said sharply. "Did you think me some ignorant boy who could be treated like a fool?"

"Master, I'm sure we can rectify these errors…" Samine said, lifting his hand, but Reez was having none of it.

"Be quiet!" he thundered, striking the table with his fist and standing abruptly. "Chrisos may be gone, but I expect to be treated with as much respect as would be given to any Master in this land. I have neglected Fiora province in order to acquire the skills to aid you, and you present me with lies and deceit. It would be just if I left you now and let you suffer the consequences of your self-seeking." Reez paced the room as he spoke, his anger palpable. "In truth, I should call the guilds to meet me here, and describe to them what their leaders have been plotting, so that you can try to explain away your actions to the people whom you represent. That way, when the situation becomes dire and the seams *do* dry up, Minra will know who to blame when there is no-one willing to help." He stopped across from the guild leaders and leaned towards them, his hands fisted on the table. "You are despicable men who would lie and cheat. Why should I ever trust you, let alone leave you free to watch over Minra province in the absence of your Master? In my view, you are not worthy of your positions and should stand down so the guilds can elect others who will represent the needs of their people fairly."

There was silence in the hall as Reez glared at the guild leaders. Eventually, Samine stood and lifted his head to meet Reez's furious gaze. "The blame is mine," he confessed. "I was the one who suggested we capitalise on your ignorance of Minra and your lack of expertise."

"To line your own pocket?" Reez asked coldly.

Samine sighed. "In part," he admitted, "but I have always been outspoken about my thoughts on restricting gold production. It is my belief that Chrisos was too careful. In the past, Masters were more liberal in allowing precious metals to be mined, and we all prospered."

"I have first-hand knowledge of how gold can affect a community," Reez said. "There would need to be a much more compelling argument than personal profit before I would countenance such a thing." Samine frowned and sat back down.

"And you two," Reez said, directing his attention toward the other men. "You agreed to this deception without a word of dissent merely to gain wealth for yourselves?"

"Hobart was not happy," Jodrel supplied after a moment's hesitation and a quick glance at Samine, "but we persuaded him. We have other reasons for requesting access to stone and ore."

"How were you to profit?"

Jodrel cleared his throat, and Reez saw a red flush

spread over his neck and face. "There is a book," he began. "It talked of blending different materials to make better alloys. One suggested blending aluminium with other chemicals to make it more resilient to seawater corrosion. I wanted to experiment, but I needed to increase production. Opening more seams solved my problem. We have already received increased orders for iron and steel. I wanted to use the opportunity to make improvements for those employed in building boats and develop better materials."

"Where is that book now?"

"In the library. I swear you will find it there. I did take it with me to read, but I replaced it before you arrived."

"I see." Reez turned next to the stone guild leader. "Do you have anything to add, Hobart?"

The big man looked up and Reez could see his jaw clenching as he considered his response. "Production would increase across the whole province if the roadways were improved. Some places are nothing more than mud tracks, others impassable in the winter cycle. I intended to use the additional stone to strengthen and fortify our existing access routes. It would speed up travel, mean fewer delays and allow bigger carriages to traverse Minra. I wanted to make improvements for a long time, but Chrisos wouldn't listen to me."

Reez pulled out a chair and sat across from them with a frown on his face. "Why didn't he agree with what you said?"

Hobart huffed. "In truth, I do not know. He never gave a reason. He would never discuss it with me."

"You make it sound as if your Master was deliberately holding you back."

"Not just him," Jodrel said belligerently. "Every Master insists we do things the way they have always been done. We are not allowed to make even the smallest change. I, too, wanted to implement new innovations, yet my ideas were rejected, and Chrisos told me not to bother him further. They call it tradition and scare us with stories of the devastation after the great war. Well, the war was the fault of Mages, not normal men. The Masters keep us reliant on them, so we are afraid to do things on our own in case we lose their favour and their aid. I did not wish his death, but the chance to live without a Master dictating every move I made was a heady dream. Believe me, if I could have discovered the answers on my own and had the skills to locate and mine the ore myself, I would not have bothered asking you to come."

Although his words were defiant, Reez could see a sheen of perspiration on Jodrel's top lip and knew that speaking his mind had not been easy. He sat back in the chair, his thoughts whirling. He had never questioned the authority of the Masters, never doubted for a moment that they had the best interests of Zelannor at heart, yet here were three men who not only had misgivings but were willing to challenge long-established traditions for the chance to live a different way. Reez wondered if this was an isolated case or whether such sentiments were more widely held. Did the inhabitants of Fiora chafe against the strictures and order that had stood for millennia? He had never heard a word of dissent, but then again, a Master was unlikely to be approached directly. What changes might they make, given the opportunity? He looked at the guild leaders who had been willing to shape a different kind of world, and he found he couldn't condemn them outright, despite their perfidiousness.

What would he do now? The three men seemed resigned to their punishment, their shoulders hunched and eyes downcast. What would Chrisos have done? Reez didn't know, although he suspected the earth Master would not have been a lenient man. He had witnessed the old Master's swift anger for himself and could well imagine the guild leaders would have been summarily castigated before being made to stand down. Instead, he thought of Wicton's willingness to listen and consider another's opinions, who had been kind and compassionate. Perhaps he should emulate his own Master's example and elicit further information before deciding what to do.

Reez took a deep breath. "You make some valid points," he conceded. Three pairs of eyes snapped to his face. "I do not approve of your intentions to increase your own coffers," he admonished, "but your ideas appear to have merit and I would like to study them carefully. Change, whether desired or not, has been forced upon us by the deaths of Chrisos and Paiter. I cannot be both here and in Fiora, so it seems natural that you should govern Minra - or at least whoever holds the post of guild leader. I have yet to decide whether any of you are fit for the role. However, any new schemes will have to be weighed carefully. They should benefit the whole of Minra, not just parts, and I will need to determine what impact this will have on the rest of Zelannor, too."

Samine nodded enthusiastically, the smile returning to

his face. "Of course, Master Reez. Perhaps if we each presented our ideas in full? We have documents with production analyses and workforce projections."

"That would be a good start. Jodrel, why don't we begin with your ideas? Return in the morning with everything you have." The men eagerly agreed and rose to leave. "Just one more thing before you leave," Reez said as they walked to the door, talking in muted excitement. They paused and turned around. "Never lie to me again. If I discover you have been sparing with the truth, I will not hesitate to deal with you. If we are to work together, I will have honesty from you."

Hobart glanced at the others before replying. "I apologise for the deception. Perhaps when you have looked at our ideas, you might think better of us."

"Perhaps," Reez said quietly. He watched the men leave before allowing himself a small smile. He leant back in his chair and ran his fingers through his hair. It was going to be tricky juggling his time between the two provinces, but his work would be much easier if the three guild leaders supported him. Hopefully, the next few days would reveal whether that would be a possibility. In the meantime, their ideas intrigued him. Apart from Samine's obvious avarice, the others seemed reasonable. He couldn't imagine why Chrisos would be so against improving the roads or strengthening metal. There didn't seem to be any disadvantages to either innovation.

All in all, he thought as he rose and returned to the keep, the meeting had actually been much more productive than he had imagined. He hoped the rest of his stay would prove just as useful.

Chapter Eleven

"Reez!" Amily exclaimed, as her brother walked through the door of the jeweller's establishment in Rathna.

Reez grinned widely and held out his arms as she rushed over and enveloped him in a hug. He had been glad to discover that one of the potential mines was situated close to where his little sister was apprenticed and immediately decided to pay her a visit. Rathna was not as large as Rudsmede or Stonaven, but its proximity to several large deposits of gemstones had meant that it boasted several jewellers and had earned a reputation for innovation and high quality. Reez extricated himself from Amily's arms and held her shoulders, pushing her back so that he could get a good look at her. Her dark hair, so like his own, was piled on top of her head and secured with pins under a fine netting. Her porcelain features were so reminiscent of his mother that he had to swallow before he could speak.

"You've grown up at last," he finally said.

She slapped him on the shoulder, and he feigned pain. "At least one of us has," she muttered before grabbing his hand and pulling him towards the back of the store. Reez glanced around at the small shop as they passed through. Open caskets in the window displayed a dazzling variety of jewellery. Reez could see rings, necklaces, and bracelets mounted on a dark velvet material which contrasted well with the brilliance of the gems. A counter stood to one side with glass on the top so that people could view the wares within. A dark drape hung over the door leading to the rear, tied back with a cord so that the jeweller and his apprentice could see anyone entering the shop and serve them.

"Master Reez, greetings," Faradan said as he stood from his bench and moved to clasp Reez's arm. "It is a pleasure to welcome you to my home."

"The honour is mine," Reez replied. "I hope my sister has not caused you too much grief."

"On the contrary," Faradan said affectionately as he regarded Amily. "She is a rare treasure, and her presence enriches our household."

Reez looked around the bright workroom lit by the south-facing windows and several lanterns hanging from the rafters. "So, this is where you learn your craft?"

"My bench is here," Amily said proudly, indicating the one to the left. Both benches were covered with metal, tools and gems, but whereas Faradan's was neatly arranged and ordered, Amily's space seemed cluttered and in utter chaos.

"I see you still haven't learnt to be tidy," he observed, earning yet another blow.

"Alas, all my attempts have failed. I have discovered, however, that despite the disarray, she can still find anything she needs with ease," Faradan said. "Her work is so exquisite that I cannot find it in my heart to force the issue."

Reez walked over and picked up the piece that Amily had obviously been working on before his arrival. It was an oval of gold about the size of his thumbnail. A tracery of flowers and vines was etched around the outside, leaving the centre clear. He turned it over in his hand and saw that she was repeating the pattern on the back. "What is this?" he asked, pointing to a small protrusion of metal on one side. Faradan smiled knowingly and lifted his brows, nodding for Amily to speak.

"Watch," she said, taking it from him. "This is a hinge. If you press like this," she pushed her nail between the fine edge opposite and the oval sprang open, revealing a hidden compartment.

"It is designed to be worn around the neck on a chain," Faradan continued. "Amily thought of the idea and we have been perfecting the design."

"You can keep a lock of hair from your beloved inside and it will stay close to your heart," Amily said proudly.

"You thought of this?" Reez asked in wonder.

Faradan moved next to Amily and put his arm around her shoulder. "That and many other things," he said fondly. "She has an instinctive understanding of gems and metals and a thousand ideas of how to use them. Our business is flourishing. Amily's designs have caught the imagination of many, and we are getting requests from Etheradia itself. It seems the ladies there are keen to be seen with the newest, brightest and best of everything, and Amily does not disappoint. In fact, we are planning a visit to the market to show off her innovations."

Reez paled. "No," he said firmly. "You can't go there. In fact, you mustn't set one foot in Bestra."

Faradan looked confused, but Amily watched Reez closely, her brown eyes understanding. "You have news from Etheradia?"

He shook his head. "Not really, but things are not right. I have heard nothing from Castor for many moons now." He looked at Faradan. "The Master of Bestra is dangerous," he breathed. "He is the one responsible for the deaths of Chrisos and Paiter, and for maiming me. There are reports of strange things happening in the province and I am worried that he is conducting experiments that might prove harmful to the people there. Please, don't take my sister anywhere near him."

"Of course not, Master Reez," Faradan said, concern etched on his face. "She is as precious to me as a daughter. We will not go if you believe it to be unsafe."

Reez nodded. Amily touched his arm gently, and he smiled wanly at her. "I'm sorry if it means you will not be able to sell your creations."

"Nonsense," she replied. "In fact, it may be a good idea to keep them exclusive." She turned to Faradan, the light back in her eyes. "We could market them as such," she said eagerly. "People will pay a higher price to have something that is not generally available." She picked up the locket and examined it. "If we added personal touches, like the name of the patron," she mused, "customers would know that it was an original."

Faradan laughed. "Trust you to discern a way to increase our profits when others would deem it a setback. Come, Master Reez. I'm sure you are hungry and weary from your journey. I will close the shop early and we can retire upstairs. My wife will be eager to meet you."

Their house was not large. The store and workshop took up the entire ground floor, and the family lived above it with Amily sleeping under the eaves. The furnishings were comfortable and the whole place exuded a warmth that Reez found most inviting. Saphira was a large woman with copper hair streaked with grey. Whereas Faradan was quiet and thoughtful, his wife was hearty and voluble. It quickly became obvious that the couple doted on Amily and she had blossomed under their attention. In everything but name, she was a beloved daughter to them, and Reez remembered Faradan's sadness when he had spoken to him of his only son moving away to Bestra. It was obvious that the couple lavished his sister with all the affection they could not bestow on their absent child. In turn, Amily had found someone who could fill the hole in her heart left by their dead mother, and a home that could replace the one she had left far behind.

Reez enjoyed a hot meal and afterwards was persuaded to sample a bottle of liquor that Faradan explained was wine with Taklar added. Reez wasn't keen to try it at first, remembering the effects of Taklar from his long ago visit to Stonehaven, but he found the taste much sweeter, and the wine muted the harsh sting of the Taklar. In all, it was a pleasant drink, and Reez resolved to search for it when he returned to Rudsmede. He was fairly certain Chrisos would have a few bottles of it in his vast cellar.

Amily, of course, wanted to know the details of his visit to Minra and pressed Reez for information. He told them of the request from the guild leaders and a little of his forays into earth magic in order to fill the void left by Chrisos' untimely demise. He decided not to mention his anger at the guild leaders or their discussions about the future. "So, you are Master of two magics now!" she exclaimed when he had finished.

"Nothing like, I'm afraid," he answered. "My knowledge of earth magic is very rudimentary. It would take many more cycles and much study before I could hope to be proficient. Unfortunately, I don't think it could ever happen. Although there is a great deal of information that I can learn from the books in the library, I fear most of the lore is locked away and might never be found. I could only hope to be a poor reflection. I think Minra will need to make some big changes to counteract my deficiencies."

"If it becomes generally known that the ore will no longer be readily available, it could cause problems," Faradan observed.

"I am working with the guild leaders to mitigate some of the issues. By making my presence known, I hope people will assume that life will continue as normal. Apart from a few seams, most mines should keep producing for decades to come. By then, I hope to have learnt enough to maintain a good flow. I am here to look for crystals in the area, as the mine you currently use may be depleted within the next few cycles."

"That doesn't sound good. We use crystals in many of our pieces," Faradan said with a small frown. "There isn't another mine anywhere close enough to reach comfortably. It will mean a journey of many days."

"Perhaps we should look to incorporating other stones in our new designs," Amily suggested. "Opals and garnets are plentiful. If we make them fashionable, the crystals will last much longer."

Faradan smiled. "See what a rare gem she is?" he said proudly. He turned back to Reez with a small smile on his face. "Tell me, what is your impression of Samine?"

"Do you know him well?" Reez asked.

Faradan pursed his lips and nodded his head to one side. "Fairly well," he hedged.

Reez decided to be diplomatic. "Our first encounters were… interesting. He strikes me as an ambitious man who holds ideas that haven't coincided with those of Chrisos."

Faradan laughed loudly. "I think you are being polite," he chuckled. "He is determined and resourceful, and it is no secret that he fought his way into the post of guild leader with every weapon in his arsenal. Having said that, I cannot fault his management. Has he asked you to release more gold?"

"In a fashion."

"We have had a few interesting discussions about it over the long cycles. Well, some of them were quite loud, in truth."

"You don't agree with him?"

"I always take an opposing view in any discussions with Samine. It keeps his wit sharpened and his tongue burnished."

"From what I gather," Reez said, "gold extraction is very carefully monitored."

"Gold is not plentiful. It is interesting because it is not a useful metal, neither is it strong, but it is beautiful and not subject to corrosion like other metals. I think that is why it has always been the base that determines the worth of any object. Gold currency is very rare these days, as you know. But the system we use to determine value is still based on it. Now, if gold becomes more plentiful, will its worth not decrease?"

"Samine says gold production has been higher in the past."

"Some Masters have taken extra for themselves. I know one of Bestra's Masters was keen to flaunt his position and, by all accounts, covered his entire palace with it."

"Not quite, but there is plenty enough to make an impression."

"You've seen it, then?"

"From afar," Reez replied.

"So then, we shouldn't be mining any more gold," Amily said, trying to follow the conversation.

"Ah, if only it were that simple," Faradan said. "Not enough gold and its price will rise, meaning that a simple galley knife could cost more than a crystal head band. Most people would not be able to afford it."

Reez rubbed his face. "This is all too complex for me. Give me a pot of earth and a seed pod any time."

"There is no straightforward answer, Master Reez." Faradan said. "My advice? Make no changes on the whim of one man. There is no harm in leaving things the way they have always been until you are better informed and sure in your own mind."

"You don't think I should listen to Samine?"

Faradan smiled. "Samine has the heart of a mountain man. These hills are his bones and the rivers his blood. He wants nothing but the best for Minra province and everything he says and does will have that end in sight. He would see Minra elevated above the others, both economically and in reputation. However, he harbours aspirations for his guild, too, and wishes that to rise above the rest. Chrisos' continued refusal to release more gold has hindered his dreams in more than one way. You might have noticed that Samine has expensive tastes and indulges himself with the finest of everything. It does not surprise me to hear that he has pleaded his case with you. It will not be the last time, I assure you. Forgive me, I do not mean to paint his character in such a bad way. He will make you a fair councillor as long as he is kept on a fine choker and not given too much freedom."

"How is it you know so much about him?" Reez asked.

Faradan shrugged. "He is my kinsman on my mother's side. We grew up together."

"Well, thank you for your timely warning. Your insights have confirmed what I had already surmised of him. Perhaps I should consult with you if I need to put him in his place. I'm sure you have a few stories that would cause him embarrassment should they be widely circulated. It might make him more circumspect."

"I'll never tell," Faradan said sombrely, but Reez detected the glint of humour in his eyes.

"Speaking of embarrassing stories," Reez said, turning to his sister with a look of mischief on his face, "I should tell you about the time Amily mistook the record keeper for my father."

Amily groaned.

They spent the rest of the evening swapping stories amid much laughter and more than a little humiliation on Amily's part. The family did not have to press hard to get him to extend his visit another day, and the following morning found Reez once more in the little workroom. He picked up one of the small tools and held it up.

"This looks like the tongs I made for myself, only much smaller," he mused.

"Many of our tools are miniature versions of those needed to work metal on a larger scale, but because our work is precise and subtle, they are small and compact," Faradan explained. "Jewellery making requires a delicate touch as opposed to the raw strength of smithing." He picked up a tiny hammer. "We use this to shape rings and give them a decorated finish. Would you like to try?"

Amily sniggered.

"Yes, I would," Reez said, pointedly ignoring his sister.

Faradan sat him at his workstation and fixed a mandrel in front of him. He slipped a band of silver metal over the top. "See this ball shape on the side? That is the part you will use. Tap it on the side of the ring; it should dent slightly. Just remember, it wants a light touch." Reez carefully took the hammer and began tapping. "That's good," Faradan said encouragingly, "but you need to apply some force, otherwise nothing will happen. Try a little harder."

Reez increased the pressure, pleased to see the metal immediately being marked as he worked.

"Stop a moment," Faradan said after he had struck the band a few times. "Take a look at the band. Can you see how the shape has deformed? That's because your strikes were too hard. What we are looking for is something in between."

Reez glared at Amily, who was smiling broadly. "No doubt your first effort wasn't perfect," he said.

"I wish that were so," Faradan said with an exaggerated sigh. "Unfortunately, your sister produced a lovely ring on her first try."

Reez ignored her as she poked her tongue out at him and turned back to the mandrel. After some time and a lot of concentration, he eventually found the right amount of force to use and was pleased to see that the latter stages of the ring were a marked improvement. He smiled to himself as he remembered his first forays into smithing with Kromar. It had taken him several days before he could swing the hammer with the right amount of force. Making jewellery, although much more delicate in nature, was very much the same in technique.

"Well done, Master Reez," Faradan said, as he removed the band and placed it in Reez's hand. "A keepsake to remember your sister by."

For the rest of the morning, he stood back and watched them both work, occasionally asking questions and making observations. All too soon, it was time for him to depart and resume his work for the guild. In one way, Reez was glad that his visit was short because he had no doubts that Amily was already concocting ways to embarrass him after his tales of the previous evening. However, it saddened him to have to say goodbye to his little sister again so soon, and he determined he would not leave it too long before his next visit. He looked fondly across at her, her face alight with pleasure as she concentrated on the delicate work on her bench, and consoled himself with the fact that she was being kept safe and happy within the shelter of the mountains of Minra.

Chapter Twelve

Reez was lost in his thoughts as he travelled across the undulating hills, enjoying the much warmer weather as he made his way further south. It was a fine day, and the breeze was pleasant on his face. He hummed to himself as he walked, not really aware of his surroundings, merely thinking back on his sojourn in Minra province.

He had met with the guild leaders several times, both as a group and individually. His initial anger at them had morphed into grudging respect as he had listened carefully and reviewed their plans to improve production and distribution, as well as introduce some innovative ideas. The detailed reports Hobart and Jodrel had submitted at such short notice made him think they had been preparing to approach Chrisos once more, or maybe even Paiter when his time came. Evidently, they had taken great care to be precise about figures and cost, benefits, and disadvantages. They had even anticipated many of the questions and objections that could be raised and answered them thoroughly. Despite not having the full workings of earth magic at his disposal, or a comprehensive knowledge of the economics involved, Reez had been impressed and, as a layman, found their proposals intriguing. Still, he remembered Faradan's advice and decided to take things slowly. The guild leaders, in turn, all agreed to keep him informed with regular, honest updates and a phased integration of the changes so that they could monitor the effects carefully. All three had decided that upgrading the road network should be their priority, much to Hobart's delight. It would benefit all the guilds to be able to transport their goods easily and safely. Neither would it upset either of the other provinces. Indeed, they could only profit from having a faster and more efficient network of roads, rather than suffering delays when carts carrying ore or metals were mired in mud.

He had also made sure that the prices of goods exported to both Bestra and Fiora were returned to their previous levels. It was no surprise to him that Samine had initiated that particular ruse, capitalising on the absence of their Master by exploiting the other provinces.

They were not evil men, Reez decided, as he ambled through the long grass. Ambitious, driven and foresighted, yes, but not bad. He wanted these men on his side, working with him, not plotting against him in the shadows, which is what he suspected might happen if they didn't feel involved. He had decided to leave all three in position, although he would keep a close eye on their progress. All in all, he was satisfied with the outcome, and suspected that the guild leaders were more than pleased to have been heard and taken seriously. He hoped it would be sufficient incentive for them to do their jobs with integrity from now on. Unfortunately, Samine's reports were still biased in favour of an increase in gold mining, and Reez had found it difficult to keep his temper as Samine had tried to persuade him to his way of thinking. Eventually, he had put an end to the discussion by reminding Samine of his place and, although the guild leader had capitulated, Reez suspected he harboured a great deal of resentment. It may even prove necessary to replace him in the future, although Reez would try to work with the man as long as possible. He hoped that, having won over Hobart and Jodrel, they would have no truck with any more of Samine's schemes and would keep him in line themselves.

#

Reez's first forays into practising his newfound skills out in the hills and mountains had been mixed. Although he could pinpoint the location of the necessary ore deposits they were seeking, he could not as yet open up a mine. He had managed to carve a crude fissure into the rock face to begin it, but had to stop when he realised he couldn't control the direction of the magic. His skills in following a seam were sadly lacking, and he had had to admit defeat. The force of the earth magic in the north had also taken him by surprise, filling him so abruptly and so powerfully that he had instinctively retreated from it. Where green magic was gentle and flowed smoothly, earth magic was wild and chaotic. Reez had balked at the intensity of the energy, fearing that he wouldn't be able to contain it. Rather than risk destroying the precious metals with his amateurish attempts, he decided to wait until he could learn more and harness the magic sufficiently. As it was, there was enough ore to see them comfortably for a few more summers, but if they needed the ore before he had mastered his technique, the people would have to dig down into the rock themselves. Opening a seam would be backbreaking work and be difficult for the miners who would need to discover ways to delve deep into the earth without putting themselves at risk. Reez had left the guild leaders with the problem, tasking them to solve the problem of how to open a mine and shore up the tunnels safely. The laborious undertaking would take time and that alone would ensure that the changes desired by the guild leaders would, by necessity, be gradual.

#

Reez's stride slowed and finally stopped as he looked around, suddenly aware of where he was. He stared at the horizon before him and swallowed, sorrow suddenly gripping his heart anew. It had been many cycles since his feet had trodden this particular path. Because of his inattention, he had wandered further east than planned as he made his way back home, and instead of avoiding this place, he had walked straight to it. Slowly, he turned his steps directly towards the clearing and stepped inside.

This had always been his Master's last stop before continuing on to the Tower of the Mages a little further to the east. Augmented over centuries by each Master, it provided all they needed for a comfortable night outside. Everything seemed hushed as Reez scanned the space, as if awaiting their arrival. Even the berry bushes were fruiting in anticipation of Wicton's return to feast on them. Wandering to the mossy beds sheltered from rain and heat beneath the trees, Reez sat down and closed his eyes, his heart aching with renewed grief. Absently, he rubbed his left arm.

In many ways, he had healed remarkably well. Physically, he had returned to strength, even though it was not the fullness of before. He could work and travel, knowing that his limp only manifested at the end of a long day. His marred features were mainly forgotten, and he had taken Wicton's mantle and made it his own. He had fulfilled his responsibilities to Fiora, as well as taking on the added burden of Minra province. Yet there was a dark place in his soul, which he kept tightly locked away during the light of day. At night, however, it often ranged free, destroying peaceful slumber and filling his mind with nightmarish visions. The horrific events of the last triumvirate haunted him still, occasionally jerking him from sleep, filmed with sweat and shaking in terror. Each time he remembered, it seemed to rip another piece of his soul and filled him again with feelings of inadequacy, fear, and loss.

He didn't want to go back to that place where so many lives had been destroyed and his own body crippled and maimed.

"Come along," Wicton said, and Reez smiled sadly at the memory.

#

"Where are we going, Master?"

Wicton grinned but didn't reply. Reez trotted along after him, running to keep up as Wicton's longer stride outpaced him as they went down the hill and through the copse of trees. He was excited and his heart raced with anticipation, wondering what new magic he was going to be shown. Despite his mind being full of questions, he stayed silent. He had learnt very early on not to badger his Master with his thoughts, knowing that no answers would be forthcoming. Wicton's method of teaching was subtle and careful, leaving Reez to puzzle through problems and solve riddles himself. He hadn't taken too much notice of their heading, but when they arrived at the shores of the lake, Reez slowed his steps. He hadn't been back there since Bilan, the Margrave's son, had almost drowned him the previous sennight during a fight. The boys had been made to apologise face to face and although he had appeared contrite, Reez had been secretly pleased to see the ugly bruising and swelling marring Bilan's features. Aydal had adamantly remained unrepentant and had refused to show any remorse for the beating he had administered after pulling Bilan away from Reez as they struggled in the shallows. As a result, as well as having to clean out the stall for the village oxen for the rest of the summer, his father had made Aydal do Bilan's chores until he recovered sufficiently from his injuries to take them on himself.

"This should do nicely," Wicton said, stopping at the edge of the pool, his green eyes watching Reez carefully. When he removed his tunic, Reez swallowed, anxiety coursing through him. "Follow me," Wicton said, dropping the rest of his clothing to the ground and wading into the water. "We have work to do."

With shaking hands, Reez stripped off his clothes and stepped towards the balmy pool. He stopped when he felt the water lap his feet, unable to go further. He turned anguished eyes up to his Master.

"I can't."

"Nonsense. Just put one foot in front of the other," Wicton replied, standing waist deep in the lake.

"Please," Reez pleaded.

"I know you are afraid, Reez," Wicton said gently, "but you cannot let fear bind you. Eventually, it will suck all the life from you and leave you an empty husk. Fear needs to be faced, confronted, and conquered. Then it will wither away and die. Now, walk to me."

Wicton waited patiently while Reez took one tentative step and then another. Eventually he stood next to his Master shivering, despite the sun blazing down from a clear blue sky.

"Good," Wicton said warmly. "A little further, I think," and he led them deeper until the water rose up to Reez's shoulders. Wicton ducked down and disappeared under the gentle swell for a moment before reappearing and wiping the droplets from his face. "So refreshing after a hard day's work," he said, slicking his long hair back from his face. He eyed his apprentice carefully and then slapped the surface between them, splashing Reez. Reez gasped and stumbled back, almost falling in his haste to retreat. Wicton grabbed his arm and steadied him.

"Careful, now," he admonished quietly.

To his horror, Reez started to cry; big wracking sobs shook his body and ugly noises wailed from his mouth. He tried to turn away and flee back to shore, but Wicton held him firmly.

"No hiding, Reez. I won't let any harm come to you here. You have my word."

"He nearly killed me!" Reez yelled, the tears blurring his vision. "I thought I was going to die. If Aydal hadn't come…"

"But he did come," Wicton said quietly. "You didn't die." He waited patiently until the shuddering sobs subsided, rubbing Reez's arm slowly until he calmed down again. "You will conquer this, Reez. We will be here every day until you do. I am a patient man. We can take as long as you need." He looked Reez in the eye and said, "Let's try again." His hand hit the water and Reez recoiled as the splash hit his face, but he didn't move. "Good," Wicton said, moving away. "I think that's enough for today. Let's swim for a while."

Every day for a sennight they walked down to the lake and played in the water. Eventually, Reez regained enough confidence to swim out of his depth and float on his back to watch the clouds meander by. He learnt he would not drown when Wicton splashed him unexpectedly and by the end of the week could even dip his face in to the water for a second. On the last day, however, when Reez waded into the water and turned, it was to see his Master still fully clothed standing on the bank.

"I will leave you now," Wicton said. Reez tried not to let the panic show on his face, but it must have been woefully obvious. "Don't be distressed, Reez. You have come a long way, but you have to take the final steps on your own."

"What if I can't?" he whispered.

"I have faith in you. I know you have the courage to face this last trial, and you will come back and tell me how you fared with a smile on your face. Be strong." Then he turned and walked back to the tower, leaving Reez alone.

For the longest time, he stood in the water, unwilling to move. He had to decide; either he ran from the lake and admitted his failure, or he accepted the challenge and returned with pride. He didn't want to concede defeat, and even though the thought was almost paralysing, Reez gradually waded deeper until the water reached his armpits. A bird called somewhere in the trees and a breeze ruffled his unruly hair. He ignored the single tear that escaped his eye and concentrated on taking long, slow breaths. A rustle in a nearby bush made him start, his heart leaping with remembered panic, but it was only a wood pigeon.

"Be strong. Be strong," he muttered to himself.

How long he stood in the water, eyes closed, murmuring the litany to himself he didn't know, but at some point he had taken a deep breath and bent his knees, allowing the cold liquid to wash over his head. It wasn't long; a few heartbeats perhaps, but when he rose from the depths, he was a different boy. As Wicton had predicted, the fear began to wither away. After that first success, he had never made himself stay under for very long and eventually had forgotten its power until he had dived under the sea on his first visit to the coast. He hadn't realised that the crippling memory still dwelt in some remote corner of his mind. Fear, it seemed, remained hidden in the mind long after you thought it had been vanquished, causing you to falter and doubt unexpectedly. He didn't want to be a slave to those feelings again.

Reez leant his head back against the tree and let the memories flow over him like those waters once had. He had never thanked Wicton for making him face his fear or for giving him back the joy and freedom of swimming in the balmy summer afternoons. The jubilant glint in Wicton's eyes, however, when he had returned with a big grin plastered on his face, made him think his Master was well aware of it, regardless. How sad he would be to think that Reez was back in the same situation, starting at noises and afraid of the shadows.

"Come along," Wicton said again, an echo in Reez's memories urging him gently down a path he had purposefully avoided.

It was still his choice. He could ignore the ghost of his Master and continue on his journey back home. No-one would ever know. No-one except him. Reez remembered cowering behind the tree at the inn, fighting the impulse to hide away. He had been brave that day, and many others after it, conquering his fears little by little and rejoining the world he imagined lost to him. He thought of the joy and happiness he now had as a result, things he never believed could be his again. Reez looked up at the sky and guessed that there was still a while to go before the sun would begin its descent, more than enough time to make the journey to the Tower of the Mages. He wiped his clammy hands on his trews. "Time to put my head under the water," he muttered, taking a deep breath and hauling himself upright. Saying a quick prayer to the First Mage for courage, he determinedly turned his face to the east and began to walk.

Chapter Thirteen

"I'm sorry it took me so long to come back," Reez said as he stood over the grave of his Master. The scent from the profusion of flowers growing on the smooth mound swirled around him, and he breathed it in deeply. By necessity, the graves were shallow, and it had taken him a long time to dig out a large enough trench and drag the remains of Wicton, Chrisos, and Paiter into it. Pain, nausea, and intense grief and fear had driven him back to the encompassing roots of the willow tree time after time, but he had laboured on, unwilling to leave his companions to rot under the heat of the sun or be scavenged by wild animals. By rights, the bodies should have been returned to their homes. Reez knew there was a huge stone ossuary near Rudsmede, where the bones of all the previous Masters were laid to rest. Perhaps one day, when the idea didn't fill him with dread, he would feel able to exhume them and send them back. Wicton had always expressed a desire to be buried near the sea he loved so much and Reez felt guilty that he had left his old Master in such a lonely place for so long.

"I miss you more than I can say," he continued. "I'm trying my best to make you proud of me." He squatted down and laid his hand on the earth, remembering how Wicton had comforted him after the sudden death of his mother. "You told me once that death was the start of a new adventure, beyond our sight. I hope you found your way through the door." He watched the humblebees dance around the blossoms for a while and allowed the peace of the clearing to seep into his soul. Despite his fears about returning, the place didn't fill him with horror; instead he could recall the happy memories of swinging in the trees with the other apprentices, splashing in the stream with Paiter, and sitting by the fire after a warm meal talking with Wicton. Verrin's betrayal had not taken away the good things. It had merely overshadowed them for a while.

Eventually, he rose and wandered over to the remains of the hut at the centre of the huge clearing. Two of the walls had been completely destroyed, exposing the stone hearth, and much of the roof had fallen in. Instead of looking ominous, however, grass and flowers gave the building a softness which obliterated much of the devastation. Seeds had obviously blown across from the graves and rooted between the boards to create a carpet over the blackened, bloodstained wood. Most of the sparse furniture was gone or was useless apart from a chest in which Reez had stored anything salvageable before he left. He lifted the lid and looked inside.

A few pots and pans had survived the fire, including the water boiler. Paiter's and Chrisos' journeyman bags were there, the tools intact. At the very bottom lay two rings belonging to a journeyman and a Master of earth magic. He brushed his finger over the outline of an anvil, remembering Paiter's excitement when he showed it to Reez that fateful day. The other depicted a hammer, the tool of a Master, the green gem seeming to flow like liquid, in exactly the same way as Reez's own ring.

Placing them carefully back into the chest, Reez took out the pans and placed them on the stone hearth. He collected up wood and kindling before setting them alight. Smiling at the ease of starting a fire with earth magic, he picked up the water boiler and walked down to the stream. "Hello, old friend," he murmured, patting the trunk of the massive willow as he passed. The fronds touched his back and face as he bent to collect water, as if to welcome him and invite him to rest. Reez chuckled. "Later," he promised. "First, I need to eat."

He brewed a herbal drink and dug up a few vegetables to make a stew. As he enjoyed his meal, he probed beneath for the magic source and was surprised by the effortless intensity of the connection. Even when drawing on it for healing and strength during his recovery, he had never experienced it so strongly before. Not for the first time, he pondered the nature of the strange phenomenon. He had experimented in the past to see how far he could travel and still access the magic, but he had barely left the clearing before the link faded away. It was frustrating to have access to an unlimited source of magic, only for it to be rooted in one of the most isolated spots in Zelannor. It would, however, be an ideal place to practice his newfound skills.

The sudden realisation made him pause. Trying to utilise the magic from the earth fires had frightened him with its intensity, to the point where he was reluctant to use it at all. But what if he could train himself without the fear of losing control to hamper him? He would be able to practice as much as he wanted. The thought of remaining in the clearing or coming back again was not as daunting as he had once imagined. He laughed softly to himself. Just this morning, he would never have imagined returning to this place, let alone staying for an extended period.

Reez inspected the remaining walls of the hut, still standing firmly thanks to the infusions of magic they had received over many cycles. He could use them as a starting point to rebuild. Grabbing one of the sides, he tried to shake it, pleased to see that the wall was perfectly steady with no sign of rot or wear. He remembered asking Wicton about the state of the hut, which never seemed to alter.

"Another little task I take care of," Wicton had replied, before explaining how the wood in the walls and roof were melded together. There were no gaps to let in draughts or inquisitive creatures, making the entire structure much stronger, as if they had hewn it from the trunk of an enormous tree.

Latterly, Wicton had taught Reez how to keep the wood dry and rid it of any fungus that would rot the structure away. Since then, it had been one of his chores to check the hut every time they visited.

If he was going to be spending an extended time at the Tower of the Mages, Reez decided, he would need to reconstruct the shelter. Sleeping in the roots of the willow would be fine in fair weather or during the summer cycle, but if he ended up staying later it might prove uncomfortable and cold. The task wouldn't be too difficult to complete, although it would take some time and effort. The floor would need to be cleared and renewed, and it would be good to have some pieces of simple furniture and a few items to make it feel more like home. He could send for some furs and blankets from Minra, so much more luxurious than the thin coverlets he was used to. It may be a small dwelling, but it didn't have to be devoid of comfort. The thought of warm bedding made him yawn widely. Deciding that he had done enough for one day, he cooled the blaze in the hearth and watched the flames die down until the fire was extinguished. Walking over to the willow, he settled himself within the familiar roots, which flexed to accommodate him. He dug his fingers into the earth, renewing his affinity to the surrounding plants, and closed his eyes. As his mind quietened, he was aware of the tree shifting slightly to cover him with its branches and protect him from the elements. Overwhelmed by feelings of peace and safety, Reez fell to sleep.

#

Sometime later, he jerked upright. Still caught in the

tendrils of his dream, it took him a moment to orientate himself and realise that he was safe in the bowl of roots. Gradually, he recognised the shapes muted in the night and willed his breathing and heartbeat to return to normal. This time, the dream had been different.

As usual, he had been watching the smiling faces surrounding him as he was initiated into his mastership when Malander's had started to melt, his features running down like wax in a candle. Paiter's jaw had widened until Reez could see the mass of bodies and legs inside waiting to explode from his eyes and nose. Wicton had turned to stone, and despite Reez's efforts, had crumbled to dust as he tried to hold him in his arms. Then, instead of being immobilised as the fire consumed the world around him, Reez had found himself crawling through pools of blood before falling down into a deep chasm that opened up beneath him, falling but never landing in eternal, inky blackness.

Groaning, Reez rubbed his face. He decided to make himself a drink, knowing that sleep would elude him for the rest of the night. Waiting for the water to heat, he propped himself against the stone of the hearth and gazed up at the darkened sky, automatically seeking the familiar constellations and recounting the stories of his childhood. A soft breeze blew across his face, still warm despite the coolness of night. Somewhere, a night lark trilled its haunting melody before silence reigned again. Despite his dream, he felt at peace, as if the horrors of the past were finally being laid to rest.

As he sipped the warm brew, Reez found his eyes

sweeping the floor of the hut again and again, as if seeking something. He felt as if he were near the edge of a precipice, desperately trying to see what was beyond it, but unable to take the last few steps that would open up the vista below. The remnants of the dream teased at the periphery of his mind, and he felt strangely restless. Instinctively, he knew there was something important that he needed to remember, but each time he came close, it skittered away and was lost. He huffed in frustration and stood, pacing the perimeter of the clearing as the sky lightened and colour returned to the world.

It was time to make a decision. He glanced to the west. He had been on his way home before his impromptu diversion. After many moons away from Maston, he was eager to return to the people he loved. He had brought back books which he hoped would unlock some more secrets to earth magic and increase his skills, and it wouldn't be long before the harvest began. They would need him for the thanksgiving ceremonies and to bless the seed for the following cycle. Yet, he reasoned, if he worked hard, there was still time to build a shelter here. He would need to get a few supplies unless he was prepared to live on nothing but fruit and vegetables or work with the few tools in the chest, but a hut wouldn't take long to construct and he could still make the celebration as required.

Reez looked across at the floor of the hut once more, wondering how much damage had been done beneath the thin carpet of grass and flowers. Strolling over, he knelt down and swept away the debris and plants with his palms to reveal the damaged wood beneath. He had cleared much of it from around the hearth when he cursed and lifted his hand. A large splinter was embedded in his thumb. It took him a little time to remove it as his nails were kept short and he had no fine pins to hook it out, and blood oozed from the hole when he finally pulled it free. He watched as it pooled and slowly dripped on to the dark earth below. His mind raced as images flashed into his head. A container with herbs and minerals inside; a small knife; an upturned bowl; blood draining through tiny cracks and disappearing into blackness. He whirled and stared at the centre of the hut, suddenly remembering how he meant to ask Wicton about the ceremony afterwards. Why use an opening ritual when there was no door to unlock? He had dismissed it from his mind, assuming it was a rite that no longer held any real significance. Now his heart raced. Perhaps it had far more meaning than any of the Masters had been aware of.

With an impatient gesture he rotted away the wooden floor and, heedless of injury, swept away the debris and soil from the exact centre, revealing white stone beneath, hidden from human sight for an untold number of cycles. Shaking with excitement, Reez chose the large slab in the centre and placed his grazed hand on it. As he pressed firmly down, he heard a low thud and he held his breath. Slowly, the slab rose until it stood proud of the others surrounding it. Exactly as he had done countless times in his own tower, Reez rotated the stone and lifted it back. He stared into the hole, revealing several ancient stone steps that began to descend before they disappeared into inky blackness. As he leaned in, he could smell the stale air laced with the scent of earth.

With excitement coursing through him at this new discovery, he descended the stairs, only to stop moments later. Despite the strengthening daylight, Reez could see nothing further than a few feet. Reluctantly, he climbed back up and knelt at the opening, looking down into the darkness below. With a frustrated sigh, he rocked back on his heels. He had no candle and no lantern or oil to burn. Pushing his hand through his hair, he thought about creating a firebrand, but wasn't sure how long one would last. He certainly didn't want to be plunged into darkness if it failed him suddenly. Swearing softly, he concluded that his exploration would have to wait until he had obtained a more reliable light source.

Mentally calculating how long it would take to get to the nearest settlement, Reez lowered the stone down, eager to begin, but stopped short of sealing it altogether. He was gripped with a terrible feeling of doubt; what if he couldn't open it again? Despite logic telling him he knew this spell and had the power to unlock it at will, an irrational part of him rebelled against closing it completely. He desperately wanted to know what was at the bottom of the staircase. Was this where the strange magic source was held? Would he be able to take it with him when he returned to Maston and keep it in his own vault? He didn't want to shut the access completely until he had a chance to reveal its secrets, but, he mused as his eyes swept around the open clearing, he also didn't want to leave it to be discovered by chance. It would only take one individual with a curious mind and an adventurous spirit to wander into the place and find it. Reez paced the ground, pulling bits of old wood and grass around to see if he could fashion an adequate disguise, but despite being able to conceal it from an idle glance, it was woefully inadequate under close scrutiny.

A low grumble from his stomach reminded Reez that he had yet to break his fast, and he reluctantly left the slab in order to prepare himself a meal. He was still mulling over the problem while he bent over the stream to clean out the pots. Instead of returning to his small fire after filling the water boiler, he leant against the rough trunk of the willow. What he needed was a deterrent; something to stop a person from coming any closer. His mind conjured up a high wall surrounding the whole clearing, but he quickly discarded the idea. Not only would it take too long, but it would be an irresistible lure to any inquisitive passer-by who would itch to know what lay behind it. Instead, his solution had to be something unremarkable that could be overlooked or ignored, yet still protect the secret entrance.

Sighing, Reez walked back to the fire, but his foot caught an errant root and he tripped, spilling the water as he tried to stay upright. Cursing softly to himself, he pushed through the fronds of the willow tree and bent back down to the stream's edge to refill the water boiler. It was then that the answer became clear. Laughing aloud, he jumped up and hurried back to the hut for his satchel, eager to get started. He knew exactly what he needed to do.

Chapter Fourteen

It took Reez almost a sennight to get to the nearest settlement, gather the supplies he needed, and return to the clearing. Owtrim was a small village, and although used to housing the Master on his journeys to and from the triumvirate, they did not have an abundance of building material at hand. Runners were hastily dispatched to the neighbouring villages and eventually, all Reez's requirements had been met. Despite his precautions, he couldn't dispel the urgency that gripped him to return and secure the site and as soon as all was ready, he left the village with the borrowed hinny and cart, and hurried back. On the journey, he kept reassuring himself that the secret door had remained undiscovered for centuries, likely since the beginning of the new age. No-one had ever approached the hut or disturbed its contents before, but the pressing need remained. His inner haste, however, meant that he made good time, and as his feet took him ever closer to the clearing, the excitement of discovering something new gripped him once more, overriding his irrational fears. He stopped only for a short time to rest the poor hinny which bore the burden of pulling the supplies, before travelling on through the night, eschewing sleep in favour of speed. As the sun began to rise, he reached the clearing and his eyes swept over his newly formed barrier. All was well.

He had worked tirelessly that last day using the seeds he had with him, along with whatever could be foraged in the surrounding area. Now an impenetrable mass of vegetation towered in front of him, enclosing the massive clearing on every side in a wall of trees, bushes, thorns and prickles that would faze the most determined of explorers. Any passers-by coming across it would just walk around without a thought. The only weakness was the stream that entered on one side, but as it exited fairly quickly on the other, he doubted anyone would try to traverse it. As a precaution, he had grown the trees low until they brushed the surface with their branches, and collected together sharp rocks where the water entered and left to deter swimmers. Afterwards, he had walked the perimeter inside and out until he was satisfied there were no gaps. The only visitors to the clearing would be the creatures able to fly over the barrier and enter from above.

Sensing his approach and the call of his plant self, the

hedge in front of him moved. Branches lifted and twisted away unnaturally, bushes shuddered to one side and thorns bowed low along the ground or snaked away to reveal a path wide enough for him to pass. As he walked through, the greenery behind him moved back into place, blocking the way and preventing anyone or anything else from following. Reez smiled to himself. During his planting of the barrier, he had adapted the blood ritual for locking doors and now the thicket answered only to him.

For the first time since discovering the secret entrance, Reez allowed himself to relax. Everything remained just as he had left it. Although he was eager to start, his plant-self reminded him he had something more pressing to do first. Stripping off his clothes, he lay down on the grass, allowing the sun's rays to bathe his skin. It began to change colour from sun-kissed bronze to a dull green, which pulsed, matching the rhythm of his heart. He closed his eyes and stretched out his arms as if to welcome the energy muted by encroaching cloud, allowing its power to flood through his body. Only when he was fully sated did he turn his attention to the food, which would satisfy his stomach.

Watching the clouds gather with impending rain, Reez reluctantly decided he would need to put off his explorations below for a little while longer. For the rest of the day, and well into the evening, he laboured on constructing a simple replica of the hut that had once stood sentinel there. Even though he had use of magic, the night had fallen, and his arms were aching when he finally decided to call a halt. The threatened storm had been raging for some time, but the ground around the exposed stone was dry thanks to the hastily erected roof. Looking around with satisfaction, he finally put away his tools and stretched his sore muscles. Starting a fire, Reez laid his wet clothes on a stool in front of the hearth to dry while beans cooked in a pot hung over the flames. He stared at the raised stone, as if his mental efforts alone could reveal its secrets. Although desperate to probe beneath and discover them for himself, he acknowledged as he rubbed his arm that he was too fatigued to make the descent that evening. He glanced out the side of the hut at the rain still teaming down, soaking the ground. It would be an uncomfortable night if he spent it outside. Foregoing his bed in the willow roots, Reez laid out his cloak and settled down in the newly constructed shelter to get some sleep. At least here, the ground was dry and the fire would keep him warm. He closed his eyes and tried to still his mind. As his thoughts tumbled over each other with possibilities, Reez sighed deeply. It was going to be a long, frustrating night.

#

Pushing aside the rest of the detritus, Reez reached down and lifted the slab. Despite the many cycles of neglect, the mechanism still worked smoothly. Rechecking his bag for the fourth time, he finally lit the linen wick in the lamp and, when the flame had settled, put his foot on the first step. In many ways, it was like descending into his own vault. The stone steps, wide enough for two people to walk side by side, circled down with the wall at his right and a metal barrier to his left to steady him. However, instead of ending after thirty steps, the stairs continued to spiral down. He risked a quick glance up, but could no longer see the opening above him. He was alone in the dark, with no clues to tell him how far he had to go. Reez breathed deeply of the air, glad to detect no trace of moisture or foul odour. Faint puffs of dust were the only evidence of his passing, and they settled quickly after his feet had moved on. He felt as if he were in a waking dream, falling forever into total darkness. He was wondering if he would ever reach the end when he suddenly came to a stop on a large, flat floor. Further along, the steps continued to descend into blackness. He moved the lantern higher. In front of him was a large ornate double door, decorated with scrolling vines which twisted and curled across the wood. Slowly, he reached forward, grasped the bronze coloured handle and pressed it down. The door opened with a soft sigh, and Reez moved inside.

There was no noise apart from his own deep breaths and the occasional hiss of the lamp, but Reez was immediately struck with the impression of being in a vast cavern. As he stepped forward, the sound of his steps seemed to whisper around him, announcing his presence to whatever waited within. As he tentatively entered, a black shape materialised in front of him, becoming a rail that stretched into the dark and disappeared on either side. Beyond was empty space, unable to be penetrated by the meagre light of his lamp. Turning, he made to move to the left and almost fell as his foot connected with something that skittered and collapsed in a sudden cacophony that echoed in the cavernous space. Looking down, Reez realised he had kicked over a pile of books. He bent down and reverently picked one up, opening it to the first page. The spidery writing announced the title as *"Elementary Manipulation of Air."* Lifting the lantern up, he could see dozens of books stacked against the rails and he let out a short laugh of disbelief which reverberated around the chamber.

Eager to discover more, Reez returned the book to the pile and continued along the gallery. All along it were haphazard piles of books which looked as if someone had dumped them in a hurry, along with several scrolls of parchment. Occasionally, Reez would come across instruments he recognised, like a scrying tool, quadrant or astrolabe. Then the shelves began. Shaking with barely contained excitement, Reez wandered around, his fingers caressing the rows upon rows of tomes. Hundreds, maybe thousands of books lined the walls, stretching up into the dark. The rail, which had been a constant to his right, stopped suddenly, and Reez could see more steps made of the black metal disappearing down. Trembling, he fumbled in his bag to draw out a second lantern and lit it, leaving it at the top of the wide staircase. When the flame was steady, he continued down.

It was only a short flight, and within moments he was walking along another gallery. No books littered the floor here, but the shelves were packed tightly with myriad volumes. When he came to yet another flight leading down, he paused. Across the vast space, he could make out his second lantern burning above and to the right. Pulling a random title from the shelf behind him, he barely glanced at it before moving to the rail and dropping it. One… two… three… then a sharp thud as if it had connected with something before a clatter and then silence.

Reez's mouth went dry. The place was immense.

Instead of moving down, he ignored further flights of stairs and had just followed the gallery round, tracking his progress by the light of his second lamp until he reached the point where he had arrived. The landing was circular, intersected by several flights of stairs that either led down into the depths or up to the door. Although he guessed the chamber would continue to follow the same pattern, he didn't want to risk getting lost in a maze of books; his oil had been growing low, and he needed to make sure he had plenty when he returned. It was with great reluctance that Reez retraced his steps. Before he shut the ornate door, he grabbed several books from the toppled pile at his feet and carried them back up the long, winding stairs.

When he reached the top, he sat on the rough floor for a long time, clutching the books to his chest, his eyes wild. Eventually, his excitement calmed somewhat, and he scanned the titles of the books he had brought back with him. Alongside the treatise on air manipulation, he held "*The Construction of Bone*," "*Theory of Matter*," and "*Understanding Emergence*." Reez's heart thumped madly at the thought of all the knowledge awaiting him in the library. All the magic in the world was his. Laying the books carefully down, he rose and slid the white slab back into position.

His mind immediately panicked as he contemplated shutting the door, refusing to acknowledge all his careful reasoning. For days he had argued with himself, concluding that his discovery was no accident and that the slab would reopen at his touch, exactly how the spell Wicton had unknowingly cast was meant to work. Now faced with the image of the way forever blocked to him, his heart sank. The thought of never being able to access it again was painful, yet he had to know. He vowed to himself that he would find a way back somehow, even if it meant melting the secret entryway and constructing another one. Taking a deep, ragged breath, he pushed down on the stone until he heard the thud of the lock engaging. He waited for a few moments before placing his palm back on to it, his relief tangible as the spell responded and the slab rose. The vast knowledge below was his for the taking.

#

Reez spent three days wandering the hidden library, mapping the entire area and familiarising himself with its layout. There were five landings in all, each crammed with books. Ladders fixed to the shelves with wheels could be manoeuvred across in order to reach the highest ledges. Each gallery housed several doors, all of which were sealed apart from those leading back out to the winding stone staircase. The bottom of the cavernous room was filled with tables, many with books and parchment opened as if the readers had merely left for a moment and would return shortly to finish their studies. In between were cabinets filled with books; creatures stuffed and mounted, some of which he couldn't recognise; trays of insects and flutterbugs pinned to a dark velvety material; instruments for observing and dissecting, as well as others Reez could only speculate about, and intricately detailed drawings of plants, flowers and trees. Even if he spent the rest of his life devouring the information contained within the library, Reez knew he would only scratch the surface of this treasure trove of information. Each time he was forced to retreat up the stone steps, he took an armful of books with him, reading by the light of the fire until his eyes watered and his head ached.

#

Reez sighed as he climbed back up to the top gallery. Time had run out. He needed to return to Fiora and his responsibilities there instead of continuing to exploring the massive library. He had emptied Paiter's journeyman bag of tools and filled it with books to take back with him, titles that appealed after he had selected them at random from the shelves. It might be many moons before he could return, and he chafed at the burden of duty that now shackled him. Reez was going to go through the open door when he paused.

Each time he had explored the library, he had automatically retraced his steps from the first day and returned the same way. Today, he had approached from the far side and as he passed the last set of shelves, his lamp had illuminated a slight reflection in his peripheral vision. He backed up and lifted the lantern higher to see it more clearly. A lever was embedded in the wall behind the door. He lifted his hand and touched it, then with a shrug, he pulled it swiftly down.

At first, nothing seemed to happen, and Reez moved to leave. A small flicker halted his steps, and he turned to look up. A globe pulsed in the ceiling, fitfully at first but gradually gaining strength. Another flashed, and another as the whole vaulted canopy above began to fill with light. Astonished, Reez moved to the rail and watched in amazement as globes appeared on each level, the glow cascading down until the entire chamber was filled with a soft light, like an early morning before the sun burnt the clouds away. He clutched the rail, his eyes raking over the sight before him, his heart thumping loudly in his chest. Around and below, illuminated by the ancient lamps, lay the complete knowledge of the Mages of old. He knew the library was vast, but to gaze at it spread out before him, instead of squinting at the little he had managed to see by the tiny lamps, took his breath away. It was magnificent.

How many Masters had sat in the little hut above, oblivious to the treasure underneath them? He thought of Wicton. Would they have discovered this together if he had lived, and Reez had piqued his curiosity with his questions? Reez closed his eyes and imagined what it would have been like to explore this place with his old Master. His eyes flew open suddenly, and he pulled the bag from his shoulder, dropping it to the floor with a thud. Where was the endless source of magic? He had been so caught up in his discovery that he had forgotten all about it. Surely now, with the room lit up, he should be able to find it? He knew it was down here somewhere. He ran down the steps, ignoring the shelves filled with books, and began to make a careful investigation of the cabinets on the ground floor, but after a long and fruitless search, he sat heavily in one of the chairs and sighed. There were many strange objects stored there, but none of them was the vessel he was looking for. He glanced at the doors leading away from the library, all of them locked. It must be behind one of them, he reasoned, hidden away from the students who used to use this place. After all, it wouldn't be safe to have it out on display for anyone to take.

    He groaned in frustration. Making his way back up the curving staircases, he picked up his bag and the lamp that still flickered. It would run out of oil very soon, and he still had to make his way up to the surface. He fought the disappointment that had gripped him. There would be many more visits, and he could spend all the time he needed to open the doors there. The lamp sputtered, and he hurriedly pushed up the lever, plunging the room into darkness once more, before closing the door firmly behind him.

Chapter Fifteen

Reez sat at the edge of the stream and tried to calm his mind. For many moons, he had studied and learnt, trying to absorb as much information as he could, his excitement growing with each new discovery. He had travelled to the Mage library several times, returning home with books and parchments crammed into his bags to spend days closeted in the tower pouring over the tomes and making notes. He had discovered a book on locating metals and opening fissures to reach them from deep in the earth, and he planned to put his newfound knowledge into action when he next visited Minra. Reez knew the guild leaders would be ecstatic, having already received missives bemoaning the length of time it was taking to create a safe tunnel underground.

He was also keen to find what the Mages described as a leading stone. After writing to Jodrel, he discovered it was unknown to them, and Reez had felt the familiar excitement of a secret uncovered. The Mages had cited several sources of it in the mountains around what he assumed to be Minra province, but Reez quickly realised that the exact locations would be difficult to pinpoint. The war, it seemed, had drastically altered the geography of the land; rivers no longer flowed the same way and other features had been obliterated altogether, but Reez was confident that he knew the general area to begin his search. Apparently, the leading stone consistently pointed in the same direction, making it a useful navigational tool. It also possessed the ability to attract other metals like iron, although Reez had yet to discover what use that might be. He was sure that somewhere in the library, there would be information on its application.

There was one thing he longed to do, however, and today he would find out if his studies had paid off. He smiled to himself as he remembered finding the book in the forbidden archives, written in Wicton's familiar hand, and wondered when he had troubled himself to learn the skill. How old was he when he made his first foray into forbidden magic? Did he feel guilty or excited?

Taking a deep breath, he ignored the whisper of magic across his skin and the deep tension in his muscles. Instead, he directed his thoughts to the places within himself that, as yet, felt uncomfortable rather than pleasurable. As he gathered the magic, he tried to ignore the tingling sensation rippling across his spine and down his arms. Instead, he allowed a picture to form in his mind before sending out the summons. "Come," he muttered to himself.

At first, nothing seemed to happen. The birds continued to chirp in the trees and the leaves fluttered in the soft wind blowing across the meadow. In some part of his awareness, Reez could feel the creak of roots and the rush of sap flooding the plants and trees around him. He heard a small splash and grinned as a filbet battled up the stream to reach him. He waited for the little fish to reach the slower running current where he sat on the bank before lowering his hand into the water and offering the berries, laughing as the filbet tickled his fingers as it swam across them. After the last berry had been nibbled or had floated downstream, Reez released the magic with a sigh and watched as the fish swam away. "Thank you," he whispered.

That night, as he sat by a small fire in the study, he related his success. "I don't know whether you would congratulate me or admonish me," he admitted to the empty chair across from him. "but as you had taken time to learn the skill, I think you would have been secretly pleased. If my sketchy research is correct, there is no limit to the creatures that you can call, as long as you understand the way they hear and can tempt them with something they need, even if you don't actually have it. The fish would have answered me with just the thought of being rewarded with berries. Can you imagine being surrounded by birds and animals, all of them heeding your summons?" He stared at the small flames flickering in the hearth and sipped the hot brew he held, letting his mind wander down imaginary paths. A fish was a simple creature with simple needs. It was easy to summon and control and didn't tax his knowledge of magic. Reez imagined bigger animals would be more difficult to coax and command, but the idea of having the village oxen at his beck and call put a wide grin on his face. He fantasised about making it follow Aydal like a lovelorn girl and laughed as he pictured his brother running down the lanes with the bull chasing behind him. He sighed happily and relaxed back in the chair.

"I'm still struggling to convert the magic, but it is getting easier the more I work," he continued after a brief silence. "I don't like the painful feelings I get when I try to utilise animal magic. It reminds me of…" He trailed into silence as he remembered Verrin taking his anger out on the two apprentices, often causing stomach cramps as he fuelled his spells. He mentally shook himself and forced the memories away. "I'm finding the animal magic very limiting. There is an abundance of green magic, and earth magic is fairly accessible too. I'm reluctant to tap into the earth fires, but I find I can still work adequately if I stick to the dirt on the surface. Apparently, that usually depletes the nutrients in the soil, though, which I don't want to do, so I will probably have to delve deeper for it. The force of the earth fire is alarming in its intensity. It fills you so quickly, like a raw bolt of power. If I ever gain control of it, it will be a dynamic source. I would much rather utilise that when performing anima magic, as I certainly don't feel comfortable using another creature to fuel my efforts." He frowned. "Even insects have a right to live. Their contribution to this world is just as important. Without them, the plants would die out and the world would be littered with dead things. It's a wonder that Bestra province survives at all when you think of how many must die to fuel their Master's magic. Of course, he could always choose something else…" His musings stopped at the thought of what Verrin might utilise. He literally had the power of life and death over every creature he came in contact with. Reez remembered how easily Verrin had incapacitated and killed all three Masters, draining them of life while bringing his twisted torments into existence. He shook his head, as if to clear the images from his mind.

Not wanting to contemplate the idea further, Reez decided to get some sleep. He swallowed the last dregs of his drink, banked the fire, and made his way up the stone steps to his own room, satisfied with the day's achievements and looking forward to all he might discover in the future.

#

"Someone needs to do somethin'!" The voice was loud and interrupted Reez's thoughts as he sat in the corner settle after enjoying a hot meal and a cup of ale. He turned his head to watch the large group of men.

"Maybe you should march into Bestra and tell its Master how to run his province, Fane," another voice chimed in. Others sniggered in agreement.

"Well, mayhap I shall!" Fane exclaimed. A half-hearted cheer went up from the table of men gathered in the far corner enjoying a few drinks after labouring in the fields. As Fane stood, swaying with the effort to take a bow, they dissolved into laughter.

"What will you tell him?" one man asked, nudging his friend in the side and nodding his head towards Fane.

Fane sat back down and took a long quaff of ale, wiping his mouth with his sleeve as his companions grinned at him. "Take back the wretches who are plaguing us. There's no more room 'ere for folks who should be minding their own 'omes," he announced. "We don't want 'em. I'd also tell 'im to get rid of those unnatural beasts terrorisin' our borders and leave us be."

"I'll drink to that!"

"You tell him!"

"That'll do it!"

Reez listened to the shouts and closed his eyes. Despite his best efforts, and those of the council, some people remained unhappy with the idea of the refugees moving in to the province. There had been scattered reports of minor thefts, vandalism of property, and even a couple of isolated cases of outright violence. Although many of the Fiorans had been welcoming and keen to help those fleeing their homes, a core of dissenters had been very vocal in their anger at being expected to feed and house those escaping Bestra province. This was the first time Reez had heard such sentiments in Maston, however. None of the refugees had come so deep into the province and the residents were unaffected by the problems faced by the border villages.

"I say we send 'em all back," Fane continued, encouraged by his audience. "Why should we look after 'em?

It's none of our business, after all." The laughter and cheering became louder, but muted, and finally stopped as Reez rose abruptly and marched towards the table. One man tried to hush Fane but, well in his cups, he was oblivious to the sudden change in atmosphere. "Filthy Bestrians. They come 'ere, eatin' all our food, and what do they give us in return? Nothin'. At the very least, they should be payin' for what they are given. They're a scourge, I tell you, like locusts ravagin' a field takin' everything they can get their grubby hands on. Why, if I were Master here…"

"Yes, Fane. Tell me what you would do," Reez interjected tersely, his face a blank mask of anger.

Fane swung around on his stool and lifted bleary eyes to focus on Reez. His face blanched as he recognised the stern face, and he began to stammer. "N… nothin', Master Reez," he said, swallowing loudly. "I was just jokin' around." Reez's eyes swept over the table, but none of the seated men were brave enough to return his gaze.

"I am disappointed," he said quietly, keeping his fury under a tight rein. All conversation in the taproom ceased as people strained to hear him. "You would turn away a frightened and unfortunate family, who have run in terror from ravaging beasts leaving everything behind, and all for the sake of coin? Where is your compassion, Fane? Where is your heart?" He leaned in close, ignoring the smell of sweat from Fane's filthy clothes. "Tell me, what happened three summers ago when blight infected your tater crop and destroyed it all? Because of your laziness and lack of attention, you didn't call me in time, and I couldn't save it. Did you and your family starve after that cycle? No. The villagers rallied round and supported you and Beryll until you could harvest your second field." Reez stared into Fane's eyes and his finger jabbed into Fane's chest. "Do you think less of us for that act of kindness?" Fane shook his head emphatically.

Reez stood up again and raised his voice so that everyone would hear it. "My duty as Master is to ensure that all people have enough food, not only in Fiora, but the rest of Zelannor. You act as if they are stealing the food from your own mouths, yet none of you are hungry or in need as a result. It matters not that they cannot pay. These are unusual circumstances, and we should open up our hearths and our hearts to those who are suffering." He turned his attention back to the men at the table, who were all looking contrite. "I believe it is time you went back to your warm homes and soft beds to spend a moment being thankful to the First Mage for the blessings you enjoy. It seems to me that you have had enough ale tonight."

Without another word, the men scrambled to their feet and, grabbing Fane by the arm, hurried out of the tavern. As Reez moved back to his seat, the hum of conversation began again.

"He'll have forgotten on the morrow," Damino said as he slipped into the settle across from Reez and placed a full tankard in front of him.

"You heard, then?"

"I think I caught most of it." Damino leant back after taking a long swallow. "It was the ale talking, nothing more."

"Don't excuse him. The drink only feeds from whatever is in him to start with." Reez sighed. "I wish I could say he was the only one, but I warrant there are folk who would agree with him. They are just too judicious to voice it aloud in my hearing."

"It's hard for us to understand the full extent of what is happening. We are so far away from it all. I know you have kept the details from us, but mayhap it's time we knew the whole story."

"People would panic if they understood the full horror of what is out there."

"Isn't listening to vicious rumours causing upset already? In my opinion, truth is preferable to ignorant rantings from people like Fane. Yes, it might make folk fearful, but it will also help us be more understanding of the refugees seeking sanctuary among us, and better prepared to face whatever else might cross over."

Reez sighed. "You could be right," he acceded.

"Fane may enjoy stirring up an ant's nest, but he's right about one thing." Reez looked across at his brother. "Something needs to be done. As to what…" he spread his hands wide. "How do you stop a Master, or take him to task?"

"Wicton would know," Reez mumbled.

"Wicton is gone. You are Master now. Perhaps you're the only one who *can* do anything."

Reez shook his head. "I can't march into Bestra and demand that he listen to me," he said bitterly. "Verrin would kill me without a thought."

"Maybe he would have once, but you are stronger now,

wiser and more capable. Wicton also gave you a way to defend yourself. It would be Verrin taken by surprise now, not you."

Reez stared at Damino. "You honestly believe that I could stand against him?"

Damino shrugged. "Only you would know that. Just consider what other options we have. There are none, unless you have a brilliant idea. The longer he is left alone to rule unopposed, the worse things will get."

"I can't," Reez said in a small voice.

"Then we deal with whatever happens," Damino replied sagely, taking a sip of his ale and letting his gaze rove over the inn.

Reez could feel the beginnings of panic bubbling up inside him, and he took a deep breath, closing his eyes against the once familiar dread that threatened to emerge. Gradually, the feelings disappeared, and he opened his eyes again. Damino was watching him closely, his eyes full of compassion.

"You all right, Weet?" he asked quietly. Reez just nodded.

After a momentary silence, the brothers turned the conversation to Damino's work at the apothecary and the latest news from Amily. They didn't speak of the troubles to the east again, but it niggled at Reez like a fly buzzing around a flower long after they parted company. He didn't want to journey into Bestra province, let alone confront his nemesis in Etheradia. Reez was certain that Verrin had other interests to occupy him other than searching for the new Master of Fiora, and he felt safe from Verrin's magic as long as he didn't leave the borders of

Fiora. He could protect his people from whatever ranged across. It would be folly to seek out trouble. He had enough work to occupy him at home.

All his reasoning stayed with him as he walked back up the lane later that evening, breathing deeply of the air redolent with fruit and the wild flowers that grew in abundance in the banks and verges. An owl hooted somewhere in the distance and a soft breeze blew against his face. The peace of the night soothed his soul and settled his heart. Whatever trouble Verrin caused wouldn't touch him here. There was no reason for him to force a confrontation.

"Come along," a voice whispered as he lay down to sleep that night. Determinedly, he ignored it, turned over and blocked the errant thought with images of filbets nibbling berries from his hand.

Chapter Sixteen

"In honour of the First Mage who brought forth fruit on the trees and under the earth, I bless the seeds of fruit to come. May they be whole and free from all pestilence, growing in strength and bringing abundance to the land." With a flourish, Reez span the seeds above him and then sent them off to the far reaches of Fiora province. The crowd oohed approvingly as a gust of wind carried them away, and Reez smiled. Manipulating air was fun and something he found incredibly easy to do.

He had pored over his new texts, devouring each scrap of information like a starving man, greedy for more. His proficiency with fire, air and water was swift, and he practised as much as possible. Unlike green magic which drew from the inherent store in each living thing and needed to be husbanded carefully, earth magic was raw, untamed and plentiful. Reez could feel the force of the earth fires below when he probed, just waiting to be released, but both wind and rushing water were stores of energy that could be used or redirected at will. It was a heady feeling to have so much power in his grasp.

Reez's understanding of philosophy and ethics, however, was not as effortless, and he struggled to understand the abstract concepts. Anyone else might have been tempted to forgo such studies and concentrate on the magic alone, but Reez had seen enough of the library to sense that it had been important to the Mages of old, so he continued to try. Late at night, he had imagined himself sitting at one of the tables, the buzz of low voices and the scratching of nibs on parchment punctuated by a sneeze or cough as dozens of students worked quietly at their tasks. He conjured up images of lounging with a group of men and women beneath the trees outside the tower, discussing the nature of the universe or the conundrum of the human mind. It was at those times that his heart would sink, and the loneliness of his reality would intrude.

He had no-one. His elation at finding the secret library had been muted by the fact that he had no companion to share it with. Nobody congratulated him as he made puffball seeds swirl in a funnel of wind or pushed the water in the lake apart. If he had questions, doubts or needed to find a solution to a problem, he had to battle them alone. He had even briefly considered taking on an apprentice of his own, knowing that he had a duty to ensure that there would be a Master to carry on his work after he was gone, but recognised that it would be many cycles before he could confide in them, if at all.

The gong sounded, breaking Reez's reverie, and the crowd cheered as the formal ceremony concluded and the real festivities could begin in earnest. Reez left the dais and walked through the throng, stopping occasionally to greet people or respond to a question. He was listening to one of the Margraves bemoaning the lack of expertise of some of the refugees when someone called his name. Looking up, he recognised the son of one of the council elders.

"Master Reez!" the boy called again, pushing his way through the crowds.

He excused himself and moved towards him. "Darwan, is something amiss?" he asked, noting the flush on the young man's face.

"There are people from Bestra at the inn asking for you by name," Darwan explained. "I came as quickly as I could."

Reez frowned. "Did they tell you who they were?"

"No, but the lady gave me this to show you." He opened his hand and Reez saw a small, yellow flower, carefully dried and pressed in a piece of fabric. Ladies Tears.

"Where are they?" Reez asked quickly.

"In the taproom. They seemed exhausted and have no possessions with them. Nula is serving them food."

"Thank you, Darwan," Reez said, patting the boy on the shoulder. "I'll go to them right away."

Reez hurried across the green and entered Phalen's inn,

his eyes eagerly scanning the packed room. The shutters had been flung wide open and a soft breeze moved through the room, dispelling the scent of sour ale and unwashed bodies. Reez finally spotted the visitors and moved across to the settle, his smile wide and his eyes alight.

"Castor!" he called in delight as he neared. His friend turned and stared at Reez's face in shock, and a soft cry came from the other side where Merrylee sat, her hands flying to her mouth to muffle her distress. He had forgotten all about his disfigurement. Merrylee jumped up and crossed over to him, enfolding him in her arms before carefully reaching up and stroking his left cheek. "What happened?" she asked, her voice laced with sorrow.

"Long story," he replied, gazing at her with affection.

"Does it hurt?" a voice asked faintly.

Reez looked across at Siril. The boy had sprouted like a weed and was as tall as Merrylee. His mousy brown hair was cropped close to his scalp, and he looked as if he hadn't eaten a proper meal in weeks.

"No, Siril, it's fine." He looked closely at the little family. All three of them were grimy and weary from their journey, but relief flooded their faces. Reez sensed that something very wrong had happened to send them travelling across two provinces with nothing but the clothes on their backs and the small bags he spied under the table. "What brings you here?" he asked, turning to Castor, who seemed older somehow, the grey in his hair much more prominent. "This doesn't look like a social visit to me."

Castor gazed at the taproom filled with patrons enjoying the celebrations and filling their bellies with ale and food. "Is there somewhere else we can speak plainly?" he asked.

Just then, Nula arrived with a tray laden with bowls and plates. "Eat first," Reez said. "We can talk after." Reez watched as they tucked into their meal with relish, wondering when they had last eaten something hot and filling. He took Nula to one side and spoke quietly to her.

"They will need a room, if you have one," he said.

"Destry has already opened up the large one at the front. She is taking up the bedding as we speak."

"You are a marvel," Reez said, kissing her cheek. "Apply to the Margrave for funds on my behalf. They are my guests."

"They say you stayed with them when you were in Etheradia," she said.

Reez grinned and tapped her nose, knowing how she relished hearing embarrassing stories about him. "I was the perfect guest," he said.

"Surely they have some interesting tales to tell."

"You'll be disappointed. Merrylee adores me and will tell you nothing but good things." He laughed as Nula screwed up her nose.

"They seem fearful," she added quietly after a moment. "What happened to them?"

"I'll find out in due course. Let them rest and eat first, and I'll hear their story upstairs. No doubt you will know everything before the day is out," he said. "Be patient."

She swatted his hand away. "Keep your secrets," she clucked. "I've got better things to do than grub through your dirt."

Reez laughed, knowing that she would interrogate Merrylee as soon as his back was turned. When the family had finished their meal, sopping up the last of the rich gravy with pieces of bread, Reez led them upstairs to their freshly prepared room.

"This is lovely," Merrylee said as she sat on one of the chairs by the window. Castor sat opposite, and Siril curled his gangly frame against the wall at his father's feet. Reez perched himself on the edge of the large bed.

"It is," Reez acknowledged. "I think it is a burden on the family that owns it, though." He turned to Castor. "Why don't you tell me what's troubling you?"

"Things haven't been right since the Ascension," he started.

Reez frowned. "Ascension?"

"When the son took on the mantle of the father and became the Eternal One," Castor explained.

Reez forced himself to breathe normally, his hands clasped in his lap. He had known that his fragile peace would be shattered eventually, but it unnerved him to have to hear first hand of Verrin again. He mentally shook himself. It had been many moons since the letters from Castor had stopped and this was a chance to discover news from the city and what had changed to send the family fleeing across the country. "Go on," he said encouragingly.

"At first, there were edicts announcing celebrations and feasting for the whole city. People were happy to lay down their work and gorge themselves with the food and drink until it became apparent that they were expected to fund it all from their own coffers. The clerics were tasked with collecting either money or goods from every household; anyone objecting was threatened and when they started to take people away, the dissenters soon quietened. It went on for several moons, and people began to get jaded. Who knew that even the hardest drinkers would grow tired of being forced to endless parties? It was a relief when the festivities ended and life returned to normal."

"It wasn't long after that the Purge began." Siril shifted uncomfortably, and Castor patted his shoulder. "All undesirables were collected from the city and made to take on honest labour or be incarcerated. At first, the clerics just took the beggars and whores. It felt good to walk down the street without being badgered and harassed, and I approved the decision. I even said so to the clerics I saw." He swallowed. "We didn't ask where they went. We didn't care." Merrylee reached across and grasped his hand in support, and he smiled thinly. "Next, they targeted the street gangs. Scores of children were rounded up and marched to the docks and the Abbey. They were carried by boats to the island, and again, I was glad that they would be given a chance to be useful, to train as a cleric or be taken to the priestesses in the Temple."

Reez stayed silent. He wasn't so sure that either option was a good thing, but as Castor and Merrylee had given up two of their own children to serve, he wasn't about to voice his criticism.

"Then people started disappearing, men and women who had been vocal against the Purge, or who were unhappy with the clerics policing the city. We quickly learnt not to speak out or express any opinion that didn't align with the clerics. Notices were nailed up, and a crier sent out saying that information about dissenters would be rewarded. Folk used it as an excuse to settle old scores or hurt their neighbours. You wouldn't recognise the place," Castor said sadly. "No one goes out after dark in case they are picked up for loitering. Suddenly, any type of festivity or celebration was banned. People were even afraid of laughing too loud. My business dried up; no-one wanted to be accused of being frivolous by having a few mugs of ale, or be charged with drunkenness and imprisoned. A few regulars would come in occasionally, but didn't stay long.

"It even affected the trade in the port. The traders from across the Endless Sea started to get wary. Most of them sailed away and never bothered to return. I don't blame them. Who would want to risk being held captive and not be able to go back home?"

"I was scared," Siril said quietly.

"I'm sure you were," Reez said.

"We all were," Castor said. "A few moons ago, they closed all the city gates except for one. We were told to apply for a permit if we needed to leave; everyone is questioned, and bags are searched when you pass through and valuables are often confiscated. I had already decided to send Merrylee and Siril here, even though they didn't want to leave me. I thought if we all left, it would look suspicious. We invented a fictitious relative who lived outside the city. We often spoke about them in the inn, so that when the two of them left for a visit, it wouldn't appear unusual. Then Jina arrived and asked to speak to me."

"You still see him?" Reez asked. The cleric had been allocated to serve Reez when he had gone to Bestra as a journeyman. By the end of the visit, Reez had been glad to call the man a friend.

"He comes in when his duties permit to make sure we are well. He always stays for something to eat," Merrylee said with a small smile.

"In truth, I think his presence helped to keep us safe, that and our association with you," Castor continued.

"Da kept reminding our customers of your visit every chance he got," Siril said proudly. "He showed them your letters, too. Everyone had been informed that the Masters and their apprentices had gone for good, but we knew differently."

"Wasn't that risky?" Reez asked.

"I showed them to those who knew you from your visit as an apprentice," Castor said. "It was enough to start the rumours. People are anxious and I think it gave some of them a little hope to think that at least one Master remains to challenge the Eternal One. Those with a vindictive bent left us alone. No one was willing to accuse people favoured by the priesthood and a journeyman of considerable ability. I even occasionally hinted that you might return and would need your old room back at short notice," he said shyly. "I hope it wasn't too much of a presumption."

"If my name meant you were protected, then I am glad," Reez replied. "Why didn't you let me know what was happening? You could have mentioned something in your letters."

Castor looked down. "There were spies everywhere. I worried that the letters would be opened. It's bad, Master Reez. You can't trust anyone."

"I understand," Reez replied. "So, Jina paid you a visit. I assume it was his news that caused you all to flee."

"He was very agitated," Castor said with a frown. "He said we needed to leave Etheradia immediately. I told him of my plans to stay, but he insisted we all go together. He made me promise to take only small bags and leave the very next day. He wouldn't tell me why it was so urgent, but it was clear he was worried. We wore as many layers of clothes as we could without it becoming obvious. We wrapped Merrylee's jewellery and all our money in bundles and tied them inside our tunics. Jina filled in a permit for us to visit Squorn, a little town to the south, and told us exactly what to say to be allowed through."

"We wouldn't have escaped if it hadn't been for him," Merrylee said.

Castor nodded. "They took the little money we had in our bags and Merrylee's jewellery."

"I only wore the pieces I didn't mind losing," she said. "It was a small sacrifice to make."

"She even cried when they took her ring, even though it

wasn't the real one," Siril said proudly.

"That was a good idea," Reez replied. "They would likely be suspicious if you carried nothing with you."

"It was Jina's idea," Merrylee said.

"So, you managed to get out of the city. Did you run into any trouble on the way here?"

"After we had been travelling a while, I planned to cut across country, but we heard stories of unnatural creatures roaming freely and attacking people. I decided to stay on the frequently travelled roads and byways. It took us a lot longer than I anticipated, and we have spent most of our money," he added dejectedly, looking at his hands, "but we stayed safe. All the way through Bestra, we came across people fleeing their towns and villages, desperately trying to get into Etheradia, but the clerics are allowing very few in. Unless you are a young woman, a healthy child, or have wealth to smooth your path, you are turned away. I heard that some were being smuggled in and a few have endeavoured to make rafts to enter from the harbour, but the currents can be treacherous and many die in the attempt."

"These creatures you mentioned. Do you know what they are? Has anyone seen them?"

Castor shook his head. "Only hearsay." He glanced at Siril, who had grown pale. "We stuck to the roads and found shelter well before night fell. Many homesteads at the borders have been deserted, so we made sure to barricade ourselves inside. When we crossed into Fiora, they wanted to send us to a different village, but I insisted we were coming here to consult with you and they reluctantly let us continue."

Reez nodded. "The border villages have been given instructions on the dispersion of refugees so the extra people can be housed and fed properly. I confess, I had expected more people to cross over, but from what you say, they seem to be seeking safety behind sturdy walls instead."

"Many of them are camped outside the city, unwilling to leave despite the fact they can't gain entry. Those that are lucky enough to be allowed through might believe they are protected from the creatures, but there are other things to be frightened of," Castor muttered ominously. "I didn't realise how afeared I was until we finally arrived here. It's such a relief to have made it."

"There is nothing that will hurt you here," Reez reassured them.

"But there aren't any walls around your town, Master Reez," Siril said quietly. "What if those creatures decide to come this way after all?"

Reez smiled at him and glanced across at Merrylee, who was stifling a yawn. "Do you think they would risk coming anywhere near a Master?" he asked. "They wouldn't dare." Siril nodded sagely. Reez patted Merrylee's hand. "Rest and eat plenty. Sleep if you like. Perhaps later you can enjoy the festivities outside; they will be continuing for a long time yet. As my guests, you can ask for anything and it will be given to you. Nula will see to your needs and I will come back tomorrow." He rose and made to leave.

"Reez?" Siril said. He stopped and turned back. "You'll make everything right, won't you?"

Reez just smiled and left them to rest, but inside he wondered whether anything would ever be right again.

Chapter Seventeen

"If Master Reez says the report is trustworthy, then we need to make further plans," the Margrave said carefully, his forehead creased with worry. He spread his hands wide. "I would very much appreciate your thoughts."

Reez gazed over the assembled people, their faces a mixture of anxiety and determination. After leaving Castor, Reez had immediately requested a meeting with the council of Elders to make them aware of the latest tidings from Bestra.

"What are you expecting to happen?" Gelad asked as she looked around the table. Head of the widow weaver's house, she was the voice of the women who had no families.

Sat on the Margrave's right-hand side, Bilan thought for a moment, elbows on the table and his fingers tucked under his ample chin. "Either we will have a flood of people entering the province for succour when they find the gates of Etheradia barred to them, or we will have these creatures crossing over the border in search of prey when the outlying villages have been ravaged and emptied."

"Perhaps both," Beran said gloomily.

The Margrave nodded and sighed. Despite being far from the border, all the settlements in Fiora would look to Maston, and in particular, Reez, to take the lead and give them wise instruction. Although the Margrave's station had been elevated even further by directing their response to the crisis, he was a wise enough man to realise that the situation was too overwhelming for one person, and he gladly deferred to the others on the council. Reez was pleasantly surprised to find Bilan to be a voice of reason and wisdom, and he grudgingly admitted that he would make a worthy successor to his father when the mantle passed on.

"Then we plan for both, and hope that we need neither," the Margrave said. "Perhaps we could divide our efforts, with half of us talking through what to do with a sudden influx of refugees, while the others consider what further defences we might need."

"Master Reez, isn't there anything you can do?" Seemer asked querulously before the Margrave could continue.

Reez frowned. "I have already done what I can. The hedges are strong enough and high enough to deter the most determined predator. If necessary, I can speed up the growth of produce to feed an expanded populace, but I would rather wait until we have need. It may well mean that the Margrave's flower garden will suffer and I'm sure he wouldn't want that unless it was absolutely necessary." There were chuckles from some of the people gathered.

"But the Master of Bestra is being deficient in his duties," Seemer persisted loudly. "Surely it is time you took him to task. He must listen to you and stop this nonsense. It isn't right that his people are coming here and asking you for help. You must demand to meet with him, then you and Master Chrisos must insist that he deal with these creatures and look after his people instead of expecting us to do it."

Beran stiffened and his face flushed red with anger, but Bilan reached over and laid a hand on his arm before he said anything. The Margrave sent Reez an apologetic look, and several people looked down at the table in embarrassment. Some on the council had questioned whether Seemer should take part in council discussions anymore as his memory was faulty and his mind seemed to wander to the past more and more rather than stay firmly rooted in the present. In the end, the elders had decided he could still continue for the time being, unless his condition deteriorated further, but that he would have no final vote or any authority to make changes. Thankfully, the Margrave had finally insisted after many cycles of argument that Seemer take on an apprentice and Darwan had been appointed in enough time to learn the trade and be able to take over the role of record keeper in all but name.

"We have already been through this, Seemer," Bilan said softly, and Reez was impressed at how calmly he handled the situation. "This Master Verrin is not one to treat with us. Remember, he killed Master Wicton and Master Chrisos many cycles ago. It was a miracle that Master Reez survived and was able to return to us. It is our responsibility to protect our lands and the people who live here."

Seemer frowned and scratched his head. "Master Wicton is dead?" he said with a hitch in his voice.

"Come, Seemer," Gelad said as she rose and took his hand. "Let us see if the Margravine has any sweet cakes in her larder."

"What about Minra province?" Dalena asked after they left, her pale blue eyes still bright after almost seventy summers. "Have they sent word of any problems?"

Reez shook his head. "I expect Fiora to be a more attractive option than Minra for both refugees and wild creatures," he said. "There have been very few people crossing over to Minra and no reports of unusual creatures as yet. Of course, that may change when the hoggets roaming the mountain reaches become the only accessible prey after the stables and barns are depleted. So far, we have only heard reports from the flatlands where the best grazing is to be found and both people and herds are plentiful."

The Margrave divided the council into two, and when Gelad returned, they began their discussions. Reez had no part to play, but decided to stay anyway in case they had any more questions for him. As the group next to him discussed the idea of arming sections of the populace, Reez sat back with a sigh. He only vaguely listened to plans to contact Minra and request weapons, and the resultant dispute about whether spears or swords would be better, as he reflected on all the changes that had happened since the deaths of Chrisos and Malander. Fiora had remained relatively untouched, but the rest of Zelannor was transforming and Reez couldn't help yearning for the peace and innocence of past cycles, when he was nothing more than an eager young boy desperate to learn magic. Looking around at the council leaders, he was saddened to think they had already been affected by the dark shadow threatening Zelannor, that seemed to grow larger every day. Life would never be the same, and Reez felt helpless. He had more chance of turning the tides on the coast than halting the situation they now found themselves in.

The weight of his responsibilities sat heavily on him and, once again, he craved a companion to share the burden with. It would be wonderful to talk through the developments happening across the land and work through the possible consequences. Even if they weren't able to find solutions, the mere thought of unburdening himself and having someone to listen to his hopes and fears would be a rare gift. With another Master stood beside him, he would't have to bear all the blame should something go wrong. Instead, he was alone. The council would do their part and his family would listen quietly, but in the end, the onus would be on Reez to fix things or make the big decisions.

He glanced up in surprise as the council members rose

from the table and began to make their way out of the room. Reez hadn't heard their final deliberations, but it mattered not, as he had no more news or advice to offer them. He stood up and made to follow them out.

"Master Reez, a word, please?"

Reez looked over at Bilan, who sat across from him. He seemed uncomfortable, yet determined. As the last of the council filed out and the door closed, Reez sat back down. "What can I do for you?" he asked.

Bilan cleared his throat and sat forward, his fingers knotted tightly on the table. "This Verrin. He did that to you," he said, pointing at Reez's face. It wasn't a question, so Reez merely nodded.

"You know him better than anyone. Could we reason with him?"

Reez wanted to laugh at the thought, but he considered for a moment before replying. "No," he said decisively. "Perhaps at one time he would have been more equitable, but he was always arrogant and considered himself above us all. It would have been hard enough to reason with the boy he used to be, let alone the man he has become. When he attacked us that day, it was as if something had snapped inside. He was wild, out of control and eager to kill and inflict pain."

"If, as you have hinted, his own Master was deficient, then he had no wise counsel to temper him," Bilan said quietly. "Perhaps since then he has come to regret his actions."

Reez looked at Bilan carefully. "What makes you think that?"

Bilan shifted in his chair. "People change. Someone can regret an action wrought in the heat of the moment."

"You imagine him feeling remorse for destroying the lives of so many? I think you are being naïve."

Bilan dragged his hand through his sandy hair and looked directly at Reez. "Did Master Wicton ever tell you about his coming to see me?"

Reez frowned and shook his head.

Unable to remain seated, Bilan stood and paced across the room. "That day at the lake," he said, glancing back to make sure Reez had remembered the incident before continuing. "You humiliated me in front of my friends, and I was ashamed beyond reason. I was so jealous of you, you know. Everyone praised you wherever I went, saying how wonderful and clever you were. I was the Margrave's son and felt I deserved the adulation, not you. I wanted you on your knees before me. I wanted to feel as if I was worthy. Instead, you reduced me to a worm crawling in the mud.

"Like Verrin, something snapped in me that day. All I could think about was vengeance, making you grovel and cry and soil yourself as you did to me. The truth is, I was mindless in my anger and I didn't stop to consider what I was doing. I just reacted." He swallowed and took a deep breath. "Master Wicton came to see me when I was abed recovering and several times over the following moons. I expected to be punished, and I was, but not by him. He would sit and gently talk with me about lots of things."

"He was a very wise man," Reez said softly. "I wish he

were here now."

Bilan nodded. "The thing is, he told me not to compare myself to others, or try to emulate someone else in order to look better. He made me look deep inside myself and encouraged me to find my own path. He said I was already worthy just because I was me; that I was unique, with my own gifts, and that I should strive to be the very best version of myself that I could." He huffed a breath and shrugged. "I'm not explaining this very well."

"I think I know what you are trying to say," Reez assured him.

Bilan dropped back into his chair and met Reez's gaze. "What if Verrin just needs a wise person to guide him?"

Reez stared at him, his face pale. "What are you saying? You think I should go to him and confront him?"

Bilan lifted his hands in apology. "I can't tell you what to do, and if you think it would be a fool's errand, then I will never speak of it again. But as soon as Aydal pulled me away from you, I knew I was wrong. I know they made me apologise, but it was from my heart. I never meant to kill you and I would have been deeply disgusted with myself if I had succeeded. The guilt would have been too heavy a burden to bear. Perhaps Verrin regretted that day when he had time to ponder it, but he has no Master Wicton to steer him down the right path. It may even be that he is struggling with the role that he coveted so much. Forgive me if I speak out of turn, but I can't help thinking of my own experiences and comparing them to him."

Reez nodded, unable to speak for a moment. He

clenched his fists and took a shaky breath. "I'll consider it," he finally managed to say.

"Well, I'll take my leave," Bilan said, standing up. When he reached the door, he paused for a moment. "If it's any consolation, I don't think Master Wicton could have done any better than you. I am glad to have you as Master." He left, closing the door behind him.

It took Reez a few moments to collect himself, but eventually, he pushed away from the table and made his way outside. He glanced across at the inn. Light shone out from the windows and he heard the faint noise of laughter. People were still out on the green enjoying the festivities, but Reez was in no mood to socialise. Instead, he kept his head down and walked swiftly back to the tower, ignoring those who tried to greet him, or waving off the obviously inquisitive people who wanted to glean some news about what had gone on in the council chambers. Heading straight to the study, he sat in his chair and stared at the empty hearth, thinking about everything Bilan had told him. It was just like Wicton to spend time with an angry young man, helping him to find his way and encouraging him to be a better person. The fact that Bilan could identify himself in Verrin made Reez take pause. Could he be right? What if Verrin was plagued by the evil he wrought that day? If he could be made to see reason and to accept wise counsel, it would be an enormous relief both for Bestra and for Reez himself.

Reez shook his head. Somehow, he couldn't envisage Verrin having any remorse for his actions, but now things had reached such a state that intervention was sorely needed. The only person with the authority and power to do it was himself. Deep down, he had recognised that there may come a day when he would have to face his nemesis again, and the thought terrified him. Even now, he felt woefully inadequate. In his heart, he didn't think that Verrin could be reasoned with, and he wanted to be able to do more to defend himself if, as he suspected, there was to be a confrontation. He would need to prepare for such an encounter and wondered what further arrangements he could make. Damino was right. He was more experienced and had the protection of Wicton's spell shielding him. He had knowledge of earth magic, too, which might prove useful. His thoughts returned to the Mage library and hope began to take seed. There had to be something within the pages of one of those books that could help him. Perhaps there were other methods to defend against an enemy attack, or a way to neutralise the effects of anima magic.

As much as he hated the idea, there was no one else who could hope to stop what was happening in Bestra. If he didn't act now, more people would die or disappear. The time for hiding away and trying to pretend all was well had gone. He must leave his home once more, and this time he would be walking directly towards the danger with his eyes open. He groaned and covered his eyes with his hands, desperately wishing for something miraculous to happen so that he wouldn't have to act.

"Damn you, Bilan," he muttered. "Why couldn't you stay silent?" Deep in his heart, however, he couldn't blame Bilan. He had merely voiced something that Reez had not wanted to acknowledge.

Sighing deeply, he picked up his candle and made his way up the stone stairs to his bed. He didn't want to think of foul creatures or Verrin anymore. He needed the blessed oblivion of sleep. There would be time enough for contemplating further courses of action in the days ahead. Yawning, he climbed into his cot, pulled the blankets over his head, and closed his eyes.

That night, the nightmares returned in force.

Chapter Eighteen

"What can I get for you, Reez? We still have some of the summer ale, or perhaps you would prefer the sowstick wine?"

"Castor, what are you doing behind the bar?" Reez asked with a grin as he walked through the door of the Inn.

"Ah well, these lovely people were being run ragged with so many folk here for the celebrations, so me and Merrylee thought we could lend a hand. Truth is, I'm glad to be in a taproom again." He rubbed the spotless surface in front of him with a rag. "Merrylee is cooking up a storm in the galley, and Siril has been fetching and carrying all morning. Only seems fair to pay our way with some hard work."

Reez laughed. "I'll have the ale, but first let me greet your lovely wife."

He rounded the bar and went through the door at the back. The galley was a hive of activity. Lileth was racing around the table singing a song to herself while Nula kneaded bread. Merrylee stood at the stove stirring a large pot whilst cradling a sleepy Lina on her hip. Siril was sat at the table peeling vegetables, his shoulders slumped, but he straightened up and waved enthusiastically when he spotted Reez.

"Da says I'm to make myself useful," he gushed.

"And he is, too," Nula said as she looked fondly at him. "I don't know how we managed without him." Siril's smile was so big, Reez imagined it would split his face in two if it were any wider.

"Well done, Siril," Reez said, his heart swelling at the look of pride on the boy's face. He wandered over to Merrylee and bussed her cheek before tickling the toddler in her arm. "How's little Reez today?"

Merrylee stopped stirring and looked at Nula in confusion. "I thought her name was Lina?"

"Pay no mind to him," Nula said, slapping Reez on the arm and leaving a white handprint behind. She took the little girl in her arms and kissed her. "He won't admit defeat."

"Boy or girl, the next one is definitely going to be named Reez."

Nula rolled her eyes. "Did you want something in particular?"

"No, I just came to say hello." He dipped his finger into the pot and lifted it to his mouth.

"You can stop that!" Merrylee exclaimed. "Who knows where your hands have been?"

Reez licked his fingers. "Not bad, but it could do with a little more seasoning, I think."

"A little more…!" Merrylee spluttered.

Reez dodged the spoon aimed at his head and skipped back towards the taproom. "I see you have everything under control," he said with a laugh as Merrylee started to berate him. "I'll leave you to your work." He ducked quickly through the door before she could find any more missiles to throw at him. Foregoing his usual seat, Reez pulled out one of the tall stools by the bar and took a sip from the mug Castor placed in front of him.

"This is a great place to live," Castor said appreciatively. "Nice people."

"I've always thought so."

"First time I've been able to breathe easily in a long while," Castor admitted, his face growing serious.

"Do you miss home?" Reez asked.

Castor sighed. "I worked hard to get the Falcon, and it was my pride and joy, but the truth is, my home is where they are," he said, indicating the kitchens.

"Maybe one day you can return."

"Perhaps."

They sat in silence for a moment. "I'll be leaving on a journey soon," Reez admitted, finally voicing the decision he had made in the early hours of the morning, "but you are my guests here. Stay for as long as you want."

"This journey," Castor said slowly. "Would it be taking you to the east?"

"I thought I might take a look for myself."

Castor nodded and sighed. "I have to admit, I was hoping you might be able to do something. Not that I want you in danger, or anything."

"To be honest, I'm not sure what I should do. I'm hoping things will become clearer to me when I get there."

"Someone needs to put a halt to the madness," Castor said with a frown. "People can't keep living in fear." He looked closely at Reez. "You can stop the Eternal One, can't you?"

Reez shrugged. "I don't know, but I have to try. There is no-one else, in truth."

"In that case, these are for the Falcon," Castor said, reaching around his neck and slipping a cord over his head. He handed it to Reez, who looked down at the two silver keys attached to it. "You'll need somewhere to stay, and it's as good a place as any. I can guarantee that your old room is free," he said with a sharp laugh.

Reez looped the cord over his own head and tucked the keys beneath his tunic. "Thank you, Castor. I promise to look after the place for you."

"Just don't drink all the best brew," he joked half-heartedly. "I was saving it for a special occasion."

"I promise to breach it only when I have something to celebrate."

"Let's hope it gets opened very soon, then," Castor said, lifting his own mug and toasting Reez.

Reez turned at the sound of the galley door opening. Destry walked through and made her way over to the bar. She stopped next to Reez and looked at him with narrowed eyes. *Merrylee wants to know if you are hungry. If you want the stew, she'll make sure she adds extra pepper to it.*

Reez laughed. *No pie today?* He asked with a wink.

She snorted. *From what I'm told, you don't deserve any.* She turned to Castor. *All well?* She asked.

He moved his fingers carefully. *Very well.*

"She's teaching you to sign?" Reez asked.

"We already knew how to say 'hello' and 'goodnight'. You taught us when you told us about your home when you first came to Etheradia, remember?"

So, are you ready to eat now? Destry asked, turning back to Reez.

What do you recommend?

She rolled her eyes. *Everything.*

That sounds too much for one person. Surprise me.

Shrugging, she sashayed back into the kitchen. Reez watched her go with an appreciative smile.

"She's a lovely lass," Castor said, his eyes knowing. "Make some lucky man a good wife, I'll wager."

Reez sighed. "I agree, but it can't be me. I can't give her what she deserves. I have too much unfinished business to take care of, and too many demands on my time as it is. A wife would be an added complication."

"You know, running an inn takes a lot of work," Castor said after thinking for a moment. "You're at the beck and call of customers at all times of the day, but you still have to make time to cook, clean, replenish the stock, make repairs and tally the takings. Too much for one person, in truth. When I was handfasted to my Merrylee, she wasn't another burden added on to my list, but a partner to help me deal with it. You talk as if having Destry as a companion would be a hardship rather than a delight. I've watched her; she's a good hard worker. My guess is she would ease your load and give you some joy in life." He looked over Reez's shoulder as the front door opened and thirsty men started to pour in. "Just think on it," he said, before moving towards the newcomers. "What can I get you fine gentlemen today? We still have a few barrels of the summer ale left, or I can breach the winter brew for you."

Reez slid down from the stool as the villagers gave their order and retired to his usual spot, nursing the rest of his ale and considering Castor's words. It was the height of madness to consider claiming Destry when he was about to journey east to an uncertain destiny, but Castor had effectively demolished all Reez's arguments. There really was nothing to stop him. Perhaps he should broach the idea with her before leaving for Bestra, although he knew in his heart what her answer would be.

Before Destry had chance to return with his food, Damino and Aydal walked in. Waving, Reez beckoned them over to join him. They chatted together amiably over their meal and it wasn't until the last of the trenchers were cleared away that Reez spoke about something that had been on his mind since his sojourn in Minra.

"Do you ever wish for change?" he asked.

Damino glanced at his older brother. "Why do you ask that?"

"In Minra, the guild leaders had ideas for increasing production, good ones too, but none of the Masters had ever listened to them. It made me wonder if they were not alone in wanting things to be different." He watched as his brothers looked at each other again. "What?"

"Lots of people have ideas," Aydal said carefully. "Would you be willing to hear them?"

"You?" Reez asked. "Did Wicton refuse to listen to you?"

"He didn't ask Wicton," Damino interjected. "Da told him he wasn't to mention it."

"You'd think I had plans to destroy our entire society, the way he carried on," Aydal grumbled, "but it was just a few ideas to increase yield and speed things up."

"Like what?" Reez asked, intrigued.

Aydal sat forward, his eagerness to share his innovations clear. "Instead of leaving a field fallow every other cycle, why not use it two cycles in a row, but with a fresh crop? Da says we need to rest the land, but I think we could use it for an extra cycle. I did some experimenting once in the garden and doubled my yield with no difference in quality. Of course, if farmers had three fields instead of two, they could still leave one fallow and work the others. We have enough empty land surrounding us to offer folk the choice. Then there's grinding corn. It takes an age to do, but what if we used the wind to turn the stones, or even water? It would mean an increase in production for very little effort."

"How would the wind be able to turn stones?" Reez asked, puzzled.

"We catch it with blades. When it pushes the blades, then they can turn the stones. I sketched a way to do it once, but Da ripped it up. I still remember the design." Aydal looked at Reez expectantly. "I could draw it out for you, if you like."

"You always hated your turn at the quern stones," Reez said with a chuckle. "No wonder you concocted a scheme to get out of it." He thought for a moment and reached a decision. "Give me your sketches. I'll have a look at them and if they seem workable, then maybe I could consult with the guild leaders in Minra about construction. Let me think about your rotation scheme, too. We don't want to deplete the land, and I can only use so much magic to help crops along, but if it has value, then I don't see why we can't implement it."

"You'll really consider it?" Aydal asked excitedly.

"After I return."

"You're going away again? But the winter cycle is coming," Damino pointed out. "Can't it wait?"

"No, I'm afraid not. Things in Bestra are worse than we imagined."

Aydal's face fell. "You're risking your life by going there. Stay here, where you are safe."

Reez took a shaky breath. "Don't assume this is a reckless decision," he said. "Believe me, if I could come up with another plan, I would. Who else can challenge a Master? But, I can't ignore what is happening anymore."

"I could come with you…" Aydal began, but Reez stopped him.

"No. This is something I must do alone. I don't want you, or anyone I love, anywhere near him. Who knows what he would do? You would be defenceless against him. At least I can protect myself against his magic, to a point. It may be enough to give me an advantage. I've spent too long making excuses and coming up for good reasons for procrastinating. Now I need to take action."

Aydal reached over and grabbed Reez's hand. "Promise me you won't take any unnecessary risks."

"I promise."

"You'll send word?"

"As often as I can."

Reez looked up as Destry bustled into the bar with an armful of plates and proceeded to hand them out to the hungry patrons. His heart warmed as he watched her work, and he remembered Castor's words. Here was another subject he had been hiding from for too long. "You must excuse me," he said, suddenly rising from his seat. "I have something I need to do." His brothers watched curiously as he crossed over to Destry and touched her arm to get her attention.

Walk out with me, he demanded.

What? Now? Reez nodded. *It's the noon meal. I can't leave.*

"Castor," Reez called loudly. "I'm walking out with

Destry. Can you cope without her?"

"Finally!" Aydal exclaimed, thumping his fist on the table.

"Of course, my friend. Take as long as you like," Castor replied, a huge grin on his face.

Now, he signed and grabbed her hand. To the sounds of mugs banging on tables, hoots and whistles, Reez pulled her out of the door.

What are you doing? Destry asked once they were outside.

Walking out with my girl, Reez replied with a smile.

Destry glanced around the square. *Are you sure?*

This is the only thing I am sure of.

Reez pulled her closer and wound an arm around her trim waist. Hesitantly, she copied him. They walked to the lanes in silence, content just to be together. When they finally stopped beneath the shade of an ancient pommor tree, Reez turned to face her, his countenance serious.

I should have done this a long time ago, he signed.

Yes, you should have.

I didn't want to hurt you. You know that life with me will be difficult for you.

She shrugged. *I keep telling you, it is my choice to make.*

I have another journey to make, he signed slowly. *I don't want to go, but there is no-one else.*

Soon?

Reez nodded. *I leave tomorrow. I have to find a way to*

stop what is happening in Bestra, maybe even confront Verrin.

Will it be dangerous?

Perhaps.

Promise me you will come home.

Reez sighed. *I promise I will try.*

Destry nodded once before rising up on tiptoe and placing a chaste kiss on his lips. Bending his head, Reez pulled her snuggly against his body and finally allowed his feelings free rein.

#

As was his custom, Reez rose very early and, after hefting his bags over his shoulder and retrieving his stout walking stick from beside the galley hearth, made fast the door behind him. Pausing, he looked around at his home. He had arranged for someone to tend to his glass house while he was gone and he had no excuses left. He had procrastinated long enough. He felt the familiar thrum of fear beginning to rise in his chest, so he turned sharply and began his descent before it had a chance to unman him.

The atmosphere was hushed as he strode through the still sleeping village, as if the whole of Fiora province held its breath. A familiar figure rose as he reached the track leading inexorably east. He knew she would be waiting. He stopped mere inches away from her. Her eyes drank him in, telling him everything that her voice and fingers could not. Gently, he reached up and cupped her face, sighing as she closed her eyes momentarily and pressed her cheek into his hand. He leaned down and feathered his lips across her mouth. With a soft cry,

Destry raised her arms and pulled him tightly to her. Eventually, Reez reluctantly stepped back, and she released him. She nodded once, her eyes filled with unshed tears, and moved aside. Neither one looked back as they went their separate ways.

Chapter Nineteen

Reez flipped the lever and sighed as the orbs began to pulse with light, illuminating the entire chamber. Somewhere within this vast library could lay the knowledge he needed to confront Verrin, but he had no idea what that might look like. Perhaps there was a way to stop Verrin from using his magic or subdue him somehow. Maybe he could discern a way to avoid the vicious creatures wandering the countryside or render himself invisible to them. Carrying a lantern in the event that the lights failed, and the bag full of books borrowed on his first visit, Reez made his way down to the lower level to start his search.

All the books had a series of four numbers engraved on

the spine, which Reez assumed was some kind of ordering system. His first task was to discover where the borrowed books fitted on the shelves and try to determine what that system might be. He reasoned that, once he understood it, he would be more likely to find the information he craved. It didn't take him long to discover that the initial number in the series determined which level the book belonged on. The ground floor held all the books beginning with one or two, with the others ranged up to the floor Reez had first entered, which held all the books starting with a seven. On closer examination, Reez identified that the lower levels held the more basic tomes, with the complexity of each subject increasing on each gallery.

Unfortunately, that proved to be the only thing he could work out. In his eyes, there was no logic to the way the books were ordered. Plant, animal and mineral were all placed beside each other along with books that didn't seem to refer to any of them. Reez had hoped that there might be a filing system somewhere, similar to the one Wicton had devised, but a search of the cabinets below had revealed nothing helpful.

Reez perched on one of the chairs and gazed at the huge volume of texts. He knew the chances of putting his hand on a useful treatise by chance was slim and his heart sank. More than anything, he had hoped to unearth some forgotten magic that would give him a clear advantage. He rubbed his eyes and realised how hungry he was. He had lost track of time down in the vault, and it had obviously been quite a while since he had last eaten. As he left the chamber, he picked up four more books at random from the haphazard piles on the top landing and made the labourious climb up to the surface.

Reez was thankful for the fire blazing in the hearth that evening, as rain poured relentlessly down from a turbulent sky, and a wild wind whistled around the enclosed clearing. He read until his eyes grew weary before rolling himself in a blanket and laying down to sleep. Whether it was the tempest raging outside or the barely restrained fears within that triggered the nightmares, Reez couldn't say, but his slumber was anything but restful and he jerked awake more than once bathed in perspiration, his heart racing. He couldn't recall any of his dreams, but the feelings of fear and hopelessness lingered long after the images had disappeared.

As the days flowed by, Reez found his attention wandering more and more. Often he would reach the end of a page in the book he was reading and not be able to recall any of it. He found it hard to concentrate, and his appetite diminished. Catching himself staring into space yet again, Reez decided to call it a day and made his way up the stone steps. He was weary to the bone and the disrupted nights were taking their toll. When he emerged from the hut, he was pleased to find the sun shining weakly. Shedding his clothes, he welcomed the rays touch on his skin, despite the coolness of the day, and decided to forgo his studies for a while. He had thought to learn more of animal magic, hoping it might provide the key to unlock his dilemma, but he soon realised it was a fruitless endeavour. He would need many cycles of study to be proficient. Even the smallest creatures were amazingly complex, and he had to admire Verrin's skill in recreating the insects that had plagued Paiter over the long cycles, even if they were short-lived. Despite his best efforts, Reez could not form a viable seed from nothing and had to deduce that there were things within it that were beyond his ability to replicate.

He plunged into the stream, the crisp water causing him to gasp aloud. He lingered long enough to clear his mind and wake himself up, but soon scrambled up the bank and into the welcoming roots of the willow, where he sat, shivering slightly, waiting for the wan sun to warm him again. Reez relaxed back against the trunk of the ancient tree and closed his eyes, enjoying the peace of the isolated spot and the song of birds perched among the branches in the trees surrounding the clearing.

#

Sometime later, Reez jerked awake, the remnants of his nightmare clinging to him like a sticky vine. His heart pounded rapidly, and he sucked in huge lungfuls of the chilly air, willing his body to quieten. He bowed his head as the feelings of dread and hopelessness overtook him. His fears were paralysing him. As much as he wanted to remain and delve deeper into the collection of knowledge in the library, he knew it was only delaying the inevitable. He needed to leave before his fear overwhelmed him completely. No matter that he was no nearer to discovering anything that would help him. He would have to make do and trust that his path would become clearer as he walked it. Not for the first time, he prayed that the First Mage would look kindly on him.

Once the decision to leave the safety of the clearing was made, Reez immediately packed up his possessions.

Although dawn was still a long way off, he turned his face resolutely towards the east and began to walk.

#

As he looked down on the settlement from a nearby hill, Reez sighed with relief. Situated in a lush valley with woodland hugging it to the north, the little town sat below three tributaries that had merged to create a wide river flowing further to the south. On either bank, Reez could see green fields stretching away, which would usually be filled with grazing herds. Now they stood empty, the normally close-cropped grass growing tall. He stared at the town itself, pleased to see people on the lanes between the houses, and made his way down, looking forward to a hot meal and a bath.

Since crossing into Bestra, Reez had found the outlying villages deserted, and he had spent uncomfortable nights in empty houses wondering whether the creatures he had heard about would make an appearance. Despite taking precautions and surrounding the places with thorns to create a barrier as he slept, his rest was fitful, and he started at every sound. Eager to be among people once more, Reez increased his pace.

As he neared, he could see the residents had utilised a variety of things to fortify the little town, creating barricades on all sides and blocking all entrance to it apart from one opening. His arrival had been noted by guards who were stationed on either side, holding poles with knives attached to them, and they watched his approach, leaning lazily against the wall of a building as he made for the gap. When he introduced himself as the Master of Fiora, the youths straightened excitedly.

"You've come to Three Rivers to see our prize?" one asked, the beard on his face barely grown.

"No," Reez said slowly. "I am journeying east. What prize is this?"

"We caught it a sennight ago," the second lad said. "Selek has it displayed in the square. He can tell you everything." He called to a young girl running nearby. "Here, Mayzee, take the Master here to Selek. Straight away, mind. No lallygagging."

Reez followed the girl through the lanes, skirting animals that had been herded behind the barriers. He had to watch his steps carefully as the way was littered with piles of dung, some still steaming in the chilly air. Eventually they came to a nondescript house set in a terrace of identical buildings, and after waving Reez to the door, his guide ran off and disappeared down an alley further down the street. Reez knocked and waited.

The man who answered was tall and muscular with several day's growth of beard. His pale blue eyes surveyed Reez, and he didn't bother to hide his irritation. "What do you want?" he asked bluntly.

Reez narrowed his eyes. "I am seeking Selek."

"Well, you've found him. State your business."

"I am Reez, Master of Fiora province," Reez said coldly. "Are you the leader here?"

"No, I mean, yes," he sputtered, glancing down at Reez's hand. When he spotted the ring on Reez's finger, he paled slightly.

Reez lifted an eyebrow. "You either are or you are not,"

he said. "Which is it?"

"I am now," the man replied, squaring his shoulders. "The mayor and his pathetic cowards left at the first sign of trouble. Those that stayed look to me to lead them in a fashion."

"In that case, I suggest you invite me in and offer me succour," Reez said. "It seems you have a tale to tell."

With a hurried bow, Selek ushered Reez inside and guided him through to a small parlour where a meagre fire smouldered in the hearth. It was sparsely furnished, boasting a single chair and a table which was strewn with paper. Reez dragged the chair round and sat in it, as Selek ran his hand agitatedly through his hair. "I'll fetch some water and bread," he said. "I've nothing else to offer, as I've yet to pull my rations for today."

Reez watched the man leave and glanced down at the papers. Numbers had been hastily scribbled and crossed out next to lists of produce. Selek appeared to be in the middle of calculating something. "I have no head for figures," Selek said as he returned, pointing at the documents. He placed a mug of water and a trencher with a heel of stale bread and a sliver of hard cheese in front of Reez. "All this stuff gives me a headache."

"What are you trying to do?"

Selek sighed and leant on the table. "We only have so much food stored here and folk who arrive often carry little with them. We saved most of the animals and we'll start butchering them soon, but the winter cycle is on us and there is no chance of supplies coming anymore. Folk in Fiora don't trade this way now; the creatures scared them, I suppose." He tapped the papers. "I was trying to work out how to stretch the foodstuffs, so we don't starve until we can replenish our stock."

Reez quickly forgave the man for his irritation at being interrupted. It was obvious that he felt responsible for the men and women within his town and was trying to look after them. "Well, it seems as if your luck has changed," Reez said kindly. "I just happen to have plenty of food with me."

Selek glanced out of the small window. "You have a cart?" he asked.

Reez laughed. "No, I have this," he said, lifting up his journeyman's bag. "I can grow you enough to see you comfortably through the winter cycle and beyond if necessary, with plenty in reserve in case other stragglers come your way."

"Well, that will be very welcome," Selek said, a smile finally crossing his face and lifting his features as he leant against the wall. "I am much obliged to you, Master Reez. If I can save some of the animals, we'll be able to breed more after the winter cycle." He glanced quickly at Reez and cleared his throat. "I don't suppose you would be able to persuade your folk to send some supplies over. We have money to pay," he added hurriedly. "I'm sure they would get a good price. I doubt we are the only ones in need."

Reez pursed his lips. "I'll bear it in mind," he said.

Selek nodded. "My thanks," he said before pausing for a moment. "I doubt you came to talk trade with me," he said finally. "What brings you this way, may I ask?"

"Word has reached me that all is not well in Bestra. We

have had folk crossing the border with grim tales, so I decided to see the truth for myself. I intend to travel to Etheradia and consult with your Master." Reez refused to admit how the thought unmanned him.

"I wish you luck with that," Selek said with a frown. "There has been no word from the capital, despite our pleas for help and succour. We're on our own here. Not that it surprises me. The Masters have never bothered themselves with us before, so why should anything be different now? We are better off without them, if you ask me." He paled slightly. "No offence," he muttered.

"None taken." There was an awkward silence, and Reez drained his mug. "When I arrived, I was told something about a prize," he prompted.

Selek grinned widely, his eyes glittering. "Aye, do you want to see it?"

#

As they walked through the congested lanes, Selek told Reez his story. "After the Mayor and his sycophants deserted, I got the rest of us organised," he began. "We stripped the houses of everything but the essentials and fashioned barricades to close in the town. The Mayor's iron bedstead makes a fine gate," he said with a short laugh. "I don't think he'll be best pleased if he ever returns. Mind you, he's not likely to be welcomed back with open arms, either." Selek cleared his throat and spat to one side.

"We brought in the herds from the fields to keep them safe, and fashioned what weapons we could. Some tools, like the pitchforks, are handy, but the knives were only good at close range. No-one wanted to get that near the creatures, so we put them on poles to give them reach. I set up a rota, so that everyone gets guard duty. Even the children have an eyrie to watch from, although it's safe inside the compound. Unfortunately, we had to put guards on the food store, too, as I got word that some spineless folk were planning to loot it. I kicked them out of the gates and left them to fend for themselves. I don't need that kind of trouble. Showed the others I wasn't going to stand for such talk. I think they got the message, but I kept the guards in place even so."

As appalled as Reez was at the thought of people being forced out of the safety of the town to an unknown fate, he could understand Selek's decision. If food was scarce, it was only fair to share it equally and eek it out through the winter cycle.

"A sennight ago," Selek continued, "a watchman spotted one of the creatures coming in from the south and raised the alarm. We closed the gates and set extra guards to patrol, but several of us were keen to have a go at it. I'd seen what they did to the livestock; carcasses ripped apart and scattered across the fields in a killing frenzy. I don't think they slaughter for food. They seem to crave blood and terror. I don't mind admitting to you I was fearful of it, but I've never been one to back down from a fight, and I wasn't going to be called craven. Four of us got together and came up with a plan to capture it.

"We set a trap using a hog as bait and waited for it to attack. It went straight for the animal, but got tangled in the ropes and netting just as we planned. I was worried the creature would just slash its way out as we hoisted it up, but it was mindless. We beat it with clubs and hammers. To be truthful, it surprised me how quick we put the thing down. Mayhap it was weakened already. After we killed it, we dragged it back here and mounted it in the square as a trophy, to remind folk that they can die, same as anything else. We broke open the mayor's wine cellar to celebrate. Best evening I've had in an age," Selek mused. "Strange thing is, the beast never uttered a sound the whole time."

They rounded a corner, and Reez slowed as Selek thrust his arm out. "Here it is," he said proudly.

The emaciated creature was nailed to a frame erected in the centre of the square, splayed out for everyone to gawk at. Reez could see ribs protruding from the sunken chest. Its twisted back legs were long and hairy, the elongated feet ended in toes with sharp talons. As Reez moved closer, he could see the bloodied misshapen head had been staked back, the maw open wide as if the creature howled silently. Huge fangs gaped from a grossly distorted muzzle that looked as if it could never fully close. Maggots crawled in the empty eye sockets, which had either been picked clean by birds or removed by the hunters. The forelimbs were shorter than the back, meaning it either walked upright or struggled to ambulate on all four limbs. They, too, ended in frightful talons, sharpened like knives. Reez felt his body convulse, and he spewed the meagre fare he had consumed at Selek's house on to the street. Despite the grotesque body and deformed head, Reez could clearly see that the creature had once been a man.

"When you do business with our Master," Selek said, idly noting Reez's distress, "make sure you tell him what we caught."

"Don't worry," Reez replied darkly, as he wiped his mouth with the back of his hand. "I'll be sure to speak to him about it."

Chapter Twenty

Reez kept his hood pulled low over his face as he walked through the streets of Etheradia.

The rest of Reez's journey from Three Rivers had been blessedly uneventful as he joined a steady stream of people making their way further east, their possessions hastily loaded into carts or tied on their backs. Although there were no further signs of the twisted beasts ravaging the countryside, the refugees always travelled during daylight, stopping well before darkness fell to make camp, or plead with any residents remaining in the settlements for a roof and a fire. At first, Reez had made good use of the Master's ring to gain food and shelter, but as he neared Etheradia and the numbers swelled, he decided to move away from the travellers and hide his identity. He did not want Verrin to catch whispers of his arrival, deciding instead to maintain the element of surprise.

He had been dismayed at the hordes of people living in hastily erected tents or squatting by meagre fires before the gates of the city. Makeshift shelters were crammed together housing men, women, and children in increasing squalor. Occasionally, a fire burned, cobbled together from discarded furniture or foraged wood, but most of the people could only huddle together for warmth as the winter cycle neared. As Castor had informed him, the gates were barred and Reez watched from a distance as scores of hopeful refugees were turned away. Even so, they chose to remain by the walls, as if their presence alone would protect them from the horrors roaming the countryside. In the chaos, thieves robbed those who toted their wealth to the gates before they could barter their way inside. Fights frequently broke out over possessions and food, and Reez had seen more than one body dumped by the roadside with fatal cuts to throat and chest.

Skirting around the walls for the better part of a day, Reez had been appalled by the misery outside the city. With little or no food, scant shelter, and only the River Rada for water, it was only a matter of time before the people died of starvation or disease. Reez had seen people drinking straight from the river, which others had used to wash their clothes or as a makeshift privy. There was nothing left to forage as all the trees and bushes had been stripped of their fruit, and Reez could see that any supplies that people had carried were dwindling fast.

Along with a few other hardy souls, Reez finally reached the coast. There were several men gathered on the rocky shore, eager to grasp the money offered for the risky passage around the curtain wall to the relative safety of the docks. As people clambered into the tiny boats, Reez wondered how many would perish on the way, either because of the journey or their shady pilots. Castor had recommended a man with a boat who might be willing to sell it for good coin, but it took Reez another day to find him. After some persuasion and even some veiled threats, he handed over the extortionate amount they finally agreed on and, under cover of darkness and with the aid of Reez's new skills with wind and water, arrived at the docks unscathed and undetected. As he made his way through the streets to the Falcon in the early morning light, Reez noticed the city was a very different place than the one he had visited many cycles earlier. The docks were devoid of all but a few ships, and Reez saw that the cleric's activities had unnerved potential traders who now avoided Etheradia. The streets themselves were still fairly crowded for the most part as people began the day's work, but the mood was subdued and nobody tried to make eye contact with Reez as he passed, his hood pulled forward to hide his face. The market square, once a huge bustling enterprise, had shrunk to half its size. As Reez passed the stalls, he noticed the wares were shoddy, the foodstuffs tired, lacking the wide variety of before, and the vendors restrained as if unwilling to call too much attention to themselves. All the life and colour had been leached from the place, leaving behind a wary sombre populace. Shaven clerics in red robes stood conspicuously on street corners, a blatant reminder to the people of their Master's watchful eye, and a warning of reprisals for those that stepped out of line or spoke out of turn.

Careful to avoid drawing unwanted scrutiny, Reez took a circular route to evade the cleric's keen eyes and arrived at the Falcon early in the afternoon. Making sure that he was unobserved, Reez quietly opened the door and let himself into the dark interior of the inn. Thankfully, the heavy drapes had been pulled across the windows before Castor had quit the place, and they now screened Reez's presence from the gaze of the curious. He trailed a finger across the empty tables, disturbing a thin layer of dust, and he grinned wryly at the thought of Merrylee's response to hearing that her furniture was less than perfect. A quick examination of the kitchen turned up very little that was edible. Having left in a hurry, Castor had not had a chance to clear the pantry; vegetables had rotted in baskets, goat's milk soured in a jug and meat had gone rancid. Setting to work, Reez disposed of the food and washed down the shelves before sitting at the table with a jar of fruit preserves and the remainder of the bread from his bag. He had enough coin left to buy supplies, but decided to wait until the following day to venture back out into the streets. He was weary and in need of rest.

Even though the night was still far off, Reez climbed the stairs and opened the door to his old room, thankful that the bed was made up. He crossed to the window and twitched the curtain to one side so that he could peek outside. All was quiet. No bawdy women toted their wares on the corner; no drunken revellers reeled down the narrow street singing drinking songs. A sorry-looking hinny pulled a lone cart piled high with night soil collected from household pits, transporting it beyond the dock where it could be dumped into the sea. Reez watched until it turned a corner and disappeared from sight before letting the drape fall back. Climbing on to the bed, he felt his body relax into the soft pillows, grateful for the comfortable mattress after many nights spent on the cold, damp ground. It wasn't long before he was fast asleep.

#

Reez sat on the bed, his knees drawn to his chest, torn with indecision. For three days he had roamed the streets but was no closer to deciding a course of action. It didn't help that his nights were tormented by grisly dreams of people he loved, twisted into nightmarish forms, screaming soundlessly and appealing to him for succour while he stood chained and helpless, unable to tear his eyes away as they writhed in agony.

In contrast to the muted suspicion in the streets, both the temple and abbey were a hive of activity, as if the citizens of Etheradia could stave off the attention of both Master and clerics by acts of piety, prayers and petitions. The huge, golden statue of Malander in the priestess' temple was festooned with flowers, and people queued almost out the door to present offerings, varying from food donated by the poor, to money and ornate gifts from the wealthy. Loud voices proclaimed the merits of the Eternal One and his righteous servants, each person trying to outdo their neighbours in excessive praise and volume. Reez also saw several children being handed over for service, wincing at the clink of coins handed over in payment. Unlike the toddler of his previous visit, these were older by several summers and were led away in silence, their haunted eyes the only sign of the fear that lurked within.

The mass of people waiting to gain entrance into the abbey to make their petitions meant Reez had no opportunity to go inside, even if he had been brave enough to risk being so close to Verrin. Instead, he walked around until he could see the whole of Verrin's palace from a distance. He stood for a long time watching the promontory, noting the occasional red robed man walk across the causeway from the abbey to disappear into the mass of buildings beyond, hidden by the wall that encompassed it on all sides. They always seemed to be in a greater hurry to leave than they were to enter. As it was unlikely that he could scale the cliff face and the wall, Reez reasoned that he would have to walk straight through the abbey itself in order to gain admittance. The only way he could do that was to reveal himself, and he didn't feel ready to make his presence known as yet.

Reez's stomach growled, reminding him he hadn't eaten since breaking his fast. Needing something to do to interrupt his fruitless brooding, he decided to go down into the galley and prepare a meal. He padded softly down the wooden stairs, shined to a polish and cool beneath his bare feet. As he neared the taproom, he paused as a soft thud sounded from the furthest corner of the room. Silently, Reez eased down the last steps and looked into the bar. He had left the drapes untouched and lit no lanterns that might announce his presence to a passerby, preferring that his stay remain unremarked. He searched the shadows for signs of the intruder and was soon rewarded with movement from one of the settles. Crouching, he crept along the bar, his feet soundless on the stone floor until he had a better view. As his eyes focused on the interloper, he noticed they wore the red robes of a cleric. Deciding to withdraw quietly and hope the person would go without investigating the inn further, he moved to leave, but hesitated when he heard a sniff and a strangled sob. Whoever it was seemed to be upset. On an impulse, Reez decided to make his presence known and confront the man.

"What business brings you here?" he demanded as he stood suddenly, his voice seeming to boom in the erstwhile silence. The cleric squealed and twisted round, his face a mask of shock and fear shining with tears. "Jina?" Reez asked as he squinted in the gloom and recognised his old friend.

"My Lord!" Jina said, leaping up and bowing low, wiping his face with the sleeve of his robe.

Reez laughed in relief and clasped the little man in a hug. "You've forgotten my name already," he said, holding the man at arm's length and searching his face. "You look older."

Jina's eyes went wide as he stared at Reez. "You look…"

"Handsome as always?" Reez supplied.

"Yes, yes, of course," he replied, trying not to stare at the scars.

"Why are you here?" Reez asked.

Jina took a deep breath and let it out shakily. "I come to think," he said. "Somehow, I feel closer to them, even when I know they are far away. I miss them."

"They reached me safely, because of your aid," Reez confirmed and watched Jina's face ease.

"Thank the Mage. But, Master Reez, why are *you* here?"

"Why don't we find something to eat and sup some of the ale I broached," Reez suggested, "then we can talk."

They chose to eat in one of the rooms at the rear of the inn and risk lighting a candle after checking that the heavy drapes were tightly closed against the encroaching night. Reez had bought meat pies fresh that day and tucked in with relish, but he noticed that Jina barely ate more than a few mouthfuls of his, instead pushing it around the plate with his fork.

"Castor told me you warned them all to leave," Reez began carefully. "Why was it so imperative that they escape Etheradia?"

"Things have changed since you were last here," Jina said quietly. "After the ascension, the chapter were told the Eternal One was the sole Master in Zelannor." He glanced up at Reez's face and frowned slightly. "I was deeply saddened at the thought of your passing, but then rumours reached us, saying that not all the Masters had left and there was still a Master in Fiora province. When Castor received your first letter, we were overjoyed. Now there are whispers of a Master in Minra province, too."

"One and the same," Reez said. "I am the only other person to survive. Verrin murdered all the Masters and Chrisos' apprentice. I was fortunate enough to discover a little of earth magic and Minra has adopted me as their own. I imagine such news would have been a shock to Verrin," Reez said tentatively. "How did he react when he heard?"

"I regret, I am not held in enough regard to be party to such information."

"Of course," Reez said wryly. "Continue with your story."

"Do you know of the Purge?" Reez nodded. "It was welcomed at first," Jina continued. "People lauded it as a way to solve increasing crime in the city, as well as making ordinary citizens safer. I wasn't part of the collection ministry, as my duties kept me within the abbey. Since my successful dealings with you, I have been elevated to more senior commissions, so I was not required to round up the people for rehabilitation, but I saw the tally increasing and began to be suspicious. When the remit changed to include the children, a few of us went to the Cardinal and expressed our unease. Two days later, after visiting the palace, he disappeared, and they appointed the High Cleric as the new Cardinal. He made a proclamation to the entire chapter that we were not to question the orders of the Eternal One, but to do our duty in obedience. None of us dare express any unhappiness now.

"They assured us that all the children were to be taken to the clerics isle for education and training to rid them of their criminal ways and restore them to society. The more promising boys were to be inducted as clerics. But I saw the dockets for transportation, and I feared we were being fed lies. Too many boys were being shipped across. The school couldn't handle such an influx. I was worried and couldn't sleep, so I started to take walks at night, to clear my head and try to think. That's when I saw them." His voice broke, and he paused. He lifted a shaking hand and wiped his eyes.

"Here," Reez said, pushing a tankard of ale over. "Drink this."

"Thank you." Jina took a long swallow before continuing. "They admitted a cart through the gates. It was a blustery night and I remember pulling my cloak tighter to shield myself from the wind as I walked. I had just decided to head for the warmth of my cell when it passed me, heading for the causeway to the palace. I moved to one side as a gust of wind buffeted me. The heavy cloth that was covering the contents came loose, and the wind whipped it away. Inside, there was a cage normally used to hold livestock, but I saw children, Master Reez. They were crammed in like animals, unable to move, naked and filthy. One girl looked straight at me, but she didn't cry or beg for help; she just stared with hopeless resignation. The driver stopped and secured the cover before driving on and I, well, I went back to my cell. The next day, I got up and returned to my duties as normal, but inside I was numb. I have never felt so useless in my entire life.

"Then I got word that the clerics were to look for more children and women of childbearing age, and I was so afraid for Castor's family. They have been so kind to me, and I was determined that they wouldn't suffer the same fate as the others. That's when I told them to flee the city. The thought of little Siril in one of those cages…"

"What do you suppose happens to them?" Reez asked tentatively.

"I don't know," Jina replied so quietly that Reez had to strain to hear him. "The only thing I am sure of is that they never come back out, or at least not many do. Sometimes there are carts that leave, but I have never seen what they contain."

"What of the rest? The ones still on the isle. Do you think they are being taught?"

Jina stared at Reez for several heartbeats before finally lowering his eyes and shaking his head.

"I asked you to tell me about the cleric's isle once before and you told me you were forbidden to speak of it," Reez said eventually. "Tell me now, Jina. I think the time has passed for secrets, don't you?"

The cleric looked up at Reez and nodded. Taking another sip of ale, he began. "I was given as an offering when I was very young. I have no recollection of parents or family; my first memory is of my branding. I was told it was an honour to be chosen and that I should bear the mark with pride, but it hurt so much, and I cried. Afterwards, I was beaten for my weakness and sent to my cell without food or water. I quickly learnt to stay small and quiet, to not draw any regard to myself for fear of being selected for special attention. Others were regularly punished for voicing an opinion or taken to the tutors' cells to be rewarded. Having a friend was prohibited, but there was one boy who I felt closer to than the others. He was so kind, older than me, with blond hair and brilliant green eyes. He occupied the cot next to mine and we would whisper to each other when the others were asleep or if we met in the corridors, and once he held me after I had hurt myself during kitchen duty and been lashed for crying. I idolised him. He was like a brother to me.

"Unfortunately, he caught the attention of our tutor of catechisms, who would take him away on any pretext. My friend diminished before my eyes, and he became withdrawn and timid. He stopped speaking to me and would hardly eat. One day, he was found hanging by his belt in the sleeping cell when we were released for prime. I didn't understand then, but as an adult, when I look back, I can guess what was happening." Jina was silent for a moment, deep in his own memories. "I lived on the near side of the isle until I reached my majority. As I excelled at my letters and was quick to learn, they placed me in the administrative offices. When I returned to the mainland, they put me to work in the abbey cataloguing petitions, and there I stayed until you arrived and changed my life."

"What you have told me is awful, Jina, but why did your tutors forbid you to speak of it?"

"We do not speak of those who were not chosen."

"I thought all the boys were offered as clerics," Reez said.

Jina shook his head. "That is what the parents are told, but the priests only select a few. The rest are transported to the far side of the isle. We never see them again. I heard rumours of one novice sneaking out at night to follow them, but he never returned either. I don't know if that was a truth, or a story circulated to prevent us from being too curious. Either way, none of us would have ever dreamed of finding out for ourselves. It didn't stop speculation, though. A few imagined they had been returned to their families, others that they had been given to slavers, or chained and sent down into mines. Some whispered that they had all been murdered and their bodies dumped into the sea."

"And now?" Reez prompted.

"I still don't know for sure, but I wouldn't imagine they were killed. In his previous incarnation, the Eternal One would visit the far side of the isle occasionally, and I suspect they played a part in his magic wielding."

"It seems from what you have told me that Verrin has his subjects brought to him instead of making the journey over to the island himself," Reez said slowly.

"Do you know what he wants with them?" Jina asked carefully.

Reez hesitated for a moment. He knew nothing for certain, but feared they might fuel Verrin's twisted experiments in some way. "Have you heard of the monsters roaming the countryside?" he asked.

Jina shook his head. "We are told nothing, and I no longer come into contact with petitioners."

"Long cycles ago, unnaturally large wolves had been let loose in the woods along the border to Fiora. We found out that Verrin was responsible, using his magic to grow them into enormous beasts. When Malander heard about it, he was beyond furious. But I doubt that any punishment would have deterred Verrin. On my way here, I passed through a small town called Three Rivers. They had captured and killed one of the creatures terrorising and slaughtering livestock and even families. They had it on display in the main square. I saw it with my own eyes. It was a fearsome, twisted nightmare of claws and fangs, but it had once been a man. I think Verrin is experimenting on people, creating these creatures and releasing them into the world for his own amusement."

Jina blanched in horror. "You don't think the Cardinal..." he began.

"I don't know, but I aim to find out," Reez said, suddenly making a decision. "As they are fully grown adults, I suspect he is using the children in other ways..." Reez trailed off, unwilling to voice such a terrible thought. "I have been sitting here for days trying to think of what to do. Perhaps I should take a clandestine trip to the Cleric's Isle first and see for myself what is going on over there."

"But how will you get across? No one is allowed over."

"I have my ways," Reez said carefully. "I already have a boat. You can help me with some information, however. Tell me more about the patrols. Are there guards on the Isle?"

The two men sat talking long into the night. When Jina finally left, and Reez made his way up the staircase to his room, his heart was lighter. The crippling fear remained, but it had muted somewhat as a plan of sorts had developed in Reez's mind. It felt good to have something to focus on instead of constantly second guessing himself, and the thought of taking action was a relief after his days of indecision. He still had no idea what he would find, or even how he would deal with any opposition, but he refused to worry himself with things over which he had no control. When he finally lay down, his sleep was dream-free.

Chapter Twenty-One

Reez corrected the trajectory of the wind blowing into his makeshift sail so that he skirted past the pier servicing the novice's school. He barely gave the manoeuvre a thought as he watched the dark shadow of the isle pass by on his right. Wind and waves were raw magic that only needed a little redirecting to be useful, leaving him free to concentrate on guiding the small craft to his goal. He felt a little guilt at depriving the few fishing boats in the distance of the wind in their sails, leaving them suddenly becalmed further out. He reasoned that his need was more important; besides, they would be able to continue when he released the air and allowed it to resume its natural course, although it would be reduced in power.

Jina's information had made it a simple matter to avoid the few patrols in the streets and reach the place where he had stowed the boat on his arrival. Apparently, fear was a great motivating factor in keeping the populace under curfew, and as the night was cold and wet, the clerics preferred to seek shelter and stay out of the rain rather than be overly zealous in their duty. The heavy clouds obscuring the moon did much to hide Reez as he crept through the city, and now hid him from the gaze of any eager acolyte who might watch the water.

When the few lights still glowing from the school were behind him, Reez moved the boat closer to the shore and looked for a place to land. Despite his misgivings, it was a relief to be doing something instead of hiding himself away, wracked with indecision and crippled by fear. He was also keen to discover the truth of what was happening to those boys sent to the far side of the isle. Spying an inlet, Reez turned towards it and was pleased to discover a tiny beach. After forcing the boat as far as it would go, Reez jumped into the cold sea and, grabbing a rope tied to the front, hauled the boat ashore, pulling it high on the shingles. His hair whipped wildly around his head for a moment as he released the wind, which began to blow in its natural direction. A quick inspection showed no path leading from the beach, forcing Reez to scramble up the rocks following a rivulet trickling through a steep depression. When he reached the top, he paused for a moment to catch his breath and orientate himself.

A wide bank of trees seemed to separate the island in

two, effectively screening the school from everything else. He could see nothing of the buildings he had passed; instead, he walked the opposite way through the wood until he emerged on the brow of a hill. The rain had stopped, and the clouds above were dispersing, allowing the soft glow of the crescent moon to illuminate the compound below.

A tall fence surrounding the buildings was interrupted by a gate at the far side, and a jetty that could berth one of the larger vessels Reez had seen docked in Etheradia on his previous visit. Six long windowless sheds were neatly arrayed in the centre with several other smaller buildings ringing them. As he watched, a figure appeared out of one of the buildings with a lantern held in front of him. He checked each of the sheds, disappearing inside for a time before emerging and moving on to the next one. After finishing, he returned to the first building which Reez could see was lit inside. Smoke curled up from a chimney hinting at a warm fire within.

Reez made his way swiftly down the hill until he reached the wooden fence. It was a simple task to warp the timber enough for him to gain entry, and he crept to the window of the only building with a light. Inside were four men. Two lay asleep on cots on one side of the room, whilst a third lounged in a chair. A fourth was helping himself to food from a pot by the fire before sitting at the small table and greedily spooning it into his mouth. All wore the familiar red robes of the clerics. Satisfied that they appeared to be settled for the moment, Reez moved silently away.

A cursory look at the smaller buildings revealed a

privy, wash house and huts full of supplies. Two small row boats were upturned by the jetty with oars propped against a shed containing nets and what looked like piles of filthy sheets. Reaching the furthest of the long sheds, Reez found that it was unlocked, and after a quick glance back at the cleric's hut, he slipped through the door and closed it quietly. It was pitch black inside, but he was immediately assailed by the pervading odour of excrement. He could hear shuffling and guessed this was where they kept the livestock to feed the clerics and novices on the island. Reaching into his bag, he pulled out a candle and tinderbox, easily coaxing a flame to light the wick. He held it up high and looked around.

The building was lined on both sides with cages, leaving an aisle down the centre wide enough for two people to easily pass each other. He moved to the nearest cage and peered inside. The floor was strewn with mouldering straw and Reez wrinkled his nose distastefully. As his eyes became accustomed to the gloom, he could see a pile of rags at the back. One moved and Reez found himself staring into the dull eyes of a young child, blinking sleepily at him. Cursing loudly, Reez reached for the door to the cage and pulled savagely, but it was firmly locked. The noise woke several others, who sat up and watched him silently. Angrily, Reez focused his magic, causing the locking mechanism to buckle and warp until the whole thing fell to the ground with a thud and the door swung ajar with a creak. Reez shoved it wide open and entered, having to duck down to avoid colliding with the top of the cage. One child whimpered and tried to move away. Reez heard metal clinking and lowered the candle down to inspect them more closely. There were five children in the cage, chained together and secured to the back by a large ring. They were dirty and thin, their clothes barely covering their wasted bodies. All of them were staring at him with horror.

"I won't hurt you," Reez said in a quiet voice, crouching down. "I've come to help you."

He heard more rustling and the chink of metal further down the hut as something else moved in the darkness.

"What's your name?" he asked the boy in front of him. When he received no answer, he continued. "My name is Reez. I'm from a place far from here called Maston in Fiora province. Have you heard of it?" The boy shook his head, but Reez perceived the fear in the boy's eyes. "How long have you been here?" Still nothing. Reez sighed and glanced over at the others, who were fixated on his face. "Ah," he said softly as he suddenly understood. He reached up and touched his left cheek. "I have looked like this for so long, I forget. I was trapped, a bit like you. I was hurt in a fire. It looks bad, doesn't it?" he added with a wry smile. One boy nodded.

"Does it hurt?" a small voice asked.

"Not anymore," he said, relieved that they were responding to him. There was more rustling and whispers in the dark.

He heard a voice from his left. "Can I see?"

Reez turned and lifted the candle. A white face peered back at him from the next cage. Reez moved the light closer and saw the boy's eyes widen a little. "That's not so bad," he said bravely.

"Shhh," someone hissed from the shadows. "They'll come back and beat us."

"What's your name?" Reez whispered to the lad.

"I'm Trane."

"Well, Trane, I need to continue my search, but afterwards I intend to come back and free you."

"Truly?"

"Yes. Let me check the other buildings first."

"If they find you, they'll hurt you. The big one is mean."

"They won't find me. I'll find them first. Stay quiet now, but pass the word on." He heard murmuring and turned to leave, but a small hand reached out and touched his arm. The first boy watched him carefully, his initial fear already receding.

"Promise?" he asked in a high voice that cracked from disuse.

"I promise," Reez said, his own voice catching. He patted the boy's hand and then left the cage, stretching gratefully. He exited the hut and shut the door quietly, glancing around to ensure he was still alone, and breathing deeply of the salty air. There could be dozens of cages in just one shed, which meant hundreds of children in the compound imprisoned like animals. Reez could feel a familiar anger simmer within him as he strode up to the next hut.

The second was similar to the first, although the boys were older. He tried to engage them in conversation, but they just stared at him as if he were an apparition rather than a real person, not even able to summon enough emotion to be frightened by him. In the third, three young men were crammed into each cage, unable to move in the cramped conditions and forced to lie in their own effluence. Approaching the first cage, he tried to ask questions and discover how long they had been chained or to elicit some information about the clerics inside the hut. In every instance, the men stared at him with vacant eyes, as if the last vestige of hope had long since fled and they were mere shells of the people they had once been.

As he left to enter the third shed, a noise from further up the compound had him flattening himself against the dark wood. He watched as one cleric exited the hut and hurried over to the privy. As soon as he entered, Reez rushed across the gap between the buildings and crouched down beside the next shed. Peering carefully around the corner, he waited until the cleric finally emerged and walked swiftly back, his arms wrapped around his body for warmth against the chilly night air. Reez let out the breath he had been holding in a huff as the door closed. He waited for a while, but observing no further movement from within, he slipped silently around the corner and entered the fourth shed.

This one held infant girls, some barely weaned. Like the young boys in the first shed, they were curious and responded positively to his promise of freedom, but they could not give him any information and Reez moved carefully in to the next shed. The fifth housed more girls, some as young as twelve summers, others older; all of them were naked and pregnant. They at least had a cage to themselves, but he saw visible marks on many of them telling of beatings and other torments. Despite his soft words, they cringed away when he approached their cages, fear and defeat in their eyes. One of them reminded him of Destry and he gripped the bars of the filthy cage in anger as his mind played images of her innocent beauty being destroyed by the four clerics.

Muttering words of encouragement and his promise to return and free them from their fetters, he left and stood outside for a long while, reining in his anger and willing his racing heart to slow. He glanced at the cleric's hut, dark now although the smoke still curled lazily up from the chimney showing that a warm fire still burned within. Reez felt sick at the thought of the clerics resting inside while being surrounded by such misery. What kind of men could sleep peacefully in such a place? He was tempted to give free rein to his anger. Instead, he took several breaths, willing himself to stay calm, before he made his way grimly to the last building.

In the final shed, Reez found women holding babes in their arms. His efforts to talk to them or elicit any kind of reaction were futile. Used and abused for who knows how long, they were silent, not even tracking his progress as he passed by. Despite not getting a response, he walked the length of the shed, whispering that he would return to unlock their chains.

By the time he emerged from the last hut, his fury was blazing fiercely, and it took all his effort to not scream his rage aloud. He marched to the building housing the clerics and looked through the window. All four were stretched out on cots, sleeping soundly whilst hundreds of souls suffered but a few strides from their comfortable warm haven. With all his heart, Reez wished he could fashion chains at will and treat them with the same inhumanity they had shown to their captives. Then his anger morphed into ice-cold decision and a feral smile stretched across his face. Reaching into his bag, he drew out a handful of seeds and began to sow them around the hut.

For a long time, all was silent within except for the deep breaths of the sleeping clerics. They were blissfully unaware as the wooden floor of the hut sagged and rotted away, leaving the hard-packed dirt exposed underneath. Green shoots appeared and quickly grow into long tendrils that slithered across the earth floor to wind thickly around the legs of the four cots. The tangleweed climbed up, twisting and curling as it grew across the forms wrapped in blankets to ward off the chill of the night, until they appeared to cover every inch of the cot, forming a mass of tangled vines. Watching from the window outside, Reez pulled the vines tighter until they immobilised all four clerics where they lay. One man woke, crying out when he realised he couldn't move, alerting the others, but by then it was too late. The tangleweed restricted them so much, they couldn't even struggle against their bonds. As Reez pulled open the door and stepped inside, he finally released the magic, confident that the vines would hold the clerics captive for as long as he needed.

Closing the door firmly against the cold, he lit the lanterns that had been extinguished for the night. He ignored the shouts and curses from the men. Instead, he reached up for a clean bowl stacked on a shelf next to the fire and helped himself to the stew, still warming over it. Sitting in the chair, he leisurely spooned the fare into his mouth, his dark eyes taking each man's measure. Only when he had finished did he put down the bowl and turn his attention fully to his captives.

"Which of you is in charge here?" he asked quietly.

The men started shouting again. "Who are you?" "What do you think you are doing?"

Reez shook his head and tutted as the cries were cut off sharply, the weed across their throats pulling tighter. "I'm the one asking the questions," he replied. "If you can't answer me, you can stay silent. Now I repeat, who is in charge here?"

"I am," a voice croaked.

Reez pulled his chair over to sit next to the cot of the one who had spoken. "Your designation?"

"13437."

"I am going to give you a name, and you will answer to it. You are now called Pariah. Tell me, Pariah," he said, leaning close to the man. "Would you be able to remember me if you saw me again?"

"Yes."

"And this," Reez said, holding up his hand so that the stone in his ring winked clearly in the dim light. It gratified him to see the man's eyes widen in fear as he viewed the jewel. "Do you know what this is?"

"Yes, Lord," Pariah said, sweat beading on his forehead.

"Good. I think we are going to get along fine." He let the vine loosen around the cleric's throat. "There, that should make it a lot easier for you to answer my questions. I urge you to speak honestly as I must admit my temper is barely under control at the moment and I don't think I am in a mood to be played with. Do you understand?"

"Of course, Lord. I live to serve."

"Excellent." Reez sat back in the chair as the tangleweed slithered around the cleric's body, dragging him upright so they were facing each other. "Are you the only clerics on this side of the island?"

"Yes, Lord."

"Are you expecting others to come here?"

"Not until the next consignment is required; maybe two or three days, or if they make a delivery."

"Consignment," Reez snapped. "Are you referring to those children you have caged in the sheds?"

The cleric hesitated for a moment before replying. "Yes, Lord."

"What is the purpose of this place, Pariah?"

"They originally built it for the Eternal One to conduct his breeding experiments," the cleric began. "He needed a vessel for his next incarnation. Potential mates were taken from the priestesses' ranks and brought here to be joined with the Master. The fruit of their union was tested and, if found worthy, were allowed to mature and be educated."

"What if they failed the test?"

"We sold them."

"Who did you sell them to?"

"Slavers from the outlands. We have an accord. They come twice each cycle to collect their cargo."

Reez rose swiftly and began to pace the cabin, his fists bunched at his side. "Why? In the name of the First Mage, why would he permit such an atrocity?" Reez shouted.

"Bestra cannot support any more heads. The population must be maintained," Pariah replied, his voice wavering. "We cannot allow it to run unchecked or the resources will be strained. The Eternal One is not due to send out a carrier for several more cycles, so the excess had to be either culled or removed."

"What do you mean by 'carrier?'"

"A plague carrier, to maintain the population of Zelannor."

Reez sat back down heavily on the chair. He remembered Wicton speaking of waves of diseases spreading across the country from time to time, and how Malander had been reluctant to interfere. He thought of his own province, which had remained the same for millennia, the population stable and the communities fixed. There had been no need to expand for many generations as, until recently, families only had enough children to take over their parents' farms or, like his brother Damino, assume a role where there was no issue to inherit. His mind whirled as he considered the peaceful world he once thought he knew. Now all he could see was stagnation. He thought of the guild leaders wanting progression but being refused an audience; he thought of his brother and his recent discussions about the need for innovation. It seemed that for all the good the Masters had done in their service to the people, they had only been maintaining the state of affairs, refusing to allow growth or change, stifling the voice of those who questioned them and even decimating the people to prevent their advancement.

All his previous understanding of the role of the Masters crumbled under this new revelation. Instead of being a champion and defender of Zelannor and its people, he was part of a system that had trammelled them, keeping them compliant and easy to control, dependent on the three magic wielders who had the power to destroy them. He thought again of his Master, so kind and patient. Had he suspected what was happening, or was he ignorant of it all? He swallowed thickly, not wanting Wicton to be complicit in any of it.

Reez stood suddenly, needing fresh air and activity. "I'm going to free those people you have chained in the sheds now. Don't bother trying to fight the vines while I'm gone. It will do you no good. I'll be back later."

He lifted the lanterns and hurried outside, leaving the clerics with the wan light of the banked fire, and walked swiftly back to the shed at the far side of the compound. He opened the door wide and placed the lanterns at intervals down the aisle. Returning to the first cage, he stooped down and squatted in front of the five boys.

"I promised I would come back, didn't I?" he said with a smile. "Now, let's take a look at those chains. I'll deal with the manacles when I have a bit more light." It was a simple matter of melting a link in the chain and pulling it through the fetters, releasing all the boys in one go. Moving to the second cage, he released them, too.

"Trane," he said, as he pulled the chain free, "do you think you can help me?" The boy nodded eagerly. "You all look hungry. Why don't you take some of the others and see if you can find where they keep the food?" Trane glanced at the door and bit his lip. "Don't worry," Reez reassured him, "the clerics are not going to come and stop you."

"Even the big one?"

"Even him."

Trane rose and left the cage, wobbling slightly on legs unaccustomed to use. When he reached the door of the shed, he glanced back at Reez once for fortitude, and, encouraged by a nod, looked out of the door, but still wouldn't leave the hut.

"Do you know where the clerics live?" Reez asked.

"Yes," Trane replied.

"Go up and take a peek and then come back for the others? I promise you, it is quite safe."

As Reez worked his way down the first row, the whispers and murmurs increased. Some of the braver boys left the cages immediately and stood at the door, waiting for Trane to come back. Others, either too weak or fearful, remained where they were. Frustrated at the time it was taking to free everyone, Reez blasted the cage doors with magic, destroying them in an instant. As the doors clattered to pieces, the cries got louder, as the children called for Reez to come to them. Then there was an excited shout at the door.

"I saw them!" Trane yelled. "They can't get out. The plants have got them."

Several of the other boys went out to see for themselves

and the noise in the shed increased as the remaining captives pulled on their chains, desperate for Reez to free them.

"Be patient a little longer," he called out. "I will get to you all."

When he finally emerged from the first shed, it was obvious that Trane or others had spread the news of their freedom, as he could see the doors of the other sheds hanging open. The more courageous children had gone to investigate Reez's claims, and he could see them staring through the window at the bound clerics. Boys who had the strength were pulling out the foodstuffs from the stores and devouring their contents. Reez had to intervene, reminding them of all the others still chained, and urging them to take food to all the people in the compound. Only when he was certain they would do as he asked did he re-enter the second shed.

Fuelled by righteous anger, Reez's magic smashed the cages and ripped through the links as he walked the aisles like a dark avatar of vengeance. Some captives were openly crying when he reached them, finally allowing themselves to have hope that their ordeal was at an end and Reez's heart broke at the sight of men and women reduced to shadows. The night was almost gone when Reez finally emerged. All around him, people were dragging themselves from their fetid cages, breathing the clean air. The children seemed better able to accept their freedom. Many of the men and women, however, still stared at him vacantly, as if unwilling to even allow hope to take root in their hearts, and remained listless in the cages. It took him some time, but he was eventually able to cajole several of the older people to cook the salted meat hanging in the stores. With Trane's eager help, the younger boys were tasked with distributing water, and Reez built and lit a few small fires around the courtyard, collapsing the first shed to fuel them. As the night wore on, more people emerged from the sheds, enticed by the promise of warmth or by the aromas of the meat. Occasionally, as he walked past, someone would call out their thanks or reached out to touch his feet. Finally satisfied that he had done what he could for the prisoners, Reez turned back to the hut containing their captors and re-entered.

"Now," he said to Pariah as he sat back down and stretched his feet out in front of him. "I think it is time for us to have a very long talk."

Chapter Twenty-Two

Reez sat watching the swell of the turquoise ocean as it lifted and fell against the rocks at the base of the small cliff face below. If he glanced to his left, he could see the sprawl of Etheradia in the distance and the jutting causeway that pointed like an accusing finger at the Master's palace. He deliberately ignored it. Breathing deeply of the salty air, he tried to let the gentle sea breeze and the plaintive cries of the birds wash his soul of the filth that remained behind him, but there was only so much peace to be found. As much as he might wish it away, the things he had seen and heard would never leave him, and he feared that the terrible revelations were not yet at an end. He scrubbed his hands across his face and sighed.

Breeders.

Originally blonde, blue-eyed women hand-picked by Malander, they now encompassed any woman of childbearing age. The first purge had focused on the prostitutes and beggars, but now women could be taken under a variety of pretexts. Their purpose was to give the Eternal One a constant supply of babies. According to the clerics, small children were the richest source of anima magic. They had an abundance within that would normally be utilised for growth and change as they matured and reached adulthood. Malander had recognised it, and had used them occasionally, but it was his son who had exploited it to the full. Whatever he was doing in that walled palace required a never-ending supply.

It soon became apparent that the process was too slow to meet the new Master's requirements. Increasing the call and raising the age for tributes didn't solve the problem, so the Purge had been widened. It also answered the question of why only young women and children were being allowed entrance through the city gates. It seemed Jina had been right to warn Castor and his family to flee.

They used all the women they had taken as breeders, one benefit that fell to the four clerics tasked with their care. Some women had been there for long cycles, raped and abused until they fell pregnant, only for it all to happen again when their babes were weaned. Pariah and his cohorts had obviously relished their duties, even retaining young girls of ten summers and breaking them in before their courses had even started.

Since Verrin's ascension, the slavers had been turned away with virtually empty holds. In the beginning, the clerics had mollified them by selling the men at a reduced price, but in the interim moons, having been badly neglected, the remaining men were too weak and ill to tempt even the worst of them. Occasionally, Verrin would require one or two, and they had sent some to supplement his insatiable need for a source of magic, but they had effectively left the rest to die in their cages. Despite the fact that they would now have access to food, Reez feared that many of them were already too sickly to survive.

Reez stood and turned, his feet reluctant to return to the compound, and his eyes roved across the devastation in front of him. The ground had been blasted clear of all vegetation, the dull earth now empty of lush grass and meadow flower. The bank of trees that had stood tall and strong for many cycles were dead, their leaves obliterated. Already, two had toppled and leant drunkenly against each other, their roots withered and no longer able to hold them upright. Further up the hill, he could see evidence that a few had survived, and he vowed to save them before leaving. His magic, fuelled by rage, had been wild and uncontrolled, and the plants had paid the price. It reminded him of Wicton's warnings of the war of the Mages and it didn't take much imagination to see how the land might have suffered, and the ravages wrought by taking magic without thought of the consequences. He felt ashamed of himself, as with time and patience, such needless destruction could easily have been avoided.

There still remained the problem of the four clerics.

Neither innocent nor ignorant, they had fully embraced their role with cruelty and sadistic pleasure and must therefore be punished. The question of how and when had yet to be determined. For the time being, he would have to chain them in one of their own cages. Reez smiled grimly at the idea of them experiencing a little of the degradation they had inflicted on so many.

The freed captives needed to be tended and returned home, and Reez decided that their first stop would be to the school on the other side of the island where food, beds and clothing would be plentiful. After that, he would need to arrange transport back to the mainland. Some of the prisoners had friends and family still in the city or further afield who would undoubtedly help them, but there would be others who had nowhere to go and no-one to care for them. They would need to be given shelter and provisions.

To Reez's surprise, the beggar boys, who he assumed would be the ones needing shelter and a place to call home, already had access to a community of sorts. Trane had told him how he had been taken in, fed and given a bed whilst being taught how to survive using his wits and light fingers. He wanted to return to the only home he now knew and had been very vocal about the benefits of the underground mismatched family that he belonged to. It was clear to Reez that some of the other boys were drawn to Trane and his stories, and he feared they would end up living a life of crime unless he could somehow provide a better alternative.

#

The compound was unusually quiet when he finally returned, despite the vast number of people sitting against the sheds or laying by the small fires wrapped in sailcloth and filthy sheets. None of them had wanted to stay inside the sheds despite the semblance of shelter, preferring to brave the cold and wind for the blessing of being outside and free. He smiled in reassurance at the gaunt captives as he passed, but no-one would meet his eyes. He frowned, wondering what had happened when earlier that morning they had been eager to touch him and thank him. Reez finally understood when he entered the hut where he had left the clerics, still wound in vines and stinking of their own urine. As soon as he opened the door, the coppery scent of blood reached his nostrils and he saw dark pools spreading across the rough floor. He lingered only long enough to confirm that all four of them were dead, their throats savagely cut, before leaving and quietly closing the door.

A few people shuffled away as he re-emerged and stood with his head bowed. It was obvious they were trying to put some distance between them, although many of the people were still too weak to move. Reez's gaze roamed across them all. A few stared at him, fear etched on their faces, and he realised they were waiting for him to punish them. He clenched his hands and lifted his face to the grey sky.

"Are you angry, Reez?" Trane asked quietly, appearing beside him.

"No," Reez said with a sigh, looking down at the young boy, "but I am very sad."

"For them?" Trane asked incredulously.

"For the ones who were driven to do such a thing."

"I wish I had done it," Trane said fiercely. He glanced at Reez before standing stiffly beside him. "Nobody will tell you who it was. It doesn't matter what you do to us."

Reez put a hand on the boy's shoulder. "I know," he said softly. "I won't ask. Murder is wrong and cloaking it under the guise of retribution doesn't make it right, but I understand."

"They didn't deserve to live," Trane said, his face red.

"Maybe so, but that must be a decision made after serious contemplation."

"After everything they did?"

"What if I decide that something you say or do is offensive or wrong? Does that give me the right to punish you, or take your life? Living that way leads to chaos, where no-one is safe. Decisions like these are best left to representatives who have been given responsibility for keeping the peace, who can judge fairly and without emotional bias."

"They hurt people. They hurt me."

Reez looked down at the young boy. Trane wanted to appear brave and strong, but he was shaking, and Reez could see that he was very close to tears. "Come on," Reez said. "Let's see if we can find something hot to eat. I'm getting pretty hungry. Then you can help me get these people somewhere warmer."

Trane gulped and smiled tremulously before grasping Reez's hand and pulling him across to one of the fires.

#

The place was in an uproar. Novices and clerics ran around the atrium like ants kicked out of a nest. Reez stood in the middle of the chaos, a dark dispenser of justice, watching as the men, women, and children from the compound were carried in on makeshift stretchers or hobbled in supported by others. Men and boys scurried around the building following Reez's command to bathe and feed the captives, and give them cots to rest in until such time as passage could be arranged across the strait back to the city. The Abbot protested ignorance, but Reez knew better and had locked him and five of the senior leaders of the school in a basement. He suspected that others may have been privy to the circumstances on the other side of the island, but he couldn't very well secure them all. Instead, he glared at the men rushing past, their red robes flying and their boots thumping across the polished floor. No one dared to look at him.

Trane had appointed himself Reez's personal assistant. Relaying information and messages as well as supplying his own commentary of thoughts and opinions. Reez found him intelligent and witty and enjoyed his company as he strode around the complex. Thanks to Trane relating to anyone in earshot all Reez had done, embellishing it each time, the clerics and their charges were decidedly uneasy, and he knew he would not encounter any trouble from them.

"Giblet says he has requested that boats be sent over in the morning to begin taking people back to Etheradia, as you directed," Trane told Reez as they walked. He had taken to giving the clerics names. Apparently, Giblet looked like a turkey's innards. "I made sure he didn't add anything else to your message, or whisper to the messenger before he left on the rowboat. It will take him some time to cross the strait and get to the Abbey. I don't think we will see any vessels until tomorrow."

"You can read, then," Reez observed as he watched several novices hurry past with arms full of drying linens.

Trane laughed. "Of course. Prime makes sure all the recruits can do their letters and make calculations."

Reez looked down at Trane. "Is he the one in charge of you?"

"He's the leader of all of the gangs. The Seconds are in charge of each individual company. I'm going to be a Second one day."

"It sounds very organised," Reez murmured.

"Prime says that without order, we have no hope of survival. We would end up fighting against each other and be easy pickings for the clerics." Trane frowned. "I think someone broke their oath of loyalty. How else would they know where to find us? When I find out who it was, I'll…" He glanced up at Reez and flushed. "Shall I finish my report?"

"You have more to tell me?"

"Sweat Bucket was complaining about giving up his cot, so I told him to speak to you about it. He won't; he's as frightened of you as the rest of them, but maybe you should wave your fingers at him or something to keep him in line."

"Which one is Sweat Bucket?" Reez asked, a bemused smile on his face.

"The fat one with the red face. His robes are damp already, and he's probably doing the least amount of work."

"Sounds like he needs to be motivated."

Trane grinned. "Can I watch?"

Reez spent a short time ensuring that all the clerics and their students were sufficiently inspired. He actually didn't have to threaten or cajole; his presence, grim and intimidating, was enough to ensure that all his instructions would be carried out to the letter. Reez stifled a yawn. He was weary and in need of sleep, but he recognised that would likely not happen if he stayed. Although the day was overcast, Reez knew that noon had long gone. It was time for him to return to the inn and rest.

"I'm leaving now," he told Trane as he picked up his bag.

Trane's face fell. "You can't go," he blurted. "What if they decide to put us back?"

"Giblet is in charge, and he fears me too much to countermand my wishes. I locked the head of the school and his lackeys below, and they will stay that way until I, or someone I trust, returns for them. There is one thing you can do for me, though," he added. Trane nodded eagerly. "You will spread the word that no-one is to mete out justice to these people. I overlooked what happened this morning because of your sufferings, but I will not tolerate vengeance in any form. Should it happen, then you will all answer to me, and I will not be pleased. I will ensure they punish the right people for their crimes; until then, no-one is to be harmed. Do I make myself clear?"

Trane lowered his eyes. "Yes."

"I trust you will make sure that everyone gets the message." He waited for Trane to agree. "Good. Now I have more work to do."

"Will I see you again?" Trane asked, his voice shaking slightly.

Reez smiled. "I'll make sure of it."

#

It didn't take him long to hike back to the cove where he had left his boat. He stumbled a few times on his way down, sliding through scree and rocks, his body and mind weary. It took great effort to haul the craft down to the water, and he was half soaked when he finally pulled himself inside and hoisted the little sail. The craft scudded across the undulating sea as he headed back to Etheradia, not caring whether or not he was seen. The time for hiding was over.

Perversely, his arrival at the dock and his walk back through the streets of the city sparked no interest whatsoever, and he let himself into the dark interior of the Falcon with a sigh. He could feel the skin on his face had tightened from the sea spray, and his cloak was stiff with salt. His old scars were starting to itch, and he knew he should take a bath, but his eyes were already drooping. Stopping only to eat some dry bread and strip off his clothes, he climbed into the soft bed and closed his eyes. Everything else could wait; now was the time to sleep. He would need to be fully rested as he had an early morning appointment to keep with the Cardinal on the morrow.

Chapter Twenty-Three

The streets were still deserted as Reez travelled through the city. The gloom of predawn shadowed him as he walked, limping slightly. His muscles ached and under other circumstances, he would have pulled the thick blankets over his head and slept for the rest of the day. Instead, he was heading for the Abbey, needing to reach the gates before the petitioners gathered, so that he could intercept the Cardinal before he had a chance to alert Verrin. His success on the cleric's isle had emboldened him. He realised that his status alone was enough to cow most people; for those who refused to be intimidated, he had his magic, and only now was he beginning to understand just how dynamic that was.

As he approached the Abbey gates, the massive statues of cowled clerics loomed over him as if to mock him for being small and weak. Reez marched up to the locked doors and banged loudly, knowing that he could reduce the effigies to rubble in moments if he had a mind. There was silence for a short while, and Reez rapped impatiently again, resisting the urge to destroy the entrance entirely. He heard a bolt being drawn back and a small hatch opened in the wicket gate.

"Who dares call so early in the morn?" a querulous voice demanded.

Reez moved into his line of sight. "I will see the Cardinal. Now."

The cleric hawked and spat on the ground. "The Cardinal sees no-one without an appointment," he said sharply. "Return at the break of dawn and make petition."

Reez thrust his right hand under the cleric's nose, the green stone of his ring flaring in the lantern's light within. "I will see him, and you will take me to him now," he snapped.

The cleric moved to slam the hatch closed. Reez could see the exact moment that the man's mind processed what his eyes had clearly seen. The lantern lifted higher, and the cleric's beady eyes narrowed.

"Open this door," Reez commanded, "or I will destroy it."

The light disappeared momentarily, and Reez could hear the man muttering as he drew back the hasps securing the gate and pulled it open to allow Reez to enter. The large courtyard seemed bigger than he remembered from his first visit, devoid as it was of the press of people clamouring to present their petitions. All the porticos were shadowed and empty. The only light was held in the gatekeeper's hand.

"Take me to the Cardinal," Reez said. The cleric stood undecided; his mouth fixed in a thin line. It was obvious that he was not used to being ordered around and Reez waited, his face stern. Perversely, he hoped the man would refuse so he could vent some of his anger that had started to simmer again. Instead, the cleric crossed the courtyard, and Reez followed him as he plodded across the cloister and up the steps. He led Reez down a long corridor until they reached an ornate entrance.

"The Cardinal's receiving room," he explained with a curt nod before turning away.

"One moment," Reez said, stopping the cleric in his tracks. "You will find a cleric for me. His designation is 22798. Have him brought here as soon as possible."

"Lord," the man said with a slight sneer, and made a small bow. As much as Reez disliked the fawning of the clerics, he knew enough to know that this one was displaying barely concealed contempt.

"Another thing," Reez said coldly, "before you leave." He noticed the cleric roll his eyes. "I find your attitude disturbing. It seems to me that you are not fit to wear those robes." With a feral grin, Reez stared at the man as he perished the weave of the cloth and allowed the fabric to fall to the floor, exposing the cleric's pasty body. Reez felt a malicious pleasure at the man's obvious discomfort. It was time that these clerics understood who they were dealing with. "I expect a little more respect in the future. Leave that," he ordered as the cleric bent to pick up the cloth to hide his nakedness.

"Yes, Lord," the man said, his face as red as his once fine robes, bowing deeply before scuttling off. Reez watched him go and then pushed open the door without knocking and moved inside. One small lamp burned within, barely illuminating the empty cavernous room. A large ornate chair studded with gems was lifted up on a dais at the far end. Benches were arrayed against each wall underneath huge old tapestries depicting scenes of the city, ships, and life in the Abbey. Reez strolled across the white stone floor towards a door set in the wall behind the cathedra. As he neared, he could see a light shining from within and heard muted voices indicating that several people were gathered inside, even though it was not yet dawn. Opening the door silently, Reez eased in unnoticed and looked around.

The Cardinal's private quarters were sumptuous. A magnificent, dark, highly polished desk sat in front of a large window, now obscured by heavy brocade red drapes. On either side stood cases of books and shelves filled with scrolls and parchments. On the opposite side was a large table big enough to hold ten people with high-backed chairs pushed in around it. A massive golden candelabra stood in its centre. Another door led away from the room, and Reez assumed it led to the Cardinal's bedchamber. Across from Reez was the stone hearth, a fire burning brightly within. Before it were four men. Two sat in deep soft seats on either side of the fireplace; the other two standing before them, blocking their view of the door through which Reez had entered. All wore the familiar red robes of the clerics; however, these were obviously of a much higher quality. Reez could see elaborate embroidery around the hems and sleeves in gold thread. One of the men seated wore a large pendant around his neck, the Cardinal, Reez assumed.

"Who authorised it?" the Cardinal said.

One of the men stood with his back to Reez began twisting his hands together. "The Abbot, Your Eminence. At least, it bore his seal."

"And none of you questioned his need for so many boats to be readied?"

The two looked at each other. "Surely, if he requested them, he has good reason," the smaller one replied hesitantly.

"What do you think he is planning to do with them? Empty the island?" the Cardinal roared. "Send for the cleric who bore the message. I wish to speak to him myself. After that, you will go down to the docks and tell the captains to stand down until I can determine what is going on."

"No, you will stay right where you are," Reez said quietly.

The men span round. "How dare you enter the Cardinal's private quarters!" one of them blurted. "Get out now!"

Reez shut the door behind him with a soft click and pointed to the chairs across the room. "Sit down and be quiet."

"We don't take orders from you," the second one blustered. Reez narrowed his eyes before dropping his gaze to the stone floor. Suddenly, it began to roll and buck beneath their feet, sending both men sprawling across the flags.

"If you won't do it willingly, then I will have to make you." Reez said pointedly.

The Cardinal rose slowly to his feet, followed by the second man. "Who are you?" he asked, his eyes assessing Reez warily.

"I am Reez, Master of green magic and wielder of earth magic."

"There are no Masters left," the man who Reez assumed must be the High Cleric said. "The Eternal One informed us they were gone."

"The Eternal One is wrong," Reez said, pushing back his hood.

"How dare you!" one man on the ground shouted, struggling to right himself.

Reez pointed his finger at him. "I thought I told you to be silent."

The Cardinal held out a hand. "Peace, brother," he said to the prone man. He turned his attention to Reez and smiled. He bowed slightly. "Master Reez. You honour us with your presence. How may we be of assistance?"

"I have sent for a cleric," Reez began. "When he gets here, you will give him the following instructions. As many boats that can be readied are to be sent to the Cleric's Isle to bring back those who have been held captive there. They are to be housed and fed within the Abbey until such time as they can return to their families or find other accommodation. Next, the

Temple of the priestesses is to be closed and no further tributes are to be received. If any children remain within its walls, they are to be returned to their families. Any reward that was given in exchange can be kept. If they can't locate their families, they will be looked after here."

"We don't have the resources for that!" the High Cleric protested.

"Then I suggest you sell some of the treasures you undoubtedly hold and use the gold you hoard here," Reez said mildly. "The gems studding the chair in the next room would feed all of them for the next three cycles."

"My Lord," the Cardinal said, shaking his head sadly and spreading his hands wide. "I'm afraid we cannot do that. The Eternal One would never agree, and we live to serve him."

"Don't worry about Verrin. You can leave him to me."

The High Cleric made to object, but the Cardinal laid a restraining hand on his arm. "Of course, Lord. I am certain you are eager to see him. We are happy to await your return."

Reez smiled, his eyes flashing darkly. "If you imagine Verrin will deal with me as he did with your predecessor, then you are mistaken. He has no power over me; in fact, his magic is useless against me. The only advantage he had the last time we met was surprise. This time, I will be the one surprising him." He watched with satisfaction as the Cardinal's face fell. Just then, a knock sounded at the outer door and Reez looked pointedly at the Cardinal.

"Enter," he called. Reez watched as Jina came into the room and bowed low. He kept his eyes on the floor, refusing to look at Reez, although he must have been desperate for information. When the Cardinal hesitated, Reez shifted the stone slightly beneath his feet, causing him to stumble against the chair behind him. Only then did he relay Reez's instructions and dismiss the little cleric. Once Jina had gone, Reez indicated that the Cardinal and High Cleric should sit down and he crossed the floor to inspect the door leading out of the room. A quick glance inside revealed it to be a bedchamber, as he had suspected. He examined the door and frame, pleased to see that it was composed of sturdy hardwood, studded with metal. Shutting it firmly, he infused the wood with moisture, swelling the door in the frame, effectively sticking it tight so that they couldn't access the room. After ensuring that it couldn't be opened, he turned his attention to the window. Pulling back the drapes, he noted that it looked out on to the causeway leading to the palace, but there was no ground outside. If they tried to climb out, they risked a long drop to the ocean below, and would likely be shattered on the rocks. He nodded to himself before turning back to the Cardinal.

"You will remain here," he said to the four men. "I don't trust you to be at liberty, so I'm afraid you will have to be confined. As soon as I ensure your orders are being carried out, I will pay your Master a visit. When I return, there will be a great many changes." He flared the fire until it burnt so brightly, the clerics had to shield their eyes from the glare. In moments, the fuel was consumed, and the hearth went cold. Their wait would be a chilly, uncomfortable one. "Goodbye, gentlemen," he said with a grin, as he stepped through the door to the receiving room. "I suggest you use your time to contemplate your actions and make peace with the First Mage. Believe me, there will be an accounting of your actions. The people will know exactly what has happened, and who is responsible for it."

"We have done nothing wrong!" one of the clerics shouted as he turned to leave. "We have served the Eternal One faithfully."

"What about the people of Bestra?" Reez replied, his face red with anger. "You have a duty to them, too. Instead, you thought only of yourselves. What does it matter if people are suffering and dying when you are cloistered away in your little fortress? What did you care about children being drained of life when your bellies were full and your beds were soft? At least the previous Cardinal had the courage to stand up for those who had no voice."

"Yes, and it cost him his life!" the High Cleric said.

"Let me ask you something," Reez replied. "Where does Verrin's power come from?" They were silent. "It seems I need to make you aware of some truths. His power comes from living creatures, those poor souls who you have been supplying him with. What would happen if you stopped sending them? What would happen if you emptied the city instead of filling it up with vessels for his use? He would have nothing."

"He would come for us."

Reez shrugged. " Lock the gate and leave the Abbey. Unlike me, he cannot melt stone or reduce this place to rubble. He is not all-powerful. He is just a petulant child who is used to getting his own way." As he spoke, Reez felt the truth of his words settle in his heart, giving him hope he could come out of this unscathed. Had he not already contemplated the limitations of anima magic? Instead of dealing with the facts, Reez had allowed his fears to overshadow the truth.

"Everyone has a choice. Do what is right, or condone wrongdoing by staying silent. You are complicit in what has happened here and you will be punished for it." He shut the door firmly behind him, fusing the wood and melting the hinges slightly so that they no longer moved. When he was satisfied that any attempts to leave would be fruitless, he crossed the hall, ignoring the shouts and frantic hammering from the Cardinal and his men.

He found Jina hovering outside the receiving room, his face anxious. "Master Reez," he breathed in relief as Reez emerged.

"Everything is fine, Jina," Reez said, clasping the man's shoulder.

"I saw activity on the dock and was worried that they were going over to stop you," he said.

"The boats are for the prisoners. They are all free now. They will hurt no more children. Did you relay the messages?"

"Yes. Everything will be done as ordered, although many clerics are unsure. I gave the instructions to those who I felt I could trust."

"Your Cardinal and High Cleric are waiting for me to return from seeing your Master. Unfortunately, they won't be leaving that room until I free them, and I will be securing this door so that they cannot countermand my orders before I return.

I think we need to make sure everyone is informed and is ready for an influx of people. They will need food and beds until we can reunite them with their families." He patted Jina on the back. "It looks like you are in charge for the time being."

"Me?" Jina squeaked.

"I can't think of a better person. Let's inform the chapter, shall we?" Reez said with a wide grin.

Chapter Twenty-Four

Reez walked slowly but steadily across the causeway, his back straight and his head high. He was conscious of all the eyes trained on him and strove to appear confident and peerless, when inside he was quacking and full of doubt. He looked across at the edifice that was getting nearer with each step, the sun glinting off the gold covered roofs. The wall surrounding it that had seemed so big from a distance was probably less than the height of two men, and as he got closer, he could see how it had crumbled in several places. Cracks were evident in the ancient mortar and plants had grown in the holes and fissures. He didn't need to waste magic if he wanted to destroy it. The wall looked as if it would collapse under a hearty sneeze. He thought fondly of the bed at the Falcon, and the inn at Maston, wishing he was anywhere but here, the one place in the whole of Zelannor he didn't want to be.

And he had no idea what he was going to do when he arrived.

Behind him, the Abbey was a hive of activity as the chapter carried out the orders they had been given, yet no sound reached Reez apart from the waves breaking on the rocks below and the cry of seabirds circling the teaming docks in the distance, waiting for the chance to snatch a fish from the day's haul or innards cast into the sea after filleting. He had never felt so alone in his life, far from family and friends, far from the safety of his home and the security of his books. He had been shaken by the things he had seen and done over the past days, and he wished with all his heart that he could forget it all. Too much blood had been shed already, and he was heartily sick of it. Yet his feet had taken him down a path and now he was committed to seeing it through to completion, whatever the outcome. As he reached the gates that guarded the palace, Reez idly imagined them remaining closed against him, even though he knew they were no longer an obstacle to him, but they slid open with ease at his touch and he was forced to continue on.

Once within the walls and out of sight of the curious, he sagged against the crumbling stones and took a good look around. What had seemed to be one complete building when viewed from afar was apparently several buildings clustered tightly together. The majority were arrayed around the outside of a cobbled courtyard hugging the dilapidated wall and facing a tower rising from the centre which dominated the surrounding buildings. It was similar to his own, except much larger in both height and girth. To Reez's eye, it seemed as if the original structure had been added to over the centuries to make it appear much more impressive. Near its pinnacle, he could see what appeared to be a balcony running around the outside of the whole tower, affording a view of both the city and the sea. A gold covered roof, which Reez had clearly seen from the other side of the causeway, shone in the wan light of a new day. In front of the large double doors was a stone statue of a man on one knee, arms stretched out before him as if offering a blessing. From the open hands, water poured forth to tumble into a wide pool surrounding the figure, the sound giving the courtyard an air of peace and tranquillity. Once, it would have been a magnificent sight, but the long cycles and sea spray had weathered it, eroding the features entirely and pitting the rest of the stone. Beyond the tower, mostly hidden behind a screen of stunted trees, stood a long windowless shed, not unlike the ones he had liberated on the island. Unwilling to discover its contents for the moment, he turned his attention to the buildings ranged around him.

    They reminded him of the older houses in the city. At one time, they would have been a grand sight, but now they displayed the results of age and neglect. Hedera plants ran up the brickwork, almost obscuring the view from several windows on the upper floors. Many of the windows were shuttered, the wood rotting away adding to the sorry sight, although the roofs were still gilded with gold, making the structures seem more impressive from afar. All of them seemed abandoned, but Reez spied smoke rising from the back of one from a fire or stove, so he moved towards it and pushed the door open. It creaked ominously as he entered, and he expected to be greeted with further signs of neglect, but he was surprised to see that the inside was in a much better state. He walked into a substantial entrance hall with decorated tiles on the floor, faded but clean. A winding open staircase in front of him led up to the floors above, the wooden rail against the wall highly polished. Glancing through a door on the left, he saw a small parlour with two large, padded chairs arranged in front of a cold hearth. A glass cabinet held several small decorative items, and the walls were covered with faded tapestries. A corridor stretched to the back of the house through an archway beyond the stairs. Just inside it, a small door to the right revealed a storeroom full of foodstuffs, preserves, and dried herbs. Hearing noises from the rear, Reez walked quietly on.

Peering through the last door at the end of the corridor, he found two people working together in a large galley, preparing a meal. A woman was sitting at a scratched and pitted wooden table cutting vegetables. Her hair was white and pulled into a severe knot on the top of her head. Her clothes would once have been fine, but the faded green dress was ragged at the hem and cuffs and her heavily stained apron was an inadequate protection from the grime. At the hearth, a man bent over the fire, stirring a large pot. His short, grey hair was thinned at the top, revealing a shiny pate. His attire was only slightly better than his partner's. His black trews were fading and the colours on his once rich brocaded tunic had dulled. The smells of a meaty broth filled the galley, making Reez's mouth water.

Reez moved into the room and cleared his throat, making his presence known. At his entrance, both people started and turned towards him, but neither cried out nor spoke. "Excuse me," he began. "My name is Reez, Master of Fiora province. I am looking for your Master. Can you tell me where he is?"

The couple glanced at one another, and the man moved in front of his wife, as if to shield her from Reez. He shook his head.

"I won't harm you," Reez soothed, lifting his hands in a gesture of peace. "Would you tell me your names?"

Again, the man shook his head. He walked forward a couple of steps tentatively, cupping his throat with his hand and opening his mouth twice before shaking his head again.

Reez frowned. "Can you not speak?" he asked. The man shook his head vigorously, his eyes showing relief that Reez had understood him. "Neither of you?" Reez asked, glancing behind the man at the woman who was now stood half-hidden behind her husband. She just stared at Reez, her eyes betraying the fear that she could not voice. "I see," Reez said. "Have you always had this affliction?" The fire popped in the grate as the old couple looked at each other. "Surely your Master could discover the cause and…" Reez stopped as they both turned their attention back to him. "Your Master did this to you," he guessed, growing cold inside. The fact that neither of them denied it confirmed his suspicions. "Why would he do such a thing?" he muttered to himself, feeling the familiar flicker of anger begin to smoulder within. Taking a deep breath, he looked at the man stood uncertainly before him and made himself smile. "You serve Verrin, the Master," he acknowledged and was rewarded with a nod. "Can you take me to him? Show me where he is?"

The elderly man gestured that Reez should go back outside and followed him down the corridor. When they stepped outside, the man beckoned and then led Reez across the courtyard to the tower. Pushing open the door, he indicated Reez should climb up to the very top. Reez thanked him and watched as the man bowed before he retreated across the courtyard and returned to his home.

Reez advanced into the gloom beyond, but instead of making his way up the stairs, he first descended into the basement. The stone floor was swept clean and there were no boxes or shelves to clutter the room. He stared at the flagstones, easily able to determine which one should be raised to reveal the hidden knowledge underneath. Wondering whether Malander had been as careless as Chrisos in protecting the secrets of his craft, he bent and laid his hand on the slab. The stone refused to budge. Satisfied that there was nothing else to see, he ascended slowly, aware of each scrape and shuffle as his feet trod the steps. As he walked, he let the protection of his plant and mineral elements rise to the fore, masking his human attributes so that Verrin could not use him to fuel his magic. He hoped it would be enough to give him an advantage. He passed several rooms on his way up, stopping briefly at each in case the man had been wrong, but they were all devoid of life. Vaguely, he noted that each room was richly decorated and elaborately furnished. When he finally reached the top, which he assumed was the Master's chambers, a large wooden door carved with animals of every kind was the only way forward. Carefully, he lifted his hand, tinged green with the presence of his plant self, pulled it open and stepped inside.

Thick woven rugs littered the floor, covering the dense wooden beams. Heavy drapes hung over several windows that faced in each direction of the vast room, and another door was partially open, leading out to the balcony Reez had spied earlier from the courtyard. Despite the light streaming through the eastern side, several lamps still burned in alcoves around the chamber. A massive bed took up one side of the room, strewn with cushions and furs in disarray. Beside it stood a large metal rack, and Reez hissed softly. A young girl who could only have been twelve summers at most was fastened upright to it, naked and spread open, her eyes wide and fearful. Dried blood streaked the inside of her thighs and dark marks were dotted across her body. Her face was swollen and bruised and Reez could see red welts across her neck. A noise to his left caused Reez to spin round.

Verrin was standing at a large table covered in tools, books, and parchment, his back to the room. He wore a black robe heavily embroidered with gold thread and cinched at the waist by a golden sash. His fine blond hair had grown long and was now tied at the nape of his neck with a leather band. So intent was he on the work in front of him he had not heard Reez enter. As he stared at his old nemesis, Reez's mind worked furiously. He had the advantage of weight and height and could possibly subdue Verrin before he even had a chance to react. His eyes flickered across the table strewn with implements, and his hand itched to grab a knife and plunge it into the murderer's back. It would be just to kill him and avenge the deaths of Wicton, Chrisos, and Paiter, yet something gave him pause. He was not a killer. In his heart, he believed that life in all its forms was precious, even one such as Verrin's.

Verrin muttered to himself and bent closer to stare at whatever he held in his hand. Reez knew then that he had to try and reason with him and give him a chance to redeem himself. He took a deep breath and spoke softly. "Verrin."

Verrin whirled round and glared at Reez, his eyes wide and wild. The similarities to Malander were startlingly obvious now. Verrin had grown and thinned out, his face becoming angular and sharp. Reez recognised the arrogant pose and lifted chin, but where Malander's eyes had been cold and lifeless, Verrin's blazed with icy madness.

"Not now," he growled. "Just leave me alone." To Reez's amazement, Verrin started to laugh. "It's usually the other one," he giggled. "I wasn't expecting you. The fat one. I was hoping it would be him. He's easy to scare off, but you, I never did figure you out. That means I'm close if they have sent you to distract me." He turned back to the table and Reez stepped closer.

"What are you doing, Verrin?" he asked.

"Doing? What am I doing? I'm figuring it out!" Verrin

shouted. "You can't stop me, you know. I know you're not real." He focused intently on Reez for a moment before he started giggling again. "See? That proves it. I can't see you, I can't feel you, so you are not there. Risen from your grave to torment me. You even look rotten." He turned his back on Reez and began mumbling to himself.

Reez was astonished. He had come to this place expecting to plead, cajole, even fight against Verrin in order to get him to listen. Instead, Verrin was treating him as if he were nothing more than a mirage. He glanced down at his hand, which was flooded with green and stifled a laugh. Along with his mangled face, he probably did resemble a corpse, especially to someone who believed him to be long dead.

It seemed as if Verrin had indeed lost his mind, as Bilan had suggested. He looked over at the young girl again and clenched his teeth. Unfortunately, his madness had resulted in the loss of untold lives. One way or another, he had to be stopped. Until they reached an agreement, he couldn't allow Verrin to leave, so he quietly fused the door to the frame.

Hoping that he could appeal to Verrin on some level, Reez moved slowly around the wall of the chamber until he could see what held Verrin's interest. Amid the piles of paper and tomes lay what used to be an arm, but elongated to twice its size. The fingers had been grossly lengthened and the whole appendage was covered in hair. "What in the name of the First Mage is that?" Reez gasped.

"I refuse to tell you, shade. I don't care what you do, you still won't be able to stop me."

"How could I stop you?" Reez asked.

"Tricky, tricky, tricky," Verrin sang. "Not like the other one. He moans and screams, always screaming, but I can silence him. What about you? Will you scream?"

"I won't scream," Reez said.

"Good," Verrin said and smiled. "You could have been my friend, but you chose the fat one instead. I hated you for that. But you won't scream. I don't like it when they scream. It's easy to stop them. They don't scream anymore."

"Tell me what you have discovered," Reez said, pointing at the limb in front of them.

"Not yet, but I must be close," Verrin said. "I just can't find it, the link, the thing that changes them."

"Maybe I can help," Reez ventured, wanting to keep Verrin talking.

"You? You know nothing. Your magic is useless. Who wants leaves and bark when they can have feathers?"

"You're trying to make feathers?"

"Pfft, any fool can make feathers," Verrin scoffed. "I need to grow them here, instead of hair. You can't fly with hair. It's totally different, but maybe, if I look closely, I can discover a solution."

"You want to fly?" Reez guessed.

"Yes! I could fly and soar in the air like a bird. Can you imagine their faces when I swoop down on them in the city? They will be terrified." He laughed again and then stopped suddenly. "I don't want to lose my arms, though. I need to grow them another way. The bones are easy, but the feathers…" He turned back to the table. "I must be close."

"Why not rest a while?" Reez soothed. "Perhaps it will come to you then."

"Rest, yes," Verrin mumbled. "He comes to me when I sleep, the fat one. He comes and screams at me." He looked at Reez and shivered. "You don't scream, but you are worse somehow. Why is that?" He shuffled backwards and turned away. Reez watched him grab a bottle and splash some liquid into a mug before gulping it down. He upended it before throwing the empty vessel into a corner. "Bastion," he shouted, "more wine!"

"Why did you do it, Verrin? Why did you kill them all?"

Verrin sighed. "Are you here to shrive me? Very well, shade. Listen to my confession and then be gone." He turned back to Reez and narrowed his eyes. "It makes sense. It should be you. You know, it was your fault. It was supposed to be just Malander, but you made me so angry. I was the best! It should have been me in that circle, not you. But he wouldn't admit it. Out of all of them, I was the one without flaws. I was the one destined to replace him, but he wouldn't go. He called me wilful and twisted and said he'd beat it out of me. Said he had no patience to start again. It should have been me, not you. I hated you then. I hated all of you. So, you had to go. First him, so superior, so clever. He didn't even realise until it was too late." Verrin giggled. "Then the fat one. That was fun." His face dropped. "He won't stop screaming, though. Always screaming." Finally, he looked back at Reez. "There, I'm done.

Now leave." He flicked his hand at Reez in dismissal.

"What about her?" Reez said, pointing to the young girl bound on the rack. "She can come with me."

"No!" Verrin shrieked and raced over to her. "I need her."

"She's just a child, Verrin. Let her go."

"She's my vessel. It's an honour to serve me, they all know. They offer themselves to me." Reez started to walk towards him, but Verrin squealed. "No, no further! Don't come. I don't want to see you. Dead, all dead. They can't hurt me now."

"I'm not going to hurt you."

"I know," Verrin said, laughing again. "I won't let you. Where is the Cardinal? He can rid me of you. I thought it would be the other one. Fat pig. I can always get rid of him."

Suddenly, the girl arched her back and her mouth gaped open soundlessly. Hundreds of spiders erupted from the floor and surged towards Reez like a wave rushing to shore. He forced himself to stand his ground as they swarmed across his feet and up his legs.

"Cease this, Verrin," Reez said sharply. The insects disappeared as quickly as they had arisen and the girl sagged back, panting, her head dropping to her chest.

"He would have been gone by now," Verrin grumbled. "Why can't you just disappear?"

"This needs to stop," Reez asserted. "Your actions are hurting people."

"I can do what I like. I am Master here, now. This is my

domain."

"You have an obligation to the people to protect them and watch over them."

"The people are mine to use as I see fit," Verrin shouted. "They are nothing to me. They never cease their complaints and demands. I refuse to listen to them anymore. The Cardinal can deal with their endless petitions. I have more important things to do."

"You are Master of anima magic," Reez countered. "You have a duty…"

"Oh, stop it! Always duty with you. I will no longer be dictated to by Masters long dead. This is my time, and I will do whatever I want."

"I understand the need for change, but you go too far."

"No, you go too far!" Verrin spat. A sly look crossed his face, and Reez saw movement in his peripheral vision. Turning, he only barely managed to duck as a clawed arm slashed down. Stumbling backwards, Reez watched in horror as the nightmarish figure lumbered towards him. Almost twice his size, the creature had huge razor-sharp talons on the end of its long, muscular arms. Its maw was dripping with saliva and filled with pointed teeth. Two massive horns protruded from its head, similar in look to the oxen in Maston. Its powerful physique rippled as the monster moved towards him on legs like tree trunks. Instead of feet, the thing had cloven hooves.

Reez was barely conscious of Verrin's squeals of delight as he desperately tried to flee. Unsure of which way to move, his hesitation proved to be disastrous as the creature lunged at him, the talons ripping through his right arm. Crying out, Reez fell, ducking behind a chair as the monster attacked again, sending the seat flying across the room. Thinking quickly, Reez scrambled across the floor towards Verrin and grabbed his leg. The monster swayed, trying to find a way to get to Reez without touching its creator. Verrin kicked out at him, but Reez held tightly. As suddenly as it had arrived, the creature disappeared and Reez realised it had all been an illusion. He sighed and loosened his hold. With a strangled cry, Verrin heaved himself away.

Before he had time to collect himself, Reez heard the sound of claws scuttling across the floor. From behind Verrin, he could see another creature racing towards him on eight legs. This one reminded him of a crustacean he had seen on his journey to the Endless Sea many cycles before, only much larger. Two massive pincers jutted out before it that could easily circle his wrist and crush it. Tiny eyes on stalks were focused solely on him, but it was the curved tail that drew his attention. Arching over the creature's back, it carried a wicked point at the end, dripping with liquid. Reez hauled himself up and threw himself on to Verrin's table as the tail stabbed at him, narrowly missing his legs. As the creature circled, Reez was relieved to see that it wouldn't be able to reach him, but his relief was short-lived. Realising that his creation was too small, Verrin began to increase its size. Reez scoured the surrounding area, desperately looking for something to use as a weapon as the tail loomed over the edge of the table. He edged backwards until he felt the wall at his back. He was trapped.

He watched, almost mesmerised, as the stinger swung back and forth before plunging down. Reez shifted quickly to one side, narrowly avoiding being speared. He watched it carefully as the creature moved again, readjusting its position for a killing blow. It barely missed him, but he had the advantage of height and he knew if he stayed alert, he would be able to anticipate the direction of the next strike. As the creature moved back to the centre, Reez froze as a second tail appeared above the table, removing the chance to avoid the stinger. He watched helplessly as more liquid oozed out of both tips, knowing that the next stab would thrust straight into his stomach. Verrin was laughing uncontrollably. "Time for you to leave, now," he jeered. Suddenly, the tails disappeared and Verrin roared with rage. Rushing to the young girl, now slumped lifeless against her bonds, he grabbed her hair and pulled her head back. "Bitch!" he screamed, striking her flaccid face, as if force alone could revive her.

Reez leapt down from the table and scanned the room. Nothing else stirred. He knew he needed to act swiftly before Verrin sought another source of magic nearby. Ignoring the blood flowing from his arm, he crossed the room and grabbed Verrin. "Enough!" he shouted, his fear morphing into anger. Verrin struggled against Reez's arms, trying to break free.

"Let me go!"

"I won't let you kill any more people, Verrin," Reez said.

With a howl, Verrin bit down on Reez's injured flesh and pulled away as Reez cried out. He rushed back to the table, gathering the scattered documents and papers in his arms. "You will not interfere with my work." He grabbed the deformed limb and brandished it in front of him. "I am Master here. I command you to leave."

"Neither of us are going anywhere."

Verrin's eyes grew wide. "How dare you!" he shouted, spittle dribbling from the corner of his mouth. "Cardinal! Cardinal!" He pulled on the door, but it wouldn't open. "Let me out!"

"No."

"You can't keep me here. I have important work to complete."

"Sit down, Verrin," Reez said quietly, trying to soothe his agitation.

"No. You're dead! You have no authority here. I don't have to listen to you." Verrin backed away from the door, his eyes darting wildly around the room. Reez stretched out his left hand in an attempt to calm him, but Verrin shrieked loudly at the puckered green flesh and clutched his documents tightly to his chest.

"Don't touch me!" he gibbered as he stumbled across the room. "You can't have me! I can defeat you. I can fly away!"

Twisting suddenly, Verrin launched himself across the room and out of the balcony door. Before Reez could move to stop him, Verrin raced on to the balcony and threw himself over the balustrade.

Chapter Twenty-Five

Reez ran down the steps of the tower and burst through the door at the bottom. Skirting the walls, he raced to Verrin's broken body and knelt down beside him. His limbs were twisted into unnatural shapes and blood poured from his mouth and nose. As Reez watched, Verrin took a ragged breath. He still lived. Reez's hands fluttered helplessly across the mangled torso of his nemesis. He had no knowledge of how to repair Verrin's injuries, even though he suspected that nothing he could do would aid him now.

Verrin opened his eyes. "Reez?" he whispered.

"Yes, it's me," Reez said softly. "Don't move. I need to

get help."

"Stay."

Reez moved closer. "Does it hurt?" he asked.

"No." Verrin's eyes shone in the light of the new morning. "Am I dying?" Reez nodded. "You've come to collect me, then."

Reez was about to deny it but decided not to argue.

"Is Mama waiting?" Verrin asked.

"Of course."

"She was warm. She sang to me."

Reez used his sleeve to wipe the blood away from Verrin's face. His lips were tinged with blue and his breathing was becoming more laboured.

Verrin looked past Reez to the sky above. "It's going to be a fine day," he said before sighing deeply and closing his eyes, a soft smile on his face. Moments later, he was dead.

Reez sat back on his heels and turned his face up. White clouds moved lazily across the sun, which peeked out intermittently. A flock of seabirds flew across the causeway and out to the open ocean. His shoulders relaxed, and he felt the relief of a heavy burden being lifted from him. He had carried the fear of Verrin in his mind for so long, and now it was gone. In fact, his fears had been far worse than the reality he had faced. He had let his own insecurities and doubts obscure the skills and advantages that he possessed, crippling him for so long and stopping him from moving forward.

Hearing scuffling, Reez turned to see the old couple making their way cautiously across the courtyard, their eyes fixed on Verrin's body.

"He's dead," Reez announced. He felt guilty for not being more sensitive, as tears began to stream down the womans face. She must have cared for Verrin a great deal. "I'm sorry," he added belatedly as he watched her clutch her husband tightly. The man pulled his wife closer, but his face was far from unhappy. He grinned at Reez, revealing gaps in his teeth, and nodded enthusiastically, patting his wife on the back. "Is she alright?" Reez asked tentatively. When the woman turned to look at him, her face beaming despite the tears, Reez understood that her reaction was one of relief, not sorrow.

"Are we really free?" she whispered.

Reez looked up sharply. "You can speak?"

The woman nodded. "When the Master began to silence anyone who came near him, my husband forbade me to be in his presence. He protected me." She gazed up at the old man, who patted her cheek fondly.

"Is your name Bastion?" Reez asked. The man nodded. Standing, Reez rolled his shoulders and took some deep breaths. "There is a girl upstairs. I'm afraid she is dead. Can you untie her for me? I don't like the thought of leaving her there." Bastion hesitated for a moment and reached for his wife's hand.

"I'll be fine," she whispered.

After Bastion entered the tower, Reez turned to the elderly woman. "What is your name?"

"Yola," she said so quietly that Reez strained to hear her.

"You don't need to be afraid to speak," he said gently.

"He cannot hurt you now."

"It's been so long," Yola said.

"Why don't we go back to your galley? We can have a drink and talk a while."

After they were both seated at the wooden table nursing a brew, Reez smiled encouragingly at Yola. "How long have you lived here?" he asked.

She took a sip of the hot liquid. "Since I was a child," she whispered. "My mother served the Master before me. In those days, there were many servants who provided for the Master's needs. All the houses were full, and it was a busy, bustling place. My mother was the laundress and seamstress, and I used to help her from the time I was able to walk." She smiled softly as she remembered. "I imagine I was more trouble than help to begin with, but she was always patient with me and showed me how to do each job to the very best standard. She took great pride in everything she did. When her hands became too stiff to work the needles, I took over for her."

"So, what happened to everyone else?" Reez asked. "Are all the other houses deserted?"

The smile disappeared. "The old Master dismissed them many cycles ago. I was newly hand-fasted, and he chose us to stay and do all the work. My husband used to watch over the sheds where the livestock were kept. The Master used them for the magic. One day, he came home distraught. At first, he wouldn't tell me what had upset him, but eventually he confessed the Master was keeping children instead. He would drain them, almost to the point of death, and Bastion had to nurse them back to health only for them to be used again. Eventually, there was nothing left, and the children would die."

"Did you tell anyone about this?"

Yola shook her head. "Who was there to tell? The Cardinal was the one bringing the poor mites here, and we were forbidden to leave the compound. We tried to help them as much as possible. After Bastion confessed to me, I insisted on doing my part in caring for them. I would tell them stories and sing songs to them when night fell. I was never blessed with a child of my own, despite my long summers of service." Bastion walked into the room and nodded at Reez before sitting next to his wife. He pointed to her eyes and frowned. "I was just telling Master Reez about the children," she explained. Bastion held her hand and pulled it up to his mouth, kissing her fingers.

"What can you tell me about Verrin?" Reez asked after a moment.

"The Master brought him here when he was tiny, possibly five summers or less. He was always a serious boy. We tried to befriend him, but the Master kept him close. He never ran or played like children are supposed to. He never got dirty or scuffed his trews. Instead, he read and watched everything the Master did."

"So Malander was teaching him long before he introduced him as an apprentice," Reez mused. "That explains a great deal."

"Initially, the Master was pleased with him, but after several cycles, he began to express disapproval all the time. Verrin tried hard to earn his favour, but the Master was very

harsh with him. Sometimes he would have bruises on his face."
Yola sighed. "The Master taught him to be cruel."

"Did he ever experiment on animals while Malander was still Master?" Reez asked. Bastion gestured quickly, and Yola nodded. Reez realised they had developed their own way of communicating just as Destry and Nula had, but it was very different. "He would leave the compound regularly when the Master was busy with other things. We don't know where he went, but we do know that the Master was furious with him some cycles ago. We heard him shouting about unnatural creatures and how he had shamed him in front of the others. The Master pushed him down the steps of the tower and refused to mend his broken bones. Bastion had to carry him to his room and splint his arm and leg. The Master must have relented at some point, because Verrin was up and walking several days later. It didn't stop him from leaving occasionally, although after that, he was much more surreptitious."

Bastion fetched the pot from the fire and refilled their mugs. Reez nodded his thanks. "Your life must have changed a great deal after Malander was killed."

"We never knew what happened, just that Verrin returned alone and declared himself Master. Bastion used to hear him in the night, crying out and speaking of terrible things. He refused to repeat what he heard to me. I think Verrin had nightmares constantly and they plagued him with memories of his deeds. He stopped eating and started drinking more and more wine, as if to dull his senses. Then the people started to be brought in…" Yola swallowed and looked up at her husband.

"Did you see what he was doing?" Reez asked. Yola shook her head. "Bastion knows. He had to deal with the aftermath. The Master became obsessed with becoming stronger and faster. He said he was going to transform himself into a super being. I think he was using the people to test his ideas. At first, I used to hear screams. I hid here, imaging terrible things, but after a while the screaming ceased. I was relieved until Bastion told me that the experiments hadn't stopped. Instead, the Master had prevented the people from making any noise. As for Bastion, I don't know what happened, or what he said, but one day, my husband also came back without a voice. After that, I stayed hidden away here and stopped speaking in case Verrin overheard me."

Reez turned to Bastion. "You saw what he was doing?"

Bastion nodded and gestured. "He says you should go with him," Yola said softly.

Reez got up and followed the old man as he shuffled down the dark corridor and out into the light of the day. Beckoning to Reez, he set off around the courtyard to the buildings Reez had assumed were empty. Fumbling with a key on a cord around his neck, the man opened a door and hurried inside, only stopping briefly to ensure that Reez was still trailing after him. Although the inside was dark, strands of light filtered through the broken and rotting shutters, allowing Reez to see that what had once been a grand house was now neglected and in need of repair. Dust coated every surface, and fine filaments of webbing were draped across the beams and in the corners. Ignoring the rooms, his guide hurried towards the back of the building and, after pulling open a heavy door, he ducked inside. Stairs led down into a basement and Reez was pleased to see that these at least were sturdy and well maintained as he followed Bastion down into the dimly lit cellar.

Before he reached the bottom, Reez heard the familiar rattle of chains and recognised the scent of unwashed bodies and human waste. His heart dropped at the thought of more people being held captive. However, nothing could have prepared him for the sight that greeted him when he stepped into the large room.

The place stretched under the whole of the ground floor supported by pillars and Reez could see that rough doorways had been cut into the stone leading to the basements in the other buildings. Several enormous cages dominated the space, allowing more room for their single occupants to move about, but which were otherwise devoid of comforts. Someone, presumably Bastion, had been down recently with bowls of food and water which were now discarded outside the prisons. Reez moved to the first cage and started when a figure flew at the bars, its arms thrusting through the spaces to reach for Reez. Long claws raked the air in front of his face, and he gasped in shock. It resembled the creature he had seen at Three Rivers, but the transformation was not as advanced. The face was still very clearly that of a man, but one who appeared to be in terrible agony. Despite the gaping mouth and the tears streaming down its cheeks, he didn't make a sound.

Reez shifted his attention to Bastion. "Verrin's experiments," he choked. Bastion pointed down the line of cages and then stood back, wringing his hands.

As Reez made his way along the row of pens, he felt as if he had stumbled into a waking nightmare. Men, women, and children had been tortured and deformed to satisfy some twisted reasoning of their Master. The parade of contorted and disfigured limbs, misshapen torsos, and grotesque faces should have sent him to his knees. Verrin had sliced one man open from throat to groin, exposing all his organs and yet somehow kept alive. Another had been spliced with animal parts. In another cage, a man had several bony growths jutting out of his back covered in fine hairs, much like the appendage Verrin had been studying in his chambers. Some had been driven mad with pain; others just stared at him, their eyes devoid of hope, begging for release. There were no cries for help, no groans of despair or screams of agony. Verrin had made sure that not one of them could make a sound.

Reez reeled and fell. From somewhere he heard a loud keening, thankful that at least one creature in this place could express the horror and grief in his heart. Only when he felt a hand touching his shoulder did he realise that the noise came from himself. Bastion looked at him, his eyes pleading when his voice couldn't, but Reez shook his head, tears streaming down his face. "I don't have the skills," he cried. "I don't have the skills."

#

Despite the chaos at the Abbey, Jina had been found and arrived in the palace with several clerics in tow. Most of them had heaved their hasty meals when they first witnessed the heart-breaking sight, unaware of what had been taking place behind the crumbling walls. They had found only a few children alive and whole in the animal shed behind the tower, although their experiences had damaged them in ways that couldn't just be measured in physical terms. The clerics had taken them to join the growing number of liberated prisoners arriving at the Abbey.

After packing their meagre possessions, Bastion and his wife had gladly crossed over the causeway without a backward glance, leaving the palace forever.

There was no way to heal the miserable souls caged in the basements, or repair any of the damage that had been inflicted upon them. Jina spoke softly to those who still retained their senses and sent for drafts which were administered as the clerics stood with them, holding their hands or stroking their heads. For those who no longer had the capacity for reason, poison was added to their food. Eventually, the last of Verrin's victims breathed their last.

"What do we do with them, Master?" Jina asked, his face glistening from the tears he had not bothered to wipe away. "If we take them to the burial grounds, people might see. Some of them still look human. If one of them is recognised…"

"Lay them out here," Reez decided. "I'll take care of it."

After Reez destroyed the cages, the bodies of the victims were laid side by side on the mud floor. Along with them was the young girl from the tower, drained of life in order to fuel Verrin's last mad illusions. It seemed a simple matter for

Reez to weaken the foundations and bring the houses down on top of them, burying them forever. However, as he began to reach for the earth fires to sustain his magic, his anger spiked, hot and potent, fuelled by the raging inferno far below. As he raged at the things he had seen, he could feel the power coursing through his body, enticing him to let it flow freely through him. As the old houses crashed down in a flurry of dust and dirt, Reez struggled to rein in the urge to punish and fought to regain control. Beneath his feet, the stack shook, accompanied by an ominous rumbling. As Reez wrestled against the incessant force of the earth fires, he heard shouts and distant screams. Ignoring them, he focused his mind, curtailing the desire to destroy everything that Verrin had corrupted. As the tremors finally stopped and the palace quietened, Reez took a shaky breath and opened his eyes. Those few clerics who had remained by him were staring with a mixture of fear and awe. The weak wall surrounding the compound was completely broken, parts of it fallen down into the sea below. The top part of Verrin's tower now lay to one side of the courtyard while the rest of the building shuddered, dust and debris still falling. The magnificent golden roof lay twisted and buckled next to it. Reez took a moment to calm himself, shaking from the effects of such colossal power coursing through his body. Only when he was sure that he could speak clearly did he issue more orders.

Eager to do his bidding, the clerics hastily gathered earth and spread it across the rubble of the houses. When they were done, Reez scattered flower seeds over the mass grave, and as the clerics gathered solemnly around him, he grew a host of fragrant blooms as a tribute to the dead.

He had scoured the now empty buildings and had found a few books and documents, but there was no sign of a second library like the one in Minra. Not wanting to study anything that had inspired Verrin or leave them for any other curious reader, he tossed all that he could find on a fire and burnt them to ashes. Verrin's body had been flung inside the remains of his tower. No-one had wanted him to rest alongside his victims. Reez stood in the doorway and stared at the man who had haunted his nightmares for so long. With a sigh, he bent down and straightened Verrin's shattered limbs and crossed his arms over his chest.

"It's over now," he said, looking at the serene face of his nemesis. "You never had peace here, but I hope you find it in the next life. This will be your tomb now. Perhaps one day, flowers will grow on your tomb, but there will be no-one to see. Rest easy." Reaching into his bag, Reez pulled out a handful of seeds and scattered them over Verrin's body.

He crossed the courtyard and paused at the gate. He needed to demolish this place and ensure that no-one would discover its dreadful secrets, but he was suddenly wary of the power he had wielded so freely before. Again, he had an insight into the devastation that had rocked the world during the Mage wars and was beginning to realise that the injudicious use of magic could be calamitous.

Tentatively, he reached down for the power raging below. Instead of giving free range to the anger that still burned inside, Reez filled his mind with other images: flowers growing in the meadow behind his tower. Destry's hand stroking his face. Aydal and Damino laughing in the inn. Wicton's gentle gaze. His mother singing. He stood silently for a long time, letting the peace and love flood his soul. Only then did he reach down to the earth fires.

A loud rumble heralded the start of the tower's final collapse, as the ancient structure toppled in on itself. A plume of dust rose from the rubble and blew across the site, obscuring the pile of stone for a moment before being carried away by the wind. This time, the force remained under control, and Reez could keep the seductive fires banked. Satisfied, Reez strode across the causeway towards the Abbey where Jina and his trusted clerics stood waiting. Glancing past them, he could see crowds of people watching from within, and he noticed hundreds more lining the walls around the city, which had a view of the palace. Just before reaching the Abbey he stopped and turned. With a gesture that all the spectators could see, Reez collapsed the causeway into the sea, ensuring that the stack beyond was inaccessible.

Weary to the bone, he turned and walked through the ornate doors.

"I need rest," he murmured to Jina as he passed. "Can you find me somewhere quiet to sleep?"

"Follow me, Lord," Jina said, and strode through the whispering crowds, leading Reez to his own chamber.

#

Reez woke the following day and stared at the ceiling of the tiny cell where Jina slept. As much as he wished to return home, there was still a great deal to be done in Etheradia, not least of which was how to punish those who had aided Verrin. Although it could be argued that the clerics had had no choice in supplying their Master with the people he demanded, their treatment on the island and the conditions in which the captives were kept had shown that those involved had no compassion in their hearts. An example would have to be made of the Cardinal and his cohorts at the very least, or the citizens may well take matters into their own hands.

Reez needed the clerics and the smooth running of the chapter to maintain some continuity. In many ways, Verrin would not be missed by the populace. He had done nothing for them in the long cycles of his tenure as Master, but he was still a figurehead that was known and relied on. When word eventually spread that Bestra was without a Master, it could cause untold havoc. There was also the question of what to do with all the refugees camping outside the city walls. Until the last of Verrin's creations had been dealt with, it wouldn't be safe to send them back to their settlements. Besides, they had no food to sustain them on a journey. Sighing, Reez sat up in the small cot and reached for his journeyman's bag. He still had seeds that he could utilise to grow produce, but it wouldn't be enough to feed everyone. Reez hoped there would be enough within the city walls to supplement the supply until a better solution presented itself. He swung his legs over the side of the cot and pulled on his trews. It was going to be another long day.

#

"You can't do this! You have no authority!" the old

High Cleric blustered when his sentence had been read.

Wearing the Cardinal's chain of office, Jina glanced at Reez quickly before standing. "As the newly appointed Cardinal of the Master of Bestra province, I have every right," he said. "You will be taken to the marketplace along with the others and stoned. The people will have their justice." With a nod of his head, Jina signalled that the trial was over. Two clerics hauled the prisoner off to await his fate. Jina dismissed the assembled chapter and sat back in the chair, which had already been stripped of its gems.

"I'm not sure I can do this," he said quietly.

Reez rose from his seat by the door and crossed the room. He laid a hand on Jina's shoulder. "I think you are doing a marvellous job."

"These executions don't sit well with me," Jina admitted. "Are you sure they are necessary?"

Reez sighed and lowered himself on to the dais. "Tell me," he said, "how did you feel when you discovered the truth of what has been happening here?"

"Sick, angry, distraught."

"Now multiply that by a thousand souls. Many of them may have missing family members, or friends and neighbours who were taken in the Purge. They will want retribution and, if we don't control it, they will take their rage out arbitrarily." Jina nodded. "Their fear of Verrin does not excuse the inhumane treatment of those who were imprisoned, or the long cycles of abuse that have been meted out. I actually think there were more who knew of what was going on, but either couldn't or wouldn't speak out. It is enough that the leaders will be punished, publicly and decisively. You, my friend, have only just begun your work."

Jina looked down at Reez with a frown. "What do you mean?"

"Bestra has been ravaged and needs healing. The people will look to you for guidance and leadership. You must forge a different path that will incorporate the best parts of the old order and fuse it with something new. I can stay for a while, until things are more settled, but I have duties in Fiora. When I'm gone, you will be the voice of authority here, not me."

"But I'm just a lowly cleric. I don't know anything about running a province."

Reez stood and pointed at the seal hanging around Jina's neck. "You are the Cardinal. Besides, you don't have to know everything. If I remember rightly, you get to rely on all those other lowly clerics to do your bidding. Now, let's go to your new rooms and see what wines are available. I don't know about you, but a hot fire and a warming drink will go a long way to soothing my spirit."

They walked into the Cardinal's private quarters and settled themselves by the hearth.

"Have you given any thought as to who to promote to High Cleric?" Reez asked as he poured them both a goblet of berry wine.

"I have," Jina said. "He's young, but passionate and dedicated. He worked tirelessly with the victims, and I know him to be intelligent and thoughtful."

"Your first task will be to come up with a name," Reez said. "In fact, all the clerics need to have one. I can't abide the fact that they are only known by a number."

Jina pulled the sleeve of his robe up and looked at the figures engraved on to his skin. "I have no memory of before," he said sadly. "When you gave me my name, it was the first time anyone had really noticed me as a person. I will always be grateful to you for that."

"When I first met you, you were just a representation of something I detested," Reez said. "It was nice to be reminded that you are a person, just like everyone else." They sat in companionable silence for a while, remembering their encounters at the Falcon Inn.

"I should go to bed," Jina said finally. "I have to see to the distribution of the gold on the morrow. It was good of you to salvage it for us." Reez had been able to melt the precious metal from the roofs of the houses and the toppled tower and break it into small blocks to be carted across the causeway before he cut off all access.

"You will need it to lodge all the victims until new homes are found for them."

"Some have already gone. Your friend, Trane, took quite a few of the boys and disappeared into the city. I asked him to come and see me every once in a while, so that I know they are healthy and being cared for. He seemed surprised, but I think he might stay in touch."

Reez smiled. "I don't think we've seen the last of him," he agreed. The two men drained their goblets and rose.

"This will take some getting used to," Jina observed as he looked around the room. "I slept on the floor last night; the bed was just too soft."

Reez laughed. "Don't worry, it won't take long, I promise."

Jina looked at him sadly. "I'm not sure if I will ever sleep again. All those children…"

Reez swallowed loudly. "I know what you mean. It would be easy to fall into despair. We can't unsee those people and, in a way, we shouldn't try. Their fates will impel us to make sure nothing like that happens again. If we forget them, then their deaths will have meant nothing. We should honour their memory and keep it alive for those who did not witness it."

"Yes, you are right. Do you think they will eventually leave me in peace?"

"I don't believe they will ever be able to be forgotten. Perhaps it will help to dwell on other images, beautiful ones which can take the sting out of the darkness. As you work tomorrow, look for the kind acts, the smiles on people's faces. Listen out for the birds and the sound of singing. Treasure the things that are true, right, and praiseworthy in your heart and think about them every day. We have seen evil things, but we have also got much to be thankful for. I suppose that is why I long for home," Reez said with a sigh. "When I am away, I remember friends and family, simple pleasures, and small blessings. They become a flame in your heart that can never be extinguished and a goal to work towards, so that no matter what obstacles you face, you will always strive to return."

"I have no such memories to draw upon," Jina said sadly, "but I will endeavour to search for them, Master Reez." He rose and bowed low. "With your permission, I will retire."

Reez waved his hand. "Stop it, Jina. We are friends."

Jina smiled. "Then that shall be my first happy thought," he said as he walked through the door to the bedchamber.

Chapter Twenty-Six

Reez took a deep breath of relief as he watched the rest of the Temple come crashing down in front of him. He had misjudged the amount of magic needed to level the building and had almost caused the earth fires to burst through fissures created by his work. He could still feel the tremors under his feet and hoped they were merely echoes of the destruction before him rather than a weakening of the barrier containing the force beneath. Wielding earth magic took an inner strength and a will of iron, and he was perilously short of both. He was tired and heartsore and desired nothing more than to sleep for an age.

"Somehow you knew it might come to this," he

whispered, picturing Wicton standing next to him. "I've torn it all down now, but I fear what might take its place."

Before he turned to walk back through the streets to the market square, he saw several people rush forward to collect stone from the blasted walls, a grim reminder of the other task scheduled for the day.

Although the streets were packed with people, he made his way easily through the throng, which parted reverently to let him pass. Occasionally, someone would reach out to touch his sleeve, or beg for petition, but he ignored them. As he neared the square, the noise rose until it became a cacophony of shouts, entreaties and expletives, punctuated by weeping and the occasional burst of laughter. Those close to him hushed as he passed, but the clamour continued unabated across the rest of the space.

The market stalls had gone, and they had set up a temporary dais near the centre of the square, the area cordoned off by sombre-faced clerics. As he approached, Reez saw that Jina and the rest of his new leaders were already seated. Reez climbed the steps and felt the tension and expectation increase as the people sensed that the moment had arrived.

"It's done," he said to Jina as he took his seat and let his gaze roam the crowds. "This could get ugly very quickly."

"I know," Jina replied, his face a mask of concern. "I'm hoping common sense will prevail."

"It wouldn't take much to sway them to violence."

"Then let us trust that your presence will be enough. I know you don't care for the robes, but the people recognise them." Jina had insisted that Reez wear the highly decorated dark red robes of a Master to demonstrate to the people that he had taken on Verrin's mantle.

"Then let us begin." Reez stood up and walked to the front of the dais, waiting until the mob quietened. Only then did he speak, raising his voice so that those at the very edges of the crowd had a chance to hear him. "Citizens of Etheradia, today you are witnesses to a new era. Gone are the former things; there will be no more petitions, no more offerings or tributes and no more Purge. I am Reez, Master of green magic and wielder of earth magic. From this day I am also overseer of Bestra Province and your Master. I have appointed a new Cardinal and High Cleric who have been conducting trials of the former holders of that office along with many others. My Cardinal will now address you."

Jina rose and bowed low to Reez before facing the people. His voice wavered as he listed the atrocities that had been committed in the name of the Eternal One, but as he continued, his voice grew stronger and his confidence increased. After proclaiming sentence on the last felon, Jina rolled up the parchment and looked out at the masses.

"There have been no executions for hundreds of cycles, and I hope I will never have to perform this duty again. Many of you here have lost friends and family or given up children as a tribute. I am sure you are angry at the things you have heard. Today, you will have the opportunity to carry out the sentence we have decreed, as is your right. This is a serious matter and must, therefore, be carried out with sober reflection. You have heard of those rescued from the Cleric's Isle and the terrible suffering they endured. It is fitting, therefore, that they should cast the first stones." Jina raised his hand, and a horn sounded from the direction of the Abbey. As the people shuffled aside to make a path, and the clerics ranged on the dais stood in respect, the men, women, and children Reez had freed walked into the square. A few had to be carried, or walked, supported by stout sticks. Most were thin and bore the marks of beatings. Many of the women carried small children or babes in their arms. As they took their positions at the front of the hushed crowd, Reez heard a low hum from his right. Looking over, he saw several boys pushing their way through the masses and recognised Trane among them. He rose and indicated that they, too, should be included with the victims. When the last of them had taken their place, Jina raised his hand again, and the perpetrators were led into the square by clerics, bound together and wearing only a loincloth to preserve their dignity. Reez tensed, expecting a howl of outrage from the assembled people or even that some might ignore Jina's edict and take matters into their own hands. Instead, the men were greeted with silence. Occasionally, Reez heard someone shout an insult, or expletive. Some spat at the prisoners as they passed by, but the majority watched quietly. The previous evening, Reez had sunk stakes into the ground in front of the dais and now the men were tied to them, creating a semicircle facing outward. Several of the clerics sobbed as they were secured; others begged for mercy or declared their innocence. When the last of them had been bound, the clerics who had created the cordon moved away, leaving the condemned to their judgement.

Bastion and Yola approached and stared at the former Cardinal. Instead of casting their stones, however, they dropped them where they stood and turned away, walking arm in arm back to the Abbey. A few followed their example, but most threw them, some randomly, or others targeting specific people who they recognised. Trane and his cohort had no compunctions in dishing out the sentence, melting back into the crowds after they were done. So great was the throng that the rocks continued to fly long after the men were all dead and their faces and bodies were broken beyond recognition. Many of those who approached were crying as they cast their stones. Some shouted the names of folk who had been taken. Eventually, the last stone skittered down the piles that had formed around the prisoners and the deed was done.

Jina drew in a ragged breath before ordering that the bodies be cut down and taken away to be burnt, erasing all evidence of the evil that had been done. Reez rotted the wooden stakes away, and the clerics began the task of clearing away the rubble until no trace remained of the executions. A few of the more curious people stayed behind to watch the spectacle, but most of the residents had returned to their homes or made their way back to the Abbey.

"I'll see you on the morrow," Reez said to Jina as they prepared to leave.

"You're not coming back to the Abbey?" Jina asked, his face still ashen.

"No," Reez said, holding up the key around his neck. "I

feel the need for solitude and something from Castor's cellar."

Jina nodded. "I might raid the Cardinal's... sorry, my stocks tonight. I hope it will expunge this day from my mind." They clasped arms and went their separate ways.

Reez headed towards the Falcon Inn, his heart heavy and his steps slow. Long before he reached the doors, he was aware that someone was following him, yet every time he turned around, there was no-one in sight. Rounding a corner, he ducked into the shadows of a deep doorway and waited. Moments later, a young boy of about six summers appeared, and Reez stepped out.

"Why are you following me?" he demanded.

The boy crossed his arms and frowned. "How did you know?"

"I am a Master of great power," he said darkly. "Only a fool would believe they could deceive me."

The lad brightened a little. "So, I was good?" he asked.

Reez laughed. "Yes, you were good."

"I'm going to be a spy when I'm older, or maybe an assassin," he boasted. "You need to be able to move without being seen. Trane said I should practice."

"So, did Trane send you to follow me?"

"He wanted to know where you were going. You didn't go back to the Abbey."

"Tell him I will be at the Falcon if he wants to speak to me, but he needs to come soon. I don't intend to be sober for long." With a quick nod, the boy turned and ran off, leaving Reez alone once more. With a small smile, Reez continued on until he reached the welcoming sight of Castor's inn and went inside. Closing the door, he leant back against it and shut his eyes tight, wishing the dreadful images would leave his mind. Although the deaths had been brutal and bloody, Reez was pleased with the way the people had responded. Instead of acting out of bloodlust or indiscriminate violence, justice had been served on those who had been found guilty by the clerics. By the reactions of many in the crowd, it was not something that they did lightly, nor, he suspected, was it an event that they would be quick to repeat.

He wandered behind the bar, his eyes straying to the Taklar on the shelf. He knew it would give him the temporary relief he craved, but wasn't sure if he was ready to suffer the consequences that would inevitably follow. Instead, he grabbed a bottle of berry wine and a tankard. As he sat in one of the settles, the door to the inn opened and Trane walked cautiously in.

"Your little messenger is quick," Reez observed.

Trane shrugged and jumped up on the settle opposite Reez. "He's good, too. Fades into the background."

"Why didn't you stay at the Abbey? You would have had a bed and warm food there."

"I want nothing from them," Trane said. "I have a place."

"What about the boys you took with you?"

"I promised them I would look after them. Prime was happy to see them. We're a family now."

Reez sighed. "Maybe you didn't have a choice before,

but you have one now. Cheating and stealing is wrong. If you get caught, you will be punished. Why not take the chance for a better life?"

"I like the life I have. I don't want to change it."

"The clerics would help you learn a trade so you could live independently."

Trane snorted. "If I never see a red robe again, it'll be too soon."

"They're not all bad. Jina will take care of you."

Trane's face twisted in mockery. "What makes him so different?"

"I trust him. I wouldn't have made him the Cardinal if I didn't. When I first arrived, I found him weeping over what was happening to the children in this city, and that was before he knew the entire story. He won't let anything like that happen again. Trane, the city needs people like you who can help to make it a good place to live."

"But I'm just a boy."

"And one day, you will be a man, a man with a big family. If you work with Jina, you may even be a man of influence. Think about it."

"Maybe," Trane said.

"I'll be here for a while, to make sure things stay calm and to help the clerics work out a plan for the future, but after that, I need to go back to Fiora. I think Jina would like a friend to talk to after I'm gone."

Trane laughed shortly. "Me? Friends with a cleric? Never!" He slid off the seat and walked to the door. "See you around, Reez."

"One more thing, before you go," Reez said. "Watch over this place for me when I leave. Until the owners return."

Trane nodded once and then left. Reez rose and bolted the door shut. Grabbing the bottle and the tankard, he made his way up the wooden staircase and into his room. It seemed like weeks since he had last slept there, rather than just a few days. He sat on the bed, his back against the decorated headboard, and drained the tankard dry before refilling it again.

Zelannor would never be the same, and Reez couldn't decide whether or not that was a good thing. The Masters, despite the split in magic, had reigned unchallenged for millennia, each controlling things in such a way that change was impossible. The Master of Bestra had maintained a small population, intervening when the denizens multiplied too much. Fiora and Minra had ensured that there were just enough resources to supply all the people, but not enough to encourage innovation or upset the balance. If not for Verrin's actions, Reez would have blindly taken on the role of Master without question, assuming his place in the long line of men and women who had unswervingly regulated the lives of their charges since the dawn of the age.

Now, with no-one to control the population or send plagues into the country to decimate it, the people would thrive and grow. Instead of one city, there would be many, all of them needing food and homes and a way of providing for their families. Reez was glad his brother had already approached him with his ideas to increase the yield in the fields. Before long,

Fiora would need to expand its production to feed more mouths; Minra would need to mine more ore for tools and provide more craftsmen to build and maintain dwellings. Somehow, Reez would have to oversee them all. He sighed and took another quaff of wine before closing his eyes.

Tomorrow. It could all wait until tomorrow. Tonight, he just wanted to forget.

Chapter Twenty-Seven

Reez turned the ring over in his hand. The green stone shone in the light of the library's strange lamps, revealing the outline of a fully grown figure. He wondered briefly if the person who created it had stopped to think about how an apprentice might feel being reminded that he was just a babe, or a journeyman nothing more than a child, and how much they would yearn to wear the ring of an adult instead. Carefully, he placed it alongside the rings from Minra and closed the box, his shoulders slumping. Now he was truly alone in the world. For a moment, the heavy burden of responsibility weighed him down, threatening to crush him. How was he supposed to manage something that three had once shouldered? He was stumbling in the dark, blind without direction. Perhaps not totally blind, he thought wryly as he gazed at the thousands of books around him. He may only be the Master of green magic, but he had access to all the ancient lore of the Mages of old. Given time and close study, he was sure he could be an adequate guardian for the other two provinces. Swinging up his bag loaded with information about anima magic, Reez made his way up the stairs, switching off the lamps behind him and plunging the vault into darkness. After closing the stone entry, he reshaped the wooden floor to erase all trace of the hidden doorway. Satisfied that the little hut was tidy, he walked outside into the hazy light of a winter sun.

A nicker of greeting from the shed next to the hut made Reez smile, and he pulled out an apple from his pocket. Opening the door, he stepped inside and stroked the nose of the animal within.

"Ready for the last part of our journey, Dash?" he asked as he offered the fruit.

Jina had shaken his head and laughed. "Why do you insist on giving everything a name?" he asked after gifting the animal to Reez.

"I can't just call him horse," Reez replied, "especially if he's going to be a constant companion."

Malander had been the one to take the humble hinny and, with time and experimentation, had been able to produce a creature that was both strong and fast. The custodian of the stable had kept the animals at his own homestead outside the city walls, and Verrin had never bothered with them. As a result, he had been free to manage them himself and had successfully bred them, teaching them to carry heavy loads, including a person. It had been Jina who had discovered their existence and had the idea to make them available to Reez after he had moaned about the constant travelling he would be forced to endure in overseeing the provinces. Eventually, it was proposed to create a number of Way stops throughout Zelannor so that he could move swiftly from one side of the country to the other. Mastering riding the creature had been a challenge, but despite the initial aches and pains, learning to sit astride a horse and guide it had been a strangely pleasurable task and Reez had revelled in it.

He reached for the plaited nose band on the back of the door and slipped it over Dash's muzzle, looping the soft rope over his ears and securing it under his chin. Then he attached the guiding rein. After the bags were fastened across the rump, Reez pulled himself up on to the horse's back and dug his heels into his side. After crossing the barrier of vegetation that guarded the Tower of the Mages, Reez leaned forward slightly, urging Dash into a gallop, laughing with delight as the wind whipped his hair back and the countryside raced past.

#

Thanks to Dash's speed and endurance, the journey home took a fraction of the time, and Reez soon spied the welcoming sights of Maston. He pulled up for a moment and let his eyes feast on the familiar view. The fields were empty today, the ground too hard to work. Instead, he imagined the families in front of warm fires weaving willow baskets or repairing clothes. Some would be cleaning tools or taking the opportunity to repair their houses. All of them would be enjoying the rest that the cycle gave them before sowing and planting started in earnest. Above it all in the distance, Reez could see the top of the tower, peeking through the trees, standing watch over the peaceful village, and reminding the residents of their Master's protection and aid. Eager to finish his journey, Reez clicked his tongue and flicked the rein, prompting Dash to resume, and they trotted down the lane.

Someone must have spotted his approach and spread the word, as he saw the villagers tumbling out of their houses and running to the edge of the village to greet him. When he reached them, Reez dismounted and led Dash through the small crowd of curious onlookers. Children fired questions at him and, once he had assured them it was safe, walked next to the horse, running their hands along his flanks and marvelling at his size. Reaching the inn, he secured the reins to a low fence and turned to the children.

"Dash will need a bucket of water and a handful of oats. Then he would like a nice rub down with a rag, and maybe a blanket over his back to keep him warm. Can you do that for me?"

The children ran off, arguing over who would do what task, and Reez walked through the doors of the inn. He was immediately enveloped in a crushing hug as Castor met him, followed by Merrylee and Siril.

"Welcome back, Master Reez!" Castor said, beaming.

"Are you well?" Merrylee asked, scanning his face.

"Everything is fine," Reez said, reassuring them.

"Then sit down," Castor demanded, pointing to the fire blazing in the hearth. "We'll bring you some food."

Reez started to cross to the settle when he recognised a familiar figure. "Phalen?" Reez said, spying the old innkeeper sat in a huge armchair by the fire. The man smiled crookedly and lifted his left arm up for Reez to clasp.

"Castor carries him down every day, so he can sit in the inn and see his old friends, or just watch the world go by," Merrylee said quietly.

"Ees," Phalen said carefully, "ud to shee oo."

"It's good to see you, too." Reez replied, holding Phalen's arm and grinning widely.

While the adults rushed off to get food and drink, Siril sat down on Phalen's left side and began to chatter. He explained how they had taken over running the inn at Nula's request. She had moved out and was now living in Reez's childhood home as its mistress. Grampy, as Siril called Phalen, was looked after by the little family, and Castor had persuaded him to be dressed and sit in the taproom during the day. Siril was helping him to practice his words. As he related their successes, Phalen stroked the young boy's head fondly.

"It's nicer than the Falcon," Siril confided. "The people here are friendly, and they take time to talk. I want to stay here. Do you think we can?"

"That would be up to your father and mother," Reez said. "It would be safe to go back to the Falcon again. Perhaps they will want to return."

"I hope not," Siril said with a frown.

"Then you must make sure they know your feelings on the matter," Reez advised.

Their conversation was interrupted by a commotion at the door as Aydal, Nula and the girls, along with Damino, all barrelled through after Beran, relief and joy on their faces. Questions were fired at him from all sides as they held him close, touching him often as if to reassure themselves that he was really safe and well. Soon, the inn was full and when the Margrave arrived, Reez recounted his story briefly to them all, knowing that it would be better if it was heard by everyone. Many of the horrors he had witnessed he kept to himself, and he promised to give the council a more detailed report the following day after he was rested. They, at least, should know the whole truth of his journey.

Surrounded by his family and friends and safe in the community he loved, Reez still scanned the room expectantly. One person hadn't yet appeared, and she was the one he wanted to see most of all. He waited in vain for her to appear throughout the day as he ate good food, drank Castor's winter brew, and answered the myriad questions from all and sundry. The atmosphere in the inn was festive as folk celebrated Verrin's demise and the end of the perceived threat to their way of life, but Reez's heart grew heavier as time went on. No-one seemed to know where she was. Merrylee had checked in her room upstairs but came back shaking her head. His heart sank. Had she changed her mind? He had been gone for many moons, after all. Perhaps the reminder of how lonely her life would be had made her rethink her decision. Even now, she could be holding hands with someone else, walking down the lanes and smiling up at them. Reez closed his eyes against the stab of pain that seemed to rip his heart open. He loved her, he acknowledged to himself, more than anyone else in the land. It would hurt him far more to see her with someone else than it had for him to hear about Aydal and Nula. He didn't know how he would ever bear it. At least his duties would take him away, he decided. Between looking after Minra and Bestra, and studying at the tower, he need not stay in Maston.

Eventually, Reez extricated himself from the exuberant villagers, and after making arrangements for Dash to be looked after until they could build a stable for him, he walked the last part of his journey alone. The sun was low in the sky when he reached the completed wall and opened the five-bar gate. As he glanced up towards the tower, a figure rose from the step and Reez smiled in relief. Hurrying up the track, he reached out his arms and Destry ran to him. Despite her winter clothes and the thick shawl around her shoulders, she was cold to his touch, and he drew her close, wrapping his heavy cloak around her. For the longest time, they just stood there until Reez drew back slightly and grasped her small hand in his. It was against every rule laid down in the vault. It had never been allowed in the long millennia since the division, but Reez no longer cared. Walking to the door, he pushed it open and pulled Destry inside, letting the door close with a soft thud behind them. Finally, he was home.

Epilogue

Burning fumes seared down his throat as he took yet another shallow breath, automatically filtering the noxious gases until he could process the life-preserving vapour. Spread-eagled over the earth fires, the bands across his torso flared hot, scorching his wasted flesh. Long ago, they had melted skin and muscles to lodge firmly within his body, further trapping him in their solid embrace. The chains that suspended him over the pit kept his limbs stretched taut and unyielding, unable to ease the pressure on shoulder and hip. The pain had been consigned to the back of his thoughts long since, leaving only the desire to survive. A lesser being would have perished with the punishment meted out by zealous Mages, but he had power beyond imagining and a will to endure. No doubt he would be dead if enough magic could have been summoned in his ultimate defeat; instead, they had sentenced him to this eternal imprisonment in the hope that, one day, he would eventually succumb.

He could not say what had changed at first, intent as he was on keeping his heart beating and his organs vital. Hairless and naked, scorched and scarred, he existed at the very limits of strength. More moments passed. How long he had been there, he couldn't fathom. So many cycles, perhaps even hundreds could have elapsed as he fought each moment to continue to be. Suddenly, his wrists exploded in agony as the pressure holding him firm lessened slightly and feeling poured through into his hands. He flexed what was left of his fingers, relishing the pain. This was different. This was new.

Another breath, fractionally deeper now, enabling him to harness more of the elements that sustained him. A chink invaded his hearing, accustomed only to the drumming of the deep earth, as he flexed slightly within his bonds. The spells that had held him captive for so long were weakening. Had his jailers become complacent, thinking him extinct and ceasing their long vigil over his prison? Another blistering bolt of pain, this time through his feet. He had lost the ability to scream long ago, as the heat had burnt away his mouth and tongue. Now he suffered in silence. As his mind cleared, he concentrated on the changes and made his plans. Something had altered, and Baddon Nox would not miss the chance to regain his freedom.

Coming December 2022

The Last Mage
Masters of Zelannor: Book Three

As Master of the three provinces, Reez has amassed knowledge and power unknown since the division, and his thoughts begin turn to the future and what this means for the land of Zelannor.

However, his nights are interrupted with dreams of places he has never been and people he has never known. In addition, a disturbing message comes to him from Minra which sends him hurrying north to investigate.

What he discovers sends his world crashing down around him.

Now, only Reez stands between an ancient power that seeks to rule unopposed and the people he loves, and it could cost him everything.

Acknowledgements

To all the readers who bought and read book one, thank you for your support and your enthusiastic praise for Master and Apprentice. I have been blown away by all the positive comments. You are the reason I do this.

As always, I am so grateful for my husband, Paul, who is also my biggest cheerleader. You will never know how much your support means to me. Maybe one day, your dream of "WictonWorld" will be realised!

I could not have done this without the help and support of Becky Waterman, my mentor and friend. Thank-you for sharing this adventure with me and for your endless enthusiasm. You made me believe that this dream was possible to achieve.

My thanks as always to my beta readers, Carol Rowe, Flick Goodhall, and Vix Parker. Your comments and insights have been invaluable in shaping this story and helping me to grow as a writer.

I am so grateful to my homegroup ladies, and my prayer partner Hev Brider, who have unswervingly supported me when my muse disappeared, and encouraged me to keep going.

Thank you, Mathilda Parker, for yet another great cover.

Above all, I give thanks to my Heavenly Father for his provision, his guidance, and his unfailing love.

About the Author

Susan Mansbridge was born in the north of England and lived in various places in the UK but has made Southampton her home.

Having trained as a nurse and worked in schools and colleges as both a support assistant and administrator, Susan was finally able to leave work and concentrate on her writing full time.

Her love of fantasy started very early after being given "A Wizard of Earthsea" one Christmas, and her dream has always been to write her own books.

When she is not writing, Susan enjoys reading (of course), watching movies, and solving cryptic crossword puzzles. She also enjoys walking in the New Forest with her camera and fellow clicking buddies and is an active member of Testwood Baptist Church.

You can follow Susan on Twitter @SuePMansbridge or Facebook @susanmansbridgewriter

To find out more visit Susan's website at susanmansbridge.com. You can sign up for her newsletter to get sneak peeks, background information on her books, and news of new releases. All new subscribers will receive a free short story set in the world of Zelannor.

Susan would love to hear from you. You can contact her via email at smwritersworld@outlook.com

Printed in Great Britain
by Amazon